These stories are wor incidents are fictitious a̶ ̶ ̶ ̶ ̶ ̶ ̶ ̶ ̶ to actual persons, locations, or events is coincidental.

Second Paperback Edition
ISBN: 978-1-998763-35-1

Unshod, Cackling, and Naked Copyright © 2023, 2024 Tamika Thompson

All rights reserved

Art and logos included in/on this volume Copyright © 2023, 2024 Unnerving

To Edgar, Corliss, and Deondre for being my foundation.

To Lendell, Morgan, and Ellis for being my light.

UNSHOD, CACKLING, AND NAKED

TAMIKA THOMPSON

Pauline,

Terror is more productive than revenge.

Tamika

Table of Contents

The Turn	9
Bridget Has Disappeared	28
Under the Crown	60
I did it for you	71
The Bats	79
These Parts	102
i will be glorious	115
Angry Slash of Blood	134
Mannequin Model	143
She By the Sea	158
And We Screamed	173
I Am Goddess	194
Abduction Near Knife Lake	227
About	244

The Turn

I am the worst person to document this disaster because I've never been a dog "owner." I rolled my eyes whenever folks dressed their pooches in doggie sweatshirts or carted them around in strollers or on their chests in what looked like baby carriers. It was lost on me why a person would share a bed or dinner table with a pup, considering what dogs got up to when no one was around—guzzled toilet water, riffled through trash cans, licked their bottoms and that of other dogs, ran their sandpaper tongues along the soles of shoes, and scratched and bit at their flea-infested fur. In other words, I thought the cleanest dogs had filthy traps and never wanted those mouths on me.

Having said that, I appreciated hounds from afar. Mostly I respected all they put up with from humans. I realized dogs were pack animals, but domestication still seemed an indignity—told to sit, stand, get on the couch, get off the bed, be nice, fetch. For what? The enjoyment of humans? To offer people companionship? And the dog got what, exactly?

Point is, I'm still here, and, although I never kept a dog as a pet, and, therefore, don't see myself as responsible for the events that unfolded this year, it looks as if I'm the one to tell it.

Oh, and since I was not of the dog-owner class, it took me a while to notice the news about The Turn, and, when I did, it was too late.

—

The first sign didn't seem like a sign at all. At the time, I thought it was an isolated incident. I was standing in my kitchen, eating a banana nut muffin, brewing coffee, and chatting on the phone with my on-again, off-again boyfriend, Micah. We were going through a friendship phase, which was really his way of letting me know he missed me without actually saying the words. He was the one with commitment issues, not me. But I was the one who always left to find something better, which never materialized, but he didn't need to know that.

My neighbor stood in his yard shouting, "Douglas!" and his usually spunky auburn-haired Shih Tzu was looking away from him, as if the dog had lost its hearing.

"Who's that?" Micah sounded annoyed.

"Mr. Vishtali."

"Didn't know Mr. Vishtali ever raised his voice."

"He doesn't."

Mr. Vishtali was my widowed neighbor with two kids off at college and only his dog to take walks with in the evenings. He was an agreeable man with sad eyes and a nervous smile he doled out liberally. He asked me to proof-read all correspondence he sent to the higher-ups at his university job. The assistant had been omitted from his department when the school cut funds. In return, Mr. Vishtali squashed bugs and set mouse traps for me. Nothing was ever caught in the sticky trays because I had a fear of mice with no actual rodent visitors. Didn't stop me from blaming every mysterious noise on mice. Mr. Vishtali suggested I get a cat, but I cannot make this clear enough—I didn't think animals should be pets.

"Why is he shouting? It's too early for all that."

"He's calling his dog, but the mutt won't go in the house."

"I wouldn't either if my owner screamed my name like that."

I hated when people referred to humans as animal "owners" but I let it go because my friendship with Micah was fragile. Even a small critique might scare him off, and, I had to admit, I enjoyed talking to him. Micah chuckled, and I normally would have as well to make him feel he was funny, but something strange happened and it caught my attention.

When Mr. Vishtali moved toward his dog, rounding his fingers against his lips to whistle, the dog rose on its hind legs, bared its teeth, and snapped at him.

Standing, the dog only came to Mr. Vishtali's knees on a good day, but I'd never seen Douglas behave that way. One of the few dogs I liked, Douglas never jumped on me, always wagged its tail when I came around, and would dog-smile and offer its belly to neighborhood kids who petted it.

"What's he doing now?" Micah seemed interested in the Mr. Vishtali-Douglas situation, but I wondered whether Micah was keeping the conversation going to avoid whatever he was working toward saying to me. He probably wanted to come over after work. And the answer was a resounding no. Friendship was friendship, and if he wanted more, then more was more.

"He's backing away from his dog slowly to avoid a bite."

That evening, when I pulled into the driveway, Mr. Vishtali was sitting on his front porch, leash in hand, staring down the block. Douglas was not there.

I rolled down the car window, feeling the Southern California heat pour in and overtake my air conditioning.

"Everything okay?" Yes, I was being nosey. I mean, I had heard of dogs getting senile, but Douglas was too young.

"Can't find Douglas." He explained that he'd phoned his vet, saying Douglas would no longer turn his head when his name was uttered, nor would the dog's eyes light up or convey he'd heard anything at all.

Like all dog owners I knew, Mr. Vishtali used the pronoun "he" to talk about an animal, when an "it" would have been sufficient, but I digress.

Hearing loss was the explanation Mr. Vishtali's vet had given him, or perhaps depression, since Douglas was only two, and therefore not quite old enough for a hearing loss diagnosis to make sense without an injury.

"What did the vet say you should do?"

"Get him more exercise. And a low-sodium diet. But I know that isn't it. He already has both."

It had never occurred to me that a pet could become depressed, but I guessed dogs had spent so much time with humans they'd started acting like us as well, complete with our ailments.

I chuckled to myself as I exited my car and went inside, waving goodbye to Mr. Vishtali. Since when do dogs have mortgages, divorces, and ungrateful kids? Depressed? More like coddled.

―

The second sign occurred when Micah and I were taking a walk in the park. The concrete path looped around a large pond, and it was the type of place that attracted wheels—roller blades, strollers, wheelchairs—as well as tons of dogs and their humans.

Micah took my hand and laced his fingers through mine, a gesture that used to cause a stir in me, but I felt nothing. No surge. No arousal. I wondered whether we'd make it out of the friendship phase this time.

"I hate going for walks." He said it with a smirk, which was how he delivered negative talk and backhanded compliments.

"Then why did you suggest we—"

"Because you enjoy walks, and I enjoy watching you enjoy things. But walks always depress me."

I heard a woman shout, "Sit, boy," but we were surrounded by so many people with dogs, the command did not intrigue me enough to search for the speaker.

"Of all the things to depress a person, why would exercise and fresh air make you—"

"Because when you're on a path like this, just walking in circles, it highlights for me how purposeless life might be. We like to think we're important, and life has meaning, and we have so many things to rush around doing and achieving and becoming, and yet, none of it means anything because we're all stuck on this planet, walking in circles, biding our time until we die."

Micah's discussions usually never bothered me much, but, in our friendship phase, it was quite annoying.

"Can I just enjoy my walk, in peace?"

"Heel, boy." The woman's voice had gone up an octave, but I assumed she was learning how to train her dog. I wasn't intimately familiar with obedience training, but I knew there were experts and books for that sort of thing.

Micah smiled and bumped my shoulder with his. He was thinner than the last time we'd been together. He'd also grown a goatee, which had surprised and delighted me so much when I first saw it that I'd caressed it and blurted out, "This is gorgeous," before realizing what I'd said. The compliment had made him blush.

It seemed he was again working his way up to saying something important. He stared at the ground, his glasses sliding down his nose. He pushed the lenses back up, cleared his throat, and caressed my index finger with his thumb. I waited for him to say, *When are you going to let me come over* or *When are you going to come to my place?*

But at that moment, the woman screamed. The mill-about crowd slowed and stared in the direction of her shriek.

Leash in hand, she ran toward the main road, just north of the circular path. Her blonde locks whipped about her head and one of her shoes flew off as she chased behind a medium-sized dog that came to her shins. "No!"

It was the same voice that had previously said, "Sit, boy," and "Heel, boy," only this time she sounded frightened. "Stop!"

Brakes screeched, a car slammed into another, and the woman yelled, "Buster!"

Micah tugged me away, but I released his hand and moved forward in the direction of the woman who'd stepped in front of the stopped cars, and, when I was closer, I saw blood.

Shivering, I turned to Micah's embrace. No, I wasn't a pet person, but that was because I had too much respect to impose my will on a being that should be free. I ate a plant-based diet, and avoided animal products like leather. I never visited zoos nor aquariums, and when I was a teenager, I let a bird out of its cage at a neighbor's house. Got in trouble for that one, but I didn't care. Parrots should be free.

As we walked away, I glanced over my shoulder where the woman dropped to her knees and wailed. It felt as if the sound vibrated inside of me. And my mind immediately went to Mr. Vishtali and Douglas, the moment when the dog rose on its hind legs and snapped.

The parking lot at the assisted living home where I organized activities and coordinated mealtimes for seniors became littered with missing dog flyers, some large, others small, and with varying display techniques—tacked up on telephone poles, taped to doors, and thrust under wiper blades on car windshields.

Entire windows were plastered with the signs. Some light poles held up flyers of four or five family dogs. Poodle, Pomeranian, Pekingese, and pug. No one knew where they'd gone, but the nights were filled with distant howls that lasted for hours. It was as if there was a dog convention out yonder and humans couldn't find it.

The dogs who remained with their owners grew isolated and anti-social. Folks who were used to their pooch climbing in bed with them noticed their dog would find a corner in a room all to itself and sleep there instead. Their pets no longer rose and greeted them at the door when they entered. The dogs were fine physically, eating heartily, with regular digestive systems, ran when they were outside, and interacted with one another as usual—playing, cuddling, fighting to maintain rank. They just seemed uninterested in the humans who filled their lives.

A black and rust Doberman pinscher showed up on my porch one morning and stared at me through the picture window. Eating a banana nut muffin and sipping coffee in my kitchen, I felt the dog's gaze on me before I noticed it was there. And when we locked eyes, I dropped the muffin and the mug. The shards scattered across the tile; one swiped my ankle and drew blood. When I searched the window again, the Doberman was gone.

A month later, I saw a news article about dogs dying from an odd illness in which they no longer rose to eat and play each day until eventually they just stopped breathing. Vets performed autopsies and sent samples to labs, and that's how the microbe was discovered.

Social media was filled with teary-eyed owners posting about their dead "fur babies." Some folks held doggie funerals, and others decided to make video tributes to their pups ahead of their demise. The dogs that had run away all seemed fine.

Micah and I joked that the dogs had probably developed an allergy to humans. The night-howling grew in volume, and sounded closer than what I remembered in the beginning.

Then, one evening, the residents at my job were having a Cutest Dog contest, in which they dressed up their pets in doggie gowns and tiaras and made them model down the dog run for bone-shaped biscuits. Though I'd been asked, I refused to judge the pageant and had to restrain myself from stripping off the dog's garments, opening the iron entry gates, and setting them loose.

As I cleared up morsels of beef treats, ruffled puppy boas, and squeaky rubber ball toys from the activity lounge, Mrs. Petroski nodded off in the corner but woke when she heard the distant animal calls. She rose from the rocking chair with creaking bones and an unsteady gait and attempted to hurry down the hall to her apartment.

"Everything okay, Mrs. Petroski?" I followed her. It wasn't like her to move about so quickly, and this was the most I'd seen her walk without her cane in the four years I'd worked at New Adventures Assisted Living.

"He'll scratch a hole in the wood if I don't let him out." She unlocked her apartment, and her golden retriever Henry leapt out of the front door, throwing the woman off balance, and knocking her to the ground. Henry dashed down the hallway, and, when he came to the glass double doors that led to the parking lot, he raised on his hind legs and used his front paws to push the metal bar to open them.

I rushed to Mrs. Petroski, who'd landed on her bottom hard enough to dislodge her dentures and send her wig flying to the carpet. I helped her up and into her unit. Luckily, she was uninjured. But her hands trembled.

"Whenever he hears the others, he goes crazy. It's not like he's never heard howls before. But with this, it's like they're calling him."

"Who?"

"The pack."

"Does he usually come right back?" I eased her onto the couch and grabbed her a glass of water. She shook her head, handed the glass back to me, and pointed to a bottle of cognac on her counter.

"Get two glasses." She wrung her hands as I poured shots for both of us.

"Since it all started, every night Henry raises his head at the sound, stares at the window, and then, instead of howling back like a sensible mutt, he scratches at the door until I wake up and let him out. Then, hours later, as I get myself to the bathroom for my nighttime routine, get the linens ready, and am just about to climb in bed, he's back scratching at the door."

"What do you think he does out there?"

"I don't know. But one time he returned with blood on him. I searched his fur from head to toe but didn't find any cuts. Isn't this all so strange, dear?"

Henry did not come back that evening.

Two days later, The Turn occurred.

—

The phrase came from folks long ago warning of old, cranky dogs who would "turn" on their owners and perhaps take a bite out of a hand that got too close to its bowl. The term was cautionary, but no one predicted what the phenomenon would come to mean.

Early one morning as commuters drove to work, dogs lined up shoulder to shoulder on the sidewalk, thousands deep, and stared at the vehicles as they passed. The animals didn't bare their teeth. They simply glared, and it didn't matter how tiny or large, young or old they were, they all turned on the same day.

Micah and I noticed several walls of dogs along the roads as we returned from dinner that evening. Puddles from the rain earlier in the day dotted the desolate sidewalk where nary a neighbor was in sight.

"Where is everyone?" The lights were off in all the homes, and I stared at Mr. Vishtali's, where the curtains were drawn on his lightless windows. I texted him: *Everything okay?*

"Whose dog is that?" Micah pointed ahead.

The Doberman was back on my porch, with its long muzzle, muscular physique, and shiny coat. It watched us as we pulled into my driveway, as if it were the real owner of my home and we were visitors.

I told Micah about the morning the black and rust dog showed up, how I broke my coffee mug. "No clue where it came from. It does remind me of that dog I fed last year near work."

"The one that was all thin and bruised?"

I nodded. "I figured it stopped coming around because it was better."

Moonlight glowed on the dog's face. It snarled, revealing blood on its teeth.

"You have your pepper spray?" The car ticked and hummed as it downshifted to *park* and turned off. Micah removed his seat belt and gripped his keys between his fingers. His makeshift weapon sent a jolt through my chest. With fingers that felt thick and uncoordinated, I reached into my work bag and retrieved the can of Mace attached to my keychain.

Micah got out first, escorted me inside the house, his keys and my spray held in front of us for protection.

The Doberman did not turn its head as we bypassed the porch and entered through the back door, but the dog's eyes followed us.

Too frightened to risk a dash to his vehicle, Micah suggested he stay overnight. I let him. He sat in the bedroom window staring down at the porch until the Doberman was gone, which wasn't until two a.m.

When he finally came to bed, we made love until sun-up, our movements frantic, because without actually saying it, we both seemed to sense we were running out of time.

After, wrapped in each other's arms, he finally shared what he'd been working up to say.

"I'm committed to you. To us."

Every discordant moment from the previous three years melted, as we were finally together, officially. I had what I'd been wanting and wouldn't let it slip away.

"So am I."

In the morning, when we shared a banana nut muffin and sipped cups of coffee, the Doberman returned and eyed us from the porch.

Noticing the creature, Micah sprang from his chair, knocking down the seat, where it crashed with a thwack. His bare feet pounded along the oak floors, and he went to the picture window, slapping his open palm against the glass.

"You want something to stare at?" With muffin crumbs in his goatee, he grabbed the longest umbrella from the stand, scattering the smaller ones across the foyer. When he threw open the front door, gripping the curved handle like a baseball bat, the Doberman padded to the curb.

"Stay off this damned porch!" Micah raised the umbrella above his head and screamed, the noise sounding an awful lot like a growl.

I moved to Micah's rear, made eye contact with the Doberman, placed a calming hand on Micah's shoulder, and took the makeshift weapon from him. After a two-minute stare-down, the Doberman seemed bored and strode off down the street.

Mr. Vishtali never responded to my text.

—

Animal control attempted to corral the dogs, but were only successful nabbing a few. The animals didn't fight. They either surrendered or ran away. Someone shot video of one of these round-ups, and, watching it online, I must say, it seemed like a coordinated canine uprising.

This went on for a few weeks more. Micah moved in, our lovemaking became more frequent and frenzied—on the shower floor, against the dryer, across the ottoman, behind the kitchen island—and ended with promises of "forever" and "always."

The Turn was the only thing discussed on TV. Many folks said they hadn't given their dogs the recalled gourmet treats blamed for the microbe. But experts said it was likely the infected dogs had passed along the germ to the healthy ones.

It was hard to know who to believe, but that final conclusion didn't sound right to me. That was an awful lot of dogs to become infected so quickly. The disease, which they'd dubbed Hound Disease, sounded quite sophisticated, made the dogs seem menacing, and had become pervasive.

Then, one day at work, while walking down the hall where Mrs. Petroski lived, I realized "menacing" was a gross understatement. The corridor was lit by fluorescents with that greenish hospital feel that let everyone know the occupants were not young. When my footfalls echoed off the walls, it occurred to me that the senior home was desolate like my street.

Mrs. Petroski slowly opened her door and peeked one eye out.

"Look at this." She pointed a crooked finger at grooves snaking up and down the wood, gashes that seemed to have been carved into her door with thick knife blades.

"What happened?" I wondered whether Mrs. Petroski had any enemies. It was one thing to key a car. It was another to hack up someone's front door.

"Henry." She glanced over her shoulder toward her living room, where the muted television played a news report about The Turn. I noticed a bruise on her collarbone. "Henry is not himself." She whispered this, as if her dog were standing just behind her, listening.

Mr. Vishtali did not answer my phone calls nor early morning knocks at his door.

Micah went home for more clothes, said he'd grab groceries, and return for dinner. We decided to work from home the rest of the week. Our friends thought we were overreacting, but after my conversation with Mrs. Petroski, I wasn't taking any chances.

Micah and I also hadn't discussed it, but I was afraid of the Doberman's eye contact. Once the creature focused on me, it never let up. It felt personal, as if the dog had made a decision about me and was biding its time to act.

Dinner came and went with no Micah. I called. Texted. At dusk, I turned off all my lights, and, even though it was dark outside, the fullness of the nighttime let me know something was wrong. No street light poured into the windows the way it typically did. The digital clock on my wall bore a blank display, and when I removed my cell phone from the charger again to call him once more, the device was almost dead.

At midnight, my anxiety turned to panic. I threw on jeans and a t-shirt in a hurry, planning to sneak out the back door, get in my car, and search for him, but just as I was tying my sneakers, he turned his key in the door.

I tripped over the loose laces as I ran to him, tossed my arms around his neck, and peppered his cheeks with kisses. I was relieved he was okay, but also, I didn't feel as frightened with him by my side.

Micah talked hurriedly, as if he were continuing a conversation with me.

"We have to leave." He took the stairs two at a time, pulling me by the hand as he mounted the steps. "Grab some clothes. Your computer. Whatever you can get quickly. Power's out. Folks are getting attacked everywhere."

I did as he said, knowing without asking that the dogs were

attacking humans. I grabbed my work bag, cell phone, charger, and my gym bag, which held extra clothes and toiletries. Hand in hand, we raced back down the stairs and outside where his car waited in my driveway.

The night was calm. No sound. And the moon was not shining as brightly as it had even hours before, so I was moving around based on memory and the light from Micah's phone.

"Where are we going?"

"Safe zones. Near the ocean. Folks with guns have been able to keep the dogs at bay." He was out of breath and pulling me toward his car. I noticed he didn't unlock the doors using the remote on his keychain, rather opened each one quietly with a soundless smart touch. Of all the things he did since arriving that evening, the way he whispered and avoided making noise was the thing that frightened me the most. "They set up at the ocean because infected dogs don't like water."

A scream cut through the night. My eyes followed the sound to the house next door.

"Mr. Vishtali." My whisper was gobbled up by another scream.

There was a moment in which he looked at me as if to say, *we can't,* but Micah also knew me well enough to plant a kiss on my lips, turn toward my neighbor's house, and rush up the front porch beside me. With every ounce of life, I wish I could have that moment back, to make a different decision.

I could tell by the blood trailing from the front door through the foyer that Mr. Vishtali probably didn't survive the attack, but, with our feeble weapons of pepper spray and keys, we pressed on because I had to be sure before leaving.

Mr. Vishtali's face was visible, eyes staring at the ceiling, mouth frozen in a silent scream, blood splattered across his cheeks. His stomach was ripped open, and I covered the light on Micah's phone to shield myself from seeing more. The room smelled of dry dog food, and my sneaker crunched something hard as I backed up to the door.

The noise must have scared Micah because he flashed his light over Mr. Vishtali again, and I saw Douglas's empty stainless steel feeding bowls.

A growl came from the corner behind Micah, and when he whipped his phone in the direction of the noise, he slipped, his sneakers squeaking as if he were sliding across liquid.

The light shot up to the ceiling, and I realized the growl wasn't beside us, rather above us, as Douglas pounced on Micah from a high perch covered in shadow.

Micah screamed; the light on his phone snapped off. I accidentally dropped the pepper spray and reached for a nearby bookcase to arm myself with something. Anything.

My hand came into contact with a heavy lamp. I gripped it, ran toward where Micah struggled with Douglas, and realized Micah was no longer screaming.

I couldn't see. Not even my hand in front of me. But I heard Douglas eating, the squelch of bloody flesh and muscle, the gnashing of its teeth, and huffs as it chewed, swallowed, and digested.

I brought the light fixture down on the area closest to the noise. My hand brushed against warm fur, and I continued to beat that fur until the beast whimpered and eventually stopped making sound.

I didn't even have a chance to check on Micah because claws scratched at the door, and it flew open, letting in pale moonlight. In the shadow between the porch and the living space stood a gang of a dozen or so dogs, growling at me.

I knew enough about dogs to know running away would incite a chase, but I also knew if I remained in place I'd end up like Mr.

Vishtali and Micah.

I ran.

Unfamiliar with Mr. Vishtali's house, I sprinted toward where I thought his back door would be. Behind me, high-pitched barks rang out, and nails scraped against the wooden floor as the gang of animals rushed through the house after me.

The back door was locked, but a stairwell to the left opened to a lower level. Our block was the few in the county that had basements, and I was grateful for this fact. I took those steps two at a time, and lost my balance at the bottom, plummeting forward into a door that flew open.

My head hitting the plywood wall broke my fall. I immediately turned to close the door and found the Doberman in front of the pack of animals, lunging at them, snarling, barking, tearing into their flesh until one of them whimpered. I slammed the wood, found a latch and deadbolt, realizing with growing fear that the Doberman had saved me.

The barks were frantic. Their bodies slammed against the wood. As they scraped and banged into the door, I took in the room behind me, where the only light came from a lone window near the ceiling.

A washer and dryer, a refrigerator, a shelf of books, and a couch with a television across from it filled the space. I set down my bags, unaware I had arrived in my prison.

I knelt on all fours, my body convulsing, tears and snot spilling from my face onto the cold cement floor. I remembered Micah's hand in mine, his lips on my flesh, our deep brown legs entwined. I should have gone with him to safety. When I saw the look on his face, the *we can't* he was too good-hearted to utter, I should have gotten in the blasted car and driven to the ocean with him.

My cell phone rang, and the dogs at the door stopped barking as if they were listening. I carried the device to the window and held it up to increase my reception. I had three bars, and my battery was at four percent. I answered and Mrs. Petroski was on the other end, crying.

"We're overrun with dogs. Police say they're sending someone, but they still haven't. I'm afraid the beasts are going to get in."

"Do you have a weapon?" I listened for the dogs outside the basement door behind me and they had grown silent.

"No. Can you come and help me? I'm so scared. My heart can't take this."

"I'm in the same bind."

I couldn't risk leaving. I'd already made one mistake and Micah had paid the price.

"Oh, wait, dear. I think I hear Henry."

"No." I remembered the grooves scratched into her door. "Henry won't be the same, Mrs. Petroski."

"But what if these dogs are hurting him? He's whining for me to let him in."

Picturing Mr. Vishtali's body upstairs and the squelching sounds of Douglas attacking Micah, I said, "Mrs. Petroski, listen to me. Do not let Henry in."

"But, he's my baby. I couldn't live with myself if I didn't at least check on him."

I heard shuffling that sounded like her house slippers scooting across the floor. "You can't. He'll kill you!"

A creaking noise rose through the phone, she screamed, and the line went dead. I sat on the floor as I dialed her back. She never picked up again. My screen lit up, and the word *Goodbye* flashed three times before the phone died.

That was ten days ago.

The refrigerator had been stocked for three.

I rationed wheat bread, deli turkey slices, and cheddar cheese as long as I could. The bathroom has running water, and there's a crank radio that also charges cell phones. I've been doing a lot of cranking.

The electricity has been spotty and remains off at night. Calls to 911 go unanswered. I have phoned every telephone number in my contacts list, and have yet to reach someone. I am so hungry and fear I will starve.

The first time the electricity blinked on, I snapped on the television. It remained powered up just long enough for me to hear the correspondent say The Turn was global. The next time it came on, there were no newscasts. No nothing.

I am writing this message in case humans don't stop this. I want whoever is here in the future to know what happened. The only conclusion I can draw is that, like I always suspected, the dogs no longer wanted to be pets.

This morning the Doberman arrived at the basement window. It used its paw to knock on the glass, and, when it had my attention, it backed up and dipped its muzzle toward two shiny objects. I pulled a chair to the wall, stood on it, and opened the window to get a better view.

The fresh air was cool on my face, and I imagined what it would've been like if Micah and I had gone to the ocean.

The Doberman backed up farther as I reached a trembling hand out the window where two stainless steel bowls rested on the ground. Douglas's bowls.

I pulled the dual objects close to my face so I could peer inside. The one on the left was filled with mashed-up banana nut muffin and a sniff of the bowl on the right let me know it contained coffee.

When my eyes met the Doberman's, the dog turned and headed back out of Mr. Vishtali's yard. Just before it exited the gate, it glanced at me over its shoulder before slinking off to freedom.

UNSHOD, CACKLING, AND NAKED

I gobbled up the muffin. Gulped down the coffee. My stomach cramped, but I was relieved to have food in my body again.

I grabbed a pen and began this note. I pray the ones who made it to the ocean are holding their ground. That we are mounting a counterattack with plans to restore order to the planet.

Night is falling. The howls have begun. I wish I could say I hear rescue sirens, but the electronic screams in the distance are car and home alarms, sounding our civilization's death cry. I just heard another knock at the glass pane, and, when I glanced outside the window, I found two fresh bowls waiting for me.

June 28, 2028
L. Reynolds
Valencia, California

Bridget Has Disappeared

If I begin by telling you I don't know where my wife is, that her disappearance has brought me as much consternation as it has anyone, then it will color everything I say. So, I won't begin that way.

I will simply say I met Bridget by chance when I visited my neighborhood bookstore and heard a brash woman arguing with one of the booksellers.

"I show up every time expecting something good and it's always the same—H.P. Lovecraft. Stephen King. Anne Rice."

I peered out from the non-fiction section, past the autograph line for the author reading, and saw the bespectacled bookseller, who spoke at a volume more like a rational adult, nodding obsequiously, almost bowing. But a shelf blocked my view of the woman.

Then she said, "'African American' isn't a genre. To find a horror book by a black writer, I have to leave the horror section and schlep to the African American section. Why are you segregating books?"

I could no longer listen to the woman's tirade without also seeing her. I left the non-fiction section, sans book, and one look at her made me forget I was in a bookstore.

Her crown of curls jutted toward the ceiling's track lights. She wore a black mini-skirt above long, slender legs, and a red cashmere sweater that fit like latex. A scar on her chin, a thin semicircle of deep brown, seemed to call out to me.

It was luck she didn't notice me. Gave me more time to gape at the copy of Octavia Butler's *Parable of the Talents* she was holding.

"I wouldn't really call her a horror writer."

She leveled her cypress brown eyes at me then glanced at Butler's book as if she'd forgotten what title she was palming. "I know. I just picked this up from the—."

"If you're looking for some good horror, check out Tananarive Due. Her African Immortals Ser—"

"Thanks for eavesdropping on my conversation." With manicured nails on a left hand that did not sport a ring, she tugged her diamond-studded earlobe.

"Eavesdropping?" I stepped toward her. "Everybody and their mama can hear you. You don't have to talk that loud, you know. We're not in the projects."

The bookseller, who'd moved on to restocking shelves, glanced over his glasses at me and shot me a warning look, likely because he was white and I'd told the kind of joke that could only be uttered by one black person to another without offense. He probably thought I was rude. She laughed. I was hooked. I'd never been chemically drawn to a person before this.

"Okay, smart ass. You see anything in this aisle by Tananarive Due?"

I swaggered to the horror shelf, uncomfortably conscious of how her head came to my bottom lip, how the tip of her chin sent waves through me. I. Wanted. Her. She smelled of cinnamon, and when I caught her scent, I realized I needed her too.

Scanning the authors whose last name began with D, I said, "Hmmm. She must be in the African American books section."

She laughed again, her cheeks reddening that time. "Ya think?"

We fell into a grinning stare-down. How do you tell a woman who is a strange mix of beauty queen, hipster, and bookworm, that although you are an odd cross between basketball player and journalist, the two of you will be married in a year, no matter what baggage she comes with?

You don't. You just say, "My name is Yusef. Let me read you a passage from *Parable of the Talents* at my favorite wine bar."

Three days later, she sub-leased her suburban Michigan studio apartment and moved into my one bedroom in Medford. It was a year before the first disappearance.

———

To clarify, the first disappearance I *noticed* occurred the Wednesday before our wedding. I'd just returned from work, and, upon entering our apartment, I heard Bridget drawing a bath and humming *Ease On Down the Road*. I tapped on the bathroom door. She cracked it open and poked her lips out like a fish.

"I have champagne," I said, savoring her lips on mine, her fingers tugging my beard and tracing my mustache, her kisses melting my tension.

My thumb traced the scar on her chin. I'd asked her once how she'd gotten it and she'd said it was part of her "initiation," and when I'd asked, "into what?" she'd demurred. She'd been drunk, giggly, so I'd let it go. She knew everything about me. I knew so little about her. The mysteries intensified my attraction but should have served as a warning.

"Why don't you let me inside?" I whispered, meaning both the bathroom and her.

"Bath first." She grinned and pecked my cheek. "Shouldn't take long."

She shut the door on me, but I could still smell the cinnamon from her cigarette. She smoked, and I didn't care. I'd lost my grandfather to lung cancer; I gave anyone who smoked around me a speech about the pain he suffered at the end. I'd been known to leave parties, dates, and had even thrown people out of my home for smoking. But not with Bridget.

She had one cinnamon-scented smoke each day, and she told

me the narrow, brown tube was harmless, was more like a flavored hookah. And I bought her an ashtray because obviously she and her aroma had taken over my brain. I assumed my acquiescence meant I was experiencing deep, inescapable love, the kind that weakens resolve.

In the kitchen, I popped open the champagne bottle and listened to the drip, splash, drip, and then silence as she entered the water. I wanted to join her in there, but instead, I cooked. Imagining her plump thighs wrapped around my waist, I got excited for the night ahead.

After twenty minutes of stillness coming from the bathroom, I finally said, "The food is cooling off, and so am I." I chuckled.

Silence.

With a scoop of rice on the serving spoon in my right hand, I stopped and listened. The neighbor's dog barked. A television from down the hall blared out a car commercial. The vent above me hissed as air passed through.

"Everything okay?"

Nothing from the bathroom. No splashing. No voice. No dripping.

I placed the utensil on the counter and tiptoed across our carpet to the bathroom door, wanting to be certain she hadn't fallen asleep. I imagined her leaning against the back of the tub, her head on the tile, her mouth open, and perhaps startling awake when I knocked. I rapped on the door. "Bridget?"

The door moaned open. Steam poured out, moistening my face and neck. I scanned the mirror above the sink, expecting to see the image of Bridget curled in a ball in the water. What I saw was a tub full of water and no Bridget.

Inside the bathroom, the scent of cinnamon enveloped me just as it did whenever I took her in my arms. Her robe hung on the back of the door, untouched. A new razor sat in her jeweled soap dish, unused.

I shook the shower curtain, as if she were somehow wrapped in it. I knelt and dipped my hand in the lukewarm water. I considered pulling the stopper and draining the basin, but changed my mind, as if emptying the tub was acceptance that she'd disappeared. I examined the water. Where were the soap suds and shavings?

An imprint of her foot remained in the slippers next to the tub. For a second, I slipped my feet inside. The house shoes were warm but dry.

She wasn't resting in our bedroom across the hall. She wasn't sitting in one of our side-by-side rocking chairs on the balcony. I didn't find her reclining on the black leather couch in the living room, wrapped in her chenille blanket. All of our windows were closed, locked, and were so rickety, had she opened them, they would have announced their movement to the entire apartment complex. She was nowhere. And when two people live in an eight hundred square-foot, one-bedroom apartment, it's obvious to one when the other is gone.

Uncertain what to do, I planted myself on the couch, stroked the blanket, and dialed her phone. My knees jerked up and down. My heart pumped so hard I felt it in my throat. I didn't expect an answer, but, at the time, calling her seemed logical. The phone vibrated in her handbag which hung on the back of the dining room chair, and her voicemail answered. *You've reached Bridget's phone. Leave a message. Or do like everyone else—hang up and send me a text. Either way, I'll holla. Peace.*

I didn't leave a message. What was there to say? *Hey. You mysteriously vanished. Call me.* So, I sat there, staring at the blank television screen, my knees still jumping up and down. The clock atop the TV said nine forty-five. I told myself if I didn't hear from her by midnight, I'd panic. Why midnight? Because passing into a new day with her still missing seemed ominous. In the meantime, I'd wait in our living room, with my cell phone set to vibrate in my hand in case she called. From where?

I was not religious. Spiritual, mostly, but didn't believe in ghosts, aliens, or anything remotely paranormal. I was a journalist, who dealt in facts, data, spreadsheets. I didn't know what to think about where she went, but I blamed her. I thought of the scar, the origins of which she kept hidden. It wasn't that I thought her scar was related to her disappearance, but it certainly was a sign that, as intimate as our relationship was, there were parts of her I might never know.

After an hour of intense fidgeting, I became exhausted and fell asleep.

The sound of the spoon scraping the plate woke me. I opened my eyes, and there was Bridget, barefoot, in her bathrobe, with water dripping from her hair to her delicate neck, with her cinnamon-flavored cigarette in one hand, a tablespoon in the other, serving herself from the food I'd cooked. The clock now said eleven thirty-seven p.m.

"Where the hell were you?" I stumbled to the kitchen, snatched the spoon from her, set it on the counter before her, took the cigarette from her, and placed it in that ash tray I'd bought for her. With the sting of tears in my eyes, I squeezed her face between my hands, pulled her to me, kissed her mouth, her cheeks, and eyebrows before she could answer. I tipped back her head and kissed the scar on her chin. Relief loosened the muscles in my neck and shoulders. She was real.

"In the tub." She smiled with both her mouth and eyes, but a question formed on her eyebrows.

"No, you weren't." I peppered my words into her face. "I looked for you all over the apartment. I didn't see you." I didn't mean to shake her face with every word.

She peeled away my palms and stepped back. "You must have been dreaming."

"I wasn't dreaming. I was cooking."

I took her left hand—the one sporting the flawless, round solitaire that cost all five years of my savings—and shoved it in the middle of the rice. "Feel! The food is cold."

Her eyes wide, she removed her hand and licked the flakes from her fingers.

"Sef. Chill."

"Chill? It's been almost two hours!"

"It was a long bath."

"I want the truth."

"You're scaring me."

"*I'm* scaring *you*?" I realized I was screaming.

We stared at each other, my breathing erratic. She placed her hands over her mouth and diamond-shaped tears appeared in the corners of her eyes. I'd never seen her cry and knew, if she did, I'd say or do whatever I needed to make her stop.

It was unlike any argument I'd had. I could deal with "you're always working," or "you never pay attention to me," like with my ex, Shari. I didn't know how to deal with "you went missing for a couple of hours from our window-less bathroom." How could this be happening?

Look. No woman is perfect. From that first whirlwind of a night, I figured she'd have a flaw, but I imagined it'd be something I could handle—too flirty with my friends, or too controlling, or irresponsible with money. She was none of that. She was perfect for *me*. Except, now, perhaps not.

Suddenly, I couldn't believe I'd moved in with her so quickly, proposed to her so quickly, spent all my money on her...so quickly. I loved her laugh, her quick wit, the way she lived in the moment and didn't fret about the past or future, but what was her story? Her real story?

One of those diamond tears fell, and I couldn't look at her any longer.

"Forget it."

I went to bed and lay in the dark, staring out the window. Orange headlights slid from right to left, as cars made their way down our busy street. Maybe she was right. Maybe it was me. Maybe I really had fallen asleep and dreamt it all. I had been pretty stressed at work and about the cost of our wedding.

When she got into bed, she pressed her nude body against my clothed one. She spooned me, lifting my t-shirt and placing a clammy hand on my stomach. Her skin felt warm and supple but with the sweat evaporating from her body, leaving her cool and damp. Is it possible to be warm and cool at the same time? I always loved that sensation, except for this night, when I knew she'd not taken that bath.

"I feel like you're angry with me." Her breath caressed my neck, giving me a chill and making me firm.

"I'm not," I said without turning toward her. But I *was* angry. It was a bizarre, unjustified anger that created silences and voids, that had the potential to reveal too much of how I felt when I didn't know how I felt at all.

We fell asleep that way. And that was the first night in the year I'd known her that we did not make love.

—

We married, with only our parents in attendance—at Bridget's request—on a day in which the sky was the most awesome shade of blue I'd ever seen. My parents made toasts to her, bought her a platinum bracelet, and my mom kept saying, "What an exquisite bride!"

Her parents, on the other hand, were as mysterious as she. Quiet. Never holding my gaze. Reserved in their answers. They annoyed her, she'd said. When she a) never lived up to their class standards, b) further snubbed them by becoming a public relations specialist at a university science lab, and c) married a nearly broke journalist, their relationship became d) "strained." Well, that's the story she gave me, anyway.

We bought a home, though not in the neighborhood we wanted. Economists were calling the housing market a "mega-bubble." Only the uber-wealthy could own in a city where jobs were. Everyone else rented or bought in a semi-rural neighborhood with long commute times, and needed parental support for even that. We were no different. It was stressful for me because we spent every paycheck we earned on survival—house, cars, groceries, gas.

A month into our new homeownership, our neighbor from down the road was shot to death in his house. We told ourselves he must have done something wrong like sold drugs or maybe it was a domestic dispute. I bought a gun. We ordered bullets online, but those were backordered. The world seemed to be changing rapidly. Declining actually. I considered myself lucky to have found the love of my life.

We had a son. Bridget glowed, as if having this child was exactly the thing she'd always been waiting for. The months after his birth were the happiest of my life. She'd done everything I'd asked since having him. She never smoked when she was pregnant. She had her cigarette outside at night when Ethan was asleep and her smoke couldn't get to him. She made sure I gave him a bottle for the hours after. She reassured me there was no nicotine or tobacco. Flavored water only. "Just calms me," she said. "Helps with the anxiety." And I *believed* her. We laughed. She didn't disappear. I felt so connected to her.

But as Ethan grew, she stayed inside more to nurse. "He hates the nursing cover," she'd say through tears. "Sometimes I think he hates me."

It was true our boy had a brooding spirit. He cooed and smiled sparingly, babbled often, and though he checked all the developmental boxes at the pediatrician's office, he also stared at people with menacing eyes, informed by an entire galaxy of knowledge and anger.

"Old soul," Bridget's parents called him, but from the first time I held him, I shivered peering into his black pupils, and knew "old soul" was an understatement. The feeling passed though, and I considered it new father nerves.

Then one day Bridget missed a series of my texts and it opened a chasm in our relationship I was never able to close. Panicked, I rushed home from work, and, by then, getting home in the middle of the day was no easy feat. The price of gasoline was well over twelve dollars a gallon, and the electric grids could no longer allow electric vehicle recharging, so only multimillionaires had cars. I'd started taking the train, which tripled my commute time, since everyone else did so as well. By the time I got home, I was exhausted, cranky, and checking for my wallet, relieved I still had it, with the pickpockets essentially owning the stations. It was neither my finest hour nor my finest day. We argued.

"We can't do this anymore." The words fell from my mouth sounding more final than what I'd intended, and I wasn't sure what "this" I was referring to.

"Come again?" A long curl fell onto her forehead. She tucked it behind her ear. Even in the midst of our disagreement, that dainty gesture still elicited a throb in my pants.

"I mean, we need to talk about the—the—you know."

"The what?" Her breasts were thick with milk. Amid my anger, I still longed to touch them, wished we could go back to simpler times, when I could hold her for hours just breathing her in, fully trusting her.

"Stop it, Bridget. I have Ethan to think about now."

Silence from her. Water bubbled in a pot on the stove. The smell of marinara sauce flowed from the kitchen.

And she almost told me. With Ethan still in her arms, she stared at me. A softening. I noticed the scar on her chin had darkened at some point and seemed to be raised from her skin higher than usual. I wanted to kiss it too and try one more time to get her to tell me about its origins, but our emotional distance made me feel I no longer had access to her body. And I'd never had much access to her past. Did I really love her if I didn't know her? Who was it that I was loving every day when she was such an enigma still? Thinking maybe I only loved the idea of her, I reached for her, to close the space between us.

"Bridget, it's all right."

But, for reasons I thought I'd never know, the resolve crept back into her expression, and she retreated.

Ethan buried his face in her neck. We hadn't raised our voices, but as her complexion turned red, his did as well. With our son clinging to her chest, she went into the bedroom, our bedroom, and slammed the door.

―

I should have been savoring the relentless nature of her red lip gloss, that even the dishwasher's power setting couldn't dissolve as it remained smudged on the rims of our glasses. I should have been admiring the way she sat at the foot of our bed with her pinky pointed toward the ceiling as she painted vermillion polish onto her nails, or how when she noticed something funny or interesting in the news, she'd read me the entire article start to finish, word-for-word.

Instead, I asked her the questions I should have put to her from that first day at the bookstore. Lying in bed one morning, I caressed her face, and brought up that scar.

"Fell off the monkey bars in first grade," she said. "Three stitches."

I won't lie. I often have a hard time turning off my journalist brain, but the answer differed from the one about "initiation" she'd given when she'd been inebriated. This new version, spoken in the morning light while sober, was too quick and convenient. If she really fell from a play structure, the front of her chin seemed an odd place for a scar. Maybe she'd have a gash on her knees or even her forehead if she bumped into someone underneath her on the way down. But her chin? And the mark was deep. If she'd told me someone had aimed for her mouth with a knife and missed, I would've believed her.

I probed her mother. The next day, Bridget's parents arrived as usual, their arms stuffed with trinkets, and they spent hours cradling Ethan, kissing his cheeks and nose, dressing him in the onesies and booties they'd bought for him, and shaking the rattles, stuffed bunnies, and plastic keys they'd packed in their grandparents' tote. When Bridget's mother was alone, I nonchalantly asked about the scar.

"You know, Bridget has always been so clumsy," she said while scooping Ethan's squeaking ducks from the floor and depositing them onto our shelves.

I hadn't known Bridget to be clumsy at all, quite the opposite, but I needed this information so I played along.

"Yeah. So clumsy." I forced a chuckle as I folded knit blankets.

"But it's such a deep scar. To get that deep, it would need to be a serious accident…or deliberate?"

She averted her eyes. "It was so silly, really, I'm surprised she hasn't told you already. She…fell out of the boat when we went fishing. Her chin clipped the edge as she went down. I'd told her thousands of times, 'too slippery to stand in the boat.' She learned her lesson after that one."

So, they were both lying.

I concluded Bridget's drunken answer had been the truthful one—an initiation.

At that point, I did the only reasonable thing I could think of. I recorded her. One night when she rose from bed and went out front to our porch swing, I pointed my phone's camera toward her from the living room window, and, sure enough, I captured her disappearing.

For five minutes the video shakes due to my trembling hand, and my sobs are audible. You'd think after searching for answers, I'd have been relieved upon vindication, but that wasn't the case. I thought I'd vomit, but I managed to compose myself long enough to tape her returning.

I showed it to her the next morning. She shouted at me, accused me of doctoring the video to prove my irrational point. She threatened to leave if I didn't drop this nonsense. Told me I needed to get my head checked.

For an entire day I questioned my own mental health. Her vehemence made me wonder whether I hadn't made up the entire thing out of some self-sabotaging need for an imperfect relationship. I never mentioned the recording to her again, because being without her was the worst possible outcome for me. But that didn't stop me from searching for answers. And, if I'm honest, a solution. I had to figure out how to make her stay.

From then on, every night after she fell asleep, I'd stay up a couple extra hours just watching her. And it paid off, sort of. One night, she started whispering in her sleep. I rested my head on her pillow right next to her lips, and when the warm air floated from her mouth to my ear, so did the words, "Force projection."

"No clue," she said, when I asked her about the phrase the next morning, but the way she abruptly changed the subject told me there was something more.

I bought nanny cams—one each for the nursery, living room, the dining room facing Ethan's highchair—and I monitored Bridget and Ethan from my desk at work. As she traveled about the house, I used the remote on my computer to move the camera along with her. I even added a doorbell camera so I could know when they left.

"Control freak," she called me during one particularly nasty argument, but I reiterated that we had a son, and I was doing this to make sure he was protected. After all, she was the one who didn't want a nanny or full-time help from her mom.

The monitor app netted me two more clips—in one she's asleep, disappears, and the sheets flatten out to prove it, and in the other she's reading in the living room, sets down her book on the coffee table, disappears, comes back twenty minutes later, and picks up the text and continues reading. She seems unperturbed upon return, as if no time has passed for her. Both times I was home with Ethan in other parts of the house. Not once did she disappear when she was alone with Ethan.

She refused to watch the monitor clips.

The thunderclap for me occurred one night after we'd left the queue. Crops were damaged either by droughts or freezes in places that didn't used to have droughts or freezes. There was a food shortage, and bandits held up the supply chains. We were lucky to make off that night with milk, bread, potatoes, cans of beans, rice, and frozen broccoli. No stores had meat anymore, and we didn't even try for it.

Then on the two-mile walk home, a kid about nineteen or so with a skeleton tattoo and pockmarks snaking up his arms, held us up at gunpoint. He demanded my wallet, her handbag, and "any other shit you got in them pockets." As she reached to her waist pack, she blew a puff of cinnamon cigarette smoke in his face. Entranced, the kid inexplicably lowered his gun, and when he turned to walk away, Bridget seized him from behind, and, with a force I hadn't known her capable of, she disarmed and laid out the guy on his stomach with his wrists behind his back until the police arrived.

"Where'd you learn to do that?" I asked when we were back home and placing our groceries in the refrigerator.

"What?" The glow from the dim fridge light made her face seem angular and hardened.

"Restrain a man half a foot taller than you."

"Oh, you know…one of those defense classes for women." She grinned, but the smile was stiff on her lips.

"Huh," I said. "Because you looked like a cop or something."

She threw back her head and laughed a little too long and hard for me to feel comfortable with. I asked if she had any thoughts on why the guy would just lower his gun midway through robbing us, and she said, "Good question. Don't know. Opioids?"

—

At work, my stories were getting cut right after I pitched them. Half of my department had been let go due to restructuring. There was one media company left in the country, I was lucky enough to work for some tiny corner of it, and, although the conglomerate spent money like they grew it, those funds were no longer flowing to my end of the enterprise. People protested outside our offices, and someone even threw a brick through the window with a note attached—*Evil ties, corporate lies, everyone dies.* The FBI got involved in the investigation.

So, I spent my workdays trying to figure out my wife. The internet was a trove of research on unexplained disappearances. There were the ten people who'd gone missing aboard the Mary Celeste, which launched one of the world's greatest nautical mysteries; the puzzling disappearance of writer Ambrose Bierce; and, of course, Amelia Earhart. I switched my keywords to "paranormal disappearances" then to "alternative science disappearances." As my fingers typed the words into the search field, a tingle sprouted on my head and crawled down my back. I couldn't believe I was doing it. But how else could I explain what was going on with my wife?

The results numbered in the hundred-thousands. It took two weeks to comb through the links and make phone calls. I had no idea what a reputable alternative science disappearance expert was, but I quickly concluded the quacks talked about kidnappings by fairies and aliens. The reputable people were authors or researchers who collected information and data and spoke of sleep paralysis or some marginally scientific study about out-of-body experiences.

Both the nuts and the reputable researchers spoke of Udali Wardene. He was an earthquake researcher who, as a hobby, collected data on psychic predictions of major tremblers. On the side, everyone told me, he studied what he called "reappearances."

The night I reached out to Udali, I sat opposite Bridget on the couch so she couldn't see my phone screen and my ongoing research of him and his theories. He agreed to meet me the next week in the basement of his brother's church, on the outskirts of the former mining town of Wickenburg, Utah. I used a nearby journalism conference as my way to break away from work, and I monitored Bridget and Ethan from an app on my phone.

Even getting to Utah was a harrowing experience. I took a flight paid for by the conference because I was to speak on a panel, then a train from Salt Lake City, but, upon my arrival in Wickenburg, I had to walk the three miles to the place because jackers had taken over the local commuter bus, which was supposed to have been my connection. Aside from my very real fear of losing Bridget, the world was changing so rapidly that surviving each day felt like a blessing.

"I offered to meet here because I keep my research closely guarded." We shook hands, and I noticed his frail bones protruding from a gray collared shirt. We sat opposite each other at a desk in a sun-starved room. "You think your wife is having reappearances?"

He wheezed, and I hoped he had an inhaler nearby.

"I don't know enough about reappearances to know if she is." The pain locked inside my chest escaped and seemed to be hanging in the dry air above our heads. I'd never told anyone about this. Even the sources who'd led me to Udali thought I was researching a story for the paper.

"The concept can be either simple or complex." Sweat gathered on his brow as he took a sip from a teacup I hadn't previously noticed. His wheezing abated. "In its simplest form," he continued, "someone disappears and then returns, sometimes years later. A fugue state, perhaps, as people often say they have during a seizure. Does your wife suffer from seizures, Yusef?"

"No. It's not that sort of thing." The room seemed to lack air altogether now. I needed a shower. "She and I are usually both at home when it happens. And she's just not there. Then she is there again. She's never acknowledged she's been gone. I've asked her directly about it and she said she has no clue what I'm talking about. I don't know if she's telling the truth or not, but I think she is aware."

Udali moved his hand across his body, leaned forward, and let out a slight gasp.

"I see. This is the more complex type." He returned his shoulders to the leather chair back and stared at the ceiling. He closed his eyes. "Start from the beginning."

I explained how she sometimes went to our backyard, sat on the swing beneath the elm tree, but was undetectable when I looked out the kitchen window. I described how she could climb into bed in the middle of the day for a nap, but for the duration she'd be nowhere, the blankets on the bed turned down, but flat. When I finished, I felt like crying because I'd reached the one person who might understand what was happening with Bridget, but I wasn't sure he could do anything at all. I wanted to leave, but then Udali opened his eyes.

"Does she have nightmares, Yusef?"

"Yes." The rumble of a large truck traveling down the road floated in through the window. "Doesn't everyone?"

"At some point, yes. But reappearances typically occur in people who have frequent nightmares. My research leads me to believe that this…fugue state, if you will…is actually not of this planet. The victim has work of some sort that is not bound by the constraints of our time and space."

I tried to have an open mind, but that theory left me with more questions. Did she control it? Why marry and have a child? Wouldn't it make more sense to stay single so no one would find out?

"Have you ever recorded this?"

I hesitated. I'd spent so much time repressing, not sharing, being gaslit by my wife that admitting I had proof of this seemed like I was crossing a boundary—*the* boundary Bridget had set. "I have."

Udali's face contorted. He smiled. He raised an eyebrow in shock. Then he let out a nervous giggle. "In all my years of research," as if he wanted to compose himself, he was stern-faced, but wheezing again, "I've never seen a video of a reappearance."

I removed my phone from my pocket and stared at it, unsure whether I should continue.

"I will not tell anyone about your wife, Yusef."

"It's not that. It's just…" I pulled up the clip, pressed play, and handed it to Udali, who accepted it the way a priest would palm the eucharist.

He watched as Bridget sat thinking on our porch swing, held her head back to stare at the sky, and then dissolved into nothing, the seat floating as if a ghost were riding it.

Udali brought his hand to his mouth. I thought it was to stifle a cough, but quickly realized he was choked up. "I can't believe…"

I sensed he felt relieved to have proof of something he'd spent so much of his life trying to get a handle on. It's a bit how I felt when I recorded the video.

He peered into my phone as the swing came to rest, and then in another blink, Bridget reappeared as if she'd never left the seat, her head still facing the sky, her curls, which had been in a ponytail when she vanished, now dangling down her back.

"Who have you shared this with?"

"Just you. Right now."

"Does she always look up?"

"What?"

"Before she disappears, does she always look to the sky?"

I thought back to the monitor clips. "Only one other happened while she was awake. She was reading in our living room, and now that I think of it, she does look up in that one as well. Does that tell us something?"

"Nothing concrete. Just that she might be controlling it or at least aware when it is about to happen."

That brought me both relief and anger. I didn't have to worry she'd leave Ethan, but if she controlled her comings and goings, she could stop this whole mess and choose to stay for good.

"I've met someone else like your wife." Udali stared at my phone as he handed it back, as if it pained him to release it. "An Afrikaner living in Cape Town—Eleanor Bosch. Her co-workers at the textile plant claimed she would disappear from her perch at one of the machines then reappear hours later somewhere else in the room as if nothing had happened. There was very little written of her, but from what I found, everyone believed she was stepping into a parallel dimension or time traveling. She didn't talk about it because she thought she was hallucinating."

I could hear my heart beating in my head. My temples throbbed along with the beat.

"How long ago was this?"

"Thirty years or so."

"Then the people who knew her might still be alive."

He nodded as if I'd asked a question, but it had been a statement. A declaration of hope.

—

Eleanor's sister, Heather Bosch, was not on social media. I could not find an email address nor a telephone number for her. I used my newsroom's person-finder to get her address, but her landlord would not put me in touch with her, nor would he confirm she rented from him. The only reason I was willing to leave Bridget and Ethan to track down this woman was because I knew the Cape Town area where she lived, and figured I could get there and back quickly.

I must admit it felt good to be away. The quality of my life had declined significantly, not just because I was terrified about Bridget all the time, but also because the economy was collapsing, the climate had become harsh, and violent crime was on a sharp increase. It just always felt as if, at any moment, I could be attacked or sent into financial ruin. The conference was a break from all that. I got to discuss politics and sports and the purpose of journalism, something I hadn't done since the days before I knew Bridget.

Heather's home was in the suburb of Salt River, two miles away from the radio station where I'd interned in graduate school. Table Mountain was visible under the midday sun, and cars and buses whizzed down Victoria Road like they were racing one another.

When I arrived on Fairview Avenue, every home on the street was a different color and they were stacked next to one another so tightly it looked as if someone had linked up all their shoeboxes, ensuring each one shared a wall with the next. One home was orange sherbet with matching irons around the doors and windows, another was cerulean with a satellite dish dangling off its side as if a great wind had struck it.

The home I approached was the color of a daisy, and was the only one without bars.

I knocked.

Heather Bosch would be about sixty-five. The article in which she said she'd had nothing to do with her sister's disappearance even though they were the only two at home when it occurred also included a picture of Heather holding a framed photo of Eleanor. In the image, Heather looked mid-thirties and wore a tan dress with a Bertha collar.

When she answered, her accent was so thick I wondered whether I would understand her, and she me. I explained my situation, that I'd been able to reach her colleagues, neighbors, and acquaintances, who all confirmed where she lived but who also wouldn't give me her cell number, and she sucked her teeth and started to close the door. But when I told her Udali had sent me, she softened, "You know Dr. Wardene?" and waved me inside to her kitchen, where she made me a cup of rooibos tea. I accepted the warm, red drink and the scones with cherry jam she offered as well.

"Where does your wife say she's going?" Her voice was gruff, but it betrayed a kindness I knew she didn't want me to detect. It reminded me of Bridget.

"She won't admit it's happening."

"Shame. Eleanor didn't either for a while. But when I finally got her to, she told me she had a mission."

"What kind of mission?"

"Don't know. I presume it's different for each person."

"How does this happen? Do they control it?"

"What does your wife do?"

"P.R. at a university lab."

"Izzit?" She stopped mid-sip and stared. "What does the lab do?"

"Make computer chips." It occurred to me that Bridget was very specific with me about the people at her job, but she claimed, since she worked for a lab, she had to keep many things hidden, so I didn't really know the specifics of what they did other than what they stated in press releases she wrote. I can't stress enough how maddening it was for a journalist to have questions with no answers.

"Eleanor moonlighted at a university lab here in Kaapstad. And she once traveled to a university in Jozi."

I was still getting used to Heather's accent, and it took me a moment to realize Kaapstad was Cape Town and Jozi was Johannesburg. "What were they working on?"

"Didn't say. But told me they did lots of experiments on people. And she—"

Heather stopped and stared at me as if she remembered something. She rose. With ginger steps from what seemed like a busted hip, she moved to the far side of the kitchen and opened a wooden armoire that stretched from the floor to the ceiling. The doors creaked as she opened them.

"I just—I found these after she disappeared the final time."

When she reached inside and pulled out a tin box, I noticed a tremor in her hands. She blew dust from the lid, opened it, careful with the rusty hinges, and brought it back to the table as if she were a pall bearer carrying a casket.

"We didn't have the internet all over the place back then. I never thought—"

I thought I would scream from anticipation.

"She kept saying they were doing experiments. Then she'd see the subjects in the paper."

I took the newspaper clippings from her, and each one was an article about a missing person. A thirty-seven-year-old shop owner from the Cape Flats. A nineteen-year-old taxi driver from Khayelitsha. A teacher from Dunoon.

"Who are these people?"

"Experiment subjects."

"She thought the labs were making people disappear?"

"Ja. Now that you tell me about your wife, I wonder. Eleanor must have realized. Why else did she save the papers?"

My chest tightened. I felt allergic to the box. I had the urge to check on Bridget. It was nighttime in Michigan. I opened the app on my phone and was reassured when I saw the outline of her body under the comforter on our bed.

I returned the cell to my pocket and stared at Heather. "What was the mechanism for making the subjects disappear and reappear?"

"Ag. I don't know."

"Try to remember. There's got to be something Eleanor had or had taken? A pill? An injection? The lab had to have done something to make her—"

"Needles frightened her. She didn't like pills. Was hale and hearty, that one. Loved to hike. Never touched the pork or steak I made." Heather chuckled at the memory, then she frowned, remembering. "She had one vice. She smoked."

"Smoked?" I could feel my breath catch in my throat and my stomach drop.

"These…odd cigarettes."

Cigarettes. Skinny. Brown. There from the first day I'd known Bridget. Innocuous, but perhaps not. I thought I'd fall off the chair. I wanted to run from the house, get back to Bridget and get those cigarettes away from her. All those times I acquiesced to Bridget's smoking came raining down on me—a flood of guilt. I should have said no emphatically. I was powerless with Bridget and maybe that had allowed the disappearances to continue.

"They smelled like…" Heather stared out the window as if she were seeing Eleanor smoking them.

"Cinnamon?" I asked, sweat gathering in my armpits and bubbling up on my forehead. I struggled to keep my breathing steady.

"Eish." Shocked, Heather's mouth grew into a circle. "Said it relaxed her."

"The cigarettes must be the connection."

Her hand trembled as she brought the cup of rooibos tea to her lips and sipped. "The last time was no different than any other time, that I could tell. She just disappeared, but then didn't reappear that time. I keep waiting, hoping she'll return. What if this isn't really where they're supposed to be?"

"Where?"

"Earth."

Heather's voice caught in her throat on the word "Earth." She made noises that sounded like frantic hiccups. "I'm sorry." She stood. "So, so sorry."

I stood. She slammed the box down, pushed me toward her back door.

"Totsiens," she said through sobs. The door slammed behind me and I wanted to jump through the nearby window and ask her to help me fix this situation, but I realized she'd already been gracious enough to speak with a man who showed up unexpectedly asking about her sister who'd been missing for thirty years.

The taxi couldn't get me to the airport fast enough. I'd perhaps found a way to stop this. If Bridget didn't smoke the cinnamon cigarettes—it seemed far-fetched, but so did the reappearances. I had to try something. On my dash through the terminal, I called Udali and caught him up on my visit. He was doubtful removing the cigarettes would work. He reminded me that just as she was reappearing here, she was also reappearing someplace else. He told me to treat the reappearances as if they were an untreatable illness. To go home and love my wife for the time I had left. What other option did I have? he asked.

"Cigarettes or no, the final disappearance will happen, Yusef, whether you love her or not."

—

The last time I spoke to Bridget was at seven p.m. her time. I was stuck in a nearly six-hour layover in New York's JFK airport. The flight was Cape Town to Doha to New York to Detroit, and I was kicking myself for not booking the more expensive Cape Town to London to Chicago to Detroit flight, which would have allowed me to drive the final leg from Chicago to save time.

She was cooking pasta and assembling caprese salad. We argued. She'd seen the camera blink or heard the buzz as the monitor turned on the base and it had just been the last straw. She'd tossed all the devices in the trash, saying she wouldn't tolerate the "police state" I'd created. The last thing I said to her was, "Don't smoke those cigarettes again."

Nearly eight hours later, when I arrived at our back door, it was ajar. Ethan was inside, asleep in his bed, the food was cold on the stove, Bridget's purse was still hanging on the back of the dining chair, but she was gone.

I wished I'd had time to follow Udali's advice. To concentrate on loving her even though I was gripped with fear of losing her. I couldn't help but feel my pressure to control what was happening, my final threat about the cigarettes, was the very thing that sent her away.

The police suspected me from the moment they arrived. I could hear it in their questions: "Any financial troubles for you two?" "Extramarital affairs?" "Why were you traveling?" "Arguments recently?" And in the way they looked with pity at Ethan, our framed wedding photos, and the unopened box of condoms in our bedroom.

They uncovered every detail in our house. No cell phone, credit card, nor bank transactions beyond the time of her disappearance, they said. Their unspoken theories wouldn't have bothered me had I thought them able to find her.

—

That first week after losing Bridget I went through an entire bottle of saline drops to rid my eyes of their redness from not sleeping, and I'd grown so thin only consuming water and coffee that I had to pull my belt to the next notch. I couldn't find her cigarettes anywhere in the house, and neither had the police. I spent my days shuffling through memories of her in my mind, researching mysterious words she'd spoken.

"Force projection," the phrase she'd uttered in her sleep, was when a nation-state conducted military operations at distances far from its territory. The U.S. especially liked to set up installations around the world that could be deployed at a moment's notice. The online searches were bottomless, no doubt, because they raised more questions than they answered.

I talked to a source at the police department. The investigators had discovered diary entries in which she talked about how "controlling" I was, and that she felt she couldn't breathe because of my "delusions." She mentioned the cameras and the tracking device I'd placed on her car, and how I questioned her whenever she returned. And, apparently, she'd once pondered taking Ethan and leaving but thought I'd use my journalism resources to track her down if she took my son. The investigators believed she skipped town without Ethan, thereby relieving me of the motivation to go after her.

I couldn't believe she'd made me out to be the bad guy. And where had she'd kept this journal? Certainly not in the house, because I'd have found it. I asked to see the diary, but my source apologized and said it was booked into evidence and couldn't leave the station. But, I mean, thank God a neighbor saw her enter the house that final day with Ethan, otherwise police might have thought I offed her.

The second week, I added whiskey to my diet and drank it to oblivion every night. Each morning I woke in the throes of a migraine with an aura, which was so painful and disorienting I often couldn't stand. One night after five shots of bourbon, I called Bridget's parents and asked them point blank, "Did Bridget disappear as a child? Did she go away and come back and you two have been covering for her the entire time?"

"Whatever are you talking about, Yusef?" her mother asked in that fake-sweet voice. "Do you need help? Do you need us to come over? Is Ethan okay? You're worrying us."

"Why, Mrs. Gale? Why did you let her marry me? Why did you let her have a child, if you knew?"

Her mom sobbed and her dad came to the phone. "I know you're hurting, but you can't call upsetting my wife like this."

"You two don't care about your grandson?"

"Of course, we do."

"Then tell me. Just tell me. Don't you understand? I have to know!"

He paused for several seconds, then sighed. I had a lot of doubts about her parents, I even had doubts about Bridget's love for me, but one thing I knew for certain was that Bridget's parents loved Ethan.

Her dad whispered, "Go back to bed, Sweet. I'll be up in a minute."

I heard the sound of slippers swishing across their wooden floors, the creaking open and shutting of a door.

"I told my daughter she picked the wrong possible person to marry," he whispered, sounding resigned, exhausted. "A person whose job is to ask questions, who can't leave anything uncovered."

I didn't dare speak because I was so close to finally having an answer. I swallowed and held my breath, not wanting to say or do anything that might mess it up.

"We don't know, Yusef."

"What don't you know?"

"The how or the why. But we do know the impossible position you've been in because we've been in that same position as well."

"So, she disappeared from the beginning?"

"We want to see our grandchild, Yusef. We do. But you can never ask us about this again."

"Why not? Is there something to fear? Should I be afraid?"

"Yes. We all should." Her Dad hung up on me. I stared at the silent phone wondering why I was willing to press them for answers but never Bridget.

Perhaps feeling guilty, the next week her parents offered to move in and help me with childcare or to move me and Ethan in with them, "Just until you're feeling better, Yusef." I declined. I wanted to ask them outright, *Why didn't you do more to help her? Why didn't you stop this?* But I knew I'd really be asking the question of myself.

And if Mr. and Mrs. Gale had been in my house every day, then I couldn't do what I really needed, and that was to be alone with Ethan and the memory of Bridget.

I couldn't tell them that in my grief, I was also kind of relieved. The feeling surprised even me, but no more would I have to live every day with the anxiety of losing her. The Yusef-Bridget story was complete. I had my memories—the way she curled up on my lap during horror flicks, the moist heat of her breath on my ear as she whispered, "I feel like we're getting away with something, being this in love."

Living with the pleasure of her while knowing it could be taken away, was far more painful than remembering her while longing for her return.

That's what I tell myself during the day. At night, I lie awake in bed, hoping she'll climb in beside me and fall asleep, so I can wake with her round, firm breasts pressed against my back. One night I fell asleep and dreamed she did exactly that. I smelled cinnamon. I turned to her, bursting with joy that she'd come back to me, and cried out when I realized she was still gone.

When Bridget never returned, I sold the house. I eventually moved with Ethan to a small home in rural Michigan, tucked at the end of a gravel lane, and I hope no one ever notices us.

This morning, a riot broke out in our town. I heard gunfire, and when I looked out from my attic window, I saw a dusty SUV ride down the street with a long rifle pointed out the passenger window. They opened fire on the house down the lane.

When I barricaded our home's windows with dressers and desks, a notebook fell from one of the loose drawers. It was covered in red and pink sparkles, just the sort of thing Bridget would love. She'd only written one entry, and it was about the day we met at the bookstore.

One paragraph struck me. She wrote, "The first night with him was like nothing I'd ever experienced before. The thing I'm feeling...it must be guilt. He has no clue."

I racked my brain. Turned over every word she uttered that first evening. Examined every tip of her head and rise of her brow.

And after ruminating on it all morning, after asking myself whether I could have known, could have guarded my heart when I met her, I've finally figured it out.

That first night, when I entered her, it was the greatest physical and emotional pleasure I've ever known. It was as if she'd captured me. She gripped my dreadlocks and whispered, "I am the one you've been waiting for."

When I was able to think again, I told her I loved her. And mere hours after meeting her, I meant it. But it was as if I never really had a choice in the matter.

In the afterglow, when she was lying in my arms, I asked, "What book had you really been looking for today?"

"I hadn't been looking for a book. I'd been looking for an

author."

Clinging to her voice, I was drifting to sleep. "But you weren't in line at the signing. Which author were you looking for?"

She snuggled closer to me and nibbled on my ear.

"One with a story about a being that takes the form of a woman, comes to Earth, marries, and then has a child that will eventually destroy the planet."

I laughed. "Destroy the planet, huh?" I loved witty women, and I had just nabbed one with a sense of humor too. "Why does the being, the woman, try to destroy the planet?"

"She doesn't want to. But it's her mission. She's a soldier. She rids the universe of wasteful things."

"Kind of like an intergalactic garbage woman?" Eyes closed and nose open, I laughed.

She didn't.

"Does she love the man?"

"The man?"

"The one she marries?"

"Oh. Love is a foreign concept to her until she meets him. So, her feelings are an approximation, but I guess she will grow to love him, unfortunately."

"Why unfortunately?"

The closeness of her body pressed against mine was lulling me to sleep, but I had a few grains of consciousness left.

"Because—"

She never finished that sentence, and I would give away my entire existence if I could go back in time and force her to.

"Well, I've never heard of that one. Maybe it wasn't in horror though. Sounds more sci-fi to me."

Her muscles relaxed, which made me think she was drifting too. The room filled with the smell of cinnamon. She'd lit a cigarette, and the scent ushered me to the threshold of subconsciousness.

With my final shred of wakefulness, I asked, "So, you never said."

"Never said what?"

"Who was the author?"

She snuggled even closer, as if she wanted to crawl inside my skin. She kissed me—the sweetest little fool she'd ever met—and I savored every second of her lips touching mine.

"You," she whispered. "The story will be written by you."

And after it hit me, I stumbled to my back porch, sat in my Adirondack chair, and watched my four-year-old swoop high on the swing. Bridget's words continued on a loop in my mind. *The story will be written by you. The story will be written by you.*

And then my son's eyes locked with mine. His face took on that vacant look it sometimes got since he was born. A chill rushed through me.

"Everything okay, little man?"

Ethan's face remained slack, then he threw back his head and stared at the sky. Before fully making the connection in my brain, I rose, rushed toward him, afraid to blink because I knew what was coming. I remembered the videos of Bridget on that porch throwing back her head, on our couch doing the same.

"Ethan!"

Somewhere on our street a dog began barking. Time stopped. Sound stopped. My eyes welled with tears because I refused to close them.

"Look at me, Ethan. Stay with me."

And just as I closed the gap, just as my hand reached for his shirt, he grinned. I blinked, forcing those tears down my cheeks. And before I could grab him to shelter him in my embrace, my son was gone.

Under the Crown

The newspaper headline didn't do the spectacle justice, really. Daughter no longer wanted to compete in pageants. She'd made this clear to Mother by not showing up to the Miss Elegant America registration, letting Mother stand in the auditorium's lobby alone, red-faced, wearing a crown pendant on her Kmart-bought blazer, surrounded by "sixty-some-odd girls who actually gave a damn about their futures," Mother said, after hunting down Daughter at the library.

"I told you after Miss American Beauty I want to focus on Poli sci."

"You can afford college without me?"

The remark landed with a blow that made Daughter's eyes burn with tears. With no father nor siblings, only a few friends, and practically no money, Daughter's studies were all she had. It wasn't unusual for Mother to threaten her, but she'd always thought her education was sacred.

"Do the pageant or no more tuition payments. It's that simple."

Daughter forced her refusal down her throat like a scream that, when it hit her stomach, choked and died.

—

On each of Daughter's nipples, Mother stuck half a jellybean, adhering the sugary pebbles with fabric glue.

"Not too much." Daughter hated it when she whined like a five-year-old, but she knew it would hurt when it was time to remove the red candies.

"Not my fault your nipples aren't perky." Mother blew on Daughter's nipples to dry the glue and went on to say, "You know the gown has a layer of chiffon at areola level that's just begging for some nipplage," and then cackled at her own joke, the crown pendant rising and falling with her sequined jacket.

Coach laughed through cigarette-stained teeth, though with less intensity because he had a detailed list of "checks" to get through.

Teeth check: With a flip of his blonde hair, Coach removed the whitening trays, and Daughter's mouth, raw with the taste of peroxide, zinged repeatedly with pain from too much bleach for too long.

"These babies are as white as a sheet of paper," Coach said, fingering his lips as if reaching for a cigarette when none was there.

Butt check: Hers wasn't round enough so they padded the back of the dress with a silicone insert. And since the gown was formfitting, Mother said Daughter's silhouette had to be "perfect. No. More than perfect. It had to be the mother of perfect."

It was telling that Mother thought "the mother" was more than the child.

Why these clothes of beads, chiffon, and sequins? Why this style of hair-sprayed tresses and shoulder pads? Why sexual abstinence? Why thin? Why polite? Smiling? They weren't only creating a fantasy, but also a goal—docile, grinning, and unquestioning, like Barbie, Miss America, and Cinderella, innocent and unsullied.

Wardrobe arrived and sewed Daughter into the garment. Daughter wore the gown like heavy flesh that had been added over her own to mask the imperfections. She imagined it as Mother's skin covering hers, making sure no one saw the square-shaped butt, the flat nipples, the waist not properly cinched.

In gray sweats with a plaid shawl about his shoulders, Wardrobe said the obsidian-colored beads were hand-sewn; the work had been intricate and time-consuming. Each time Daughter moved, a shiny ball dug into her skin like a bite. She felt the black orbs were tiny blood-suckers intent on making her body thin, shapely, and "perky." She pulled back her sleeve to reveal a mess of miniature cuts.

"Honey, don't tug at it." Wardrobe was breathy and sweating above the lip. "If you get one loose, the rest will unravel from the line and fall off."

The mirror was missing from the dressing room. Daughter assumed Mother had removed it, thereby forcing Daughter to rely on Mother's eyes. Daughter couldn't help but stare at the wall where the mirror should have been and imagine herself as a puppet, with strings sewn into her skin where the bead-pricks were. Daughter would tell Mother she wanted to leave, that pageants were the product of a backward society.

"My beauty!" Taking in Daughter's image, Mother placed her hand over the crown pendant near her heart as if she were going to break into a tear-filled rendition of the *Star-Spangled Banner*.

"I don't want to do this."

"Excuse me?" Wardrobe, who had been steaming the gown's chiffon train, dropped the fabric and set the steamer on the sink counter.

"Don't want to do what?" Coach asked, glancing at Wardrobe then back at her.

"Remember what we discussed, my beauty."

Daughter looked down at her wrists where blood trembled and mixed with her sweat. She had nothing to dab it with, so she simply wiped it with her palm.

The room fell silent, which seemed to raise the volume on the women rushing about the hall, shouting for pins, scissors, and hairspray. There was never enough hairspray! Coach and Wardrobe looked at Mother, who nodded, allowing the room to sigh with relief.

Seeming upset about Daughter's statement, Wardrobe shoved a pair of heels at her. The shoes were four and a half inches. Anything less would not have allowed her calves to be "pronounced," and she'd learned she couldn't go on stage with unpronounced calves when she lost her first teen pageant. Mother placed slip guards on the soles, which Daughter thought silly because it was wobble guards that she really needed since she and the other contestants had to descend twelve steps in a ball gown.

Irritated that her protest fell on sexist ears and that she was still too afraid to force the issue, she told Mother to keep the slip guards. She didn't want to risk them becoming dislodged as she strutted down the catwalk, so she just scuffed the shoe's soles by doing a few tap dancing shuffles on the concrete outside her dressing room. As she trudged down the hallway to the stage, she thought of traction. Yes, traction would keep her grounded, would keep her from slipping, or perhaps from snatching up her chiffon train and running away.

———

She was 'on,' and, at twenty-one, she had mastered turning off and on. She could smile when she wanted to cry, blow kisses at the judges when she wanted to spit on the floor, toss her hot-curled hair when she wanted to flip the bird, and sashay across the stage in a gown of death-beads when she wanted to storm out of the auditorium.

She had bested fifty-five 'girls' in three categories— swimsuit, evening gown, and a 'challenge' question— "What's the best thing about being a young lady in America today?" Apparently, that question was hard-hitting because she was the only contestant to answer it. "Opportunity," she'd said and got a standing ovation for her ability to elaborate.

Being 'on' meant that her dazzling performance had catapulted her to this moment, where the only thing standing between her and the crown was contestant number forty-two, Jessica Starr, a petite blonde with an athlete's body, a supermodel's face, and a politician's smile. Jessica was competing for the second year in a row, willing to shell out the thousand-dollar entry fee twice for a chance at the title.

With all of the disappointed delegates fanned out behind them, she and Jessica stood under a spotlight, only able to see the flash of cameras at the foot of the stage. It was dark, but there was no escaping the true spectacle— the crown. With a spotlight of its own, and covered in radiant stones, the five-inch-tall circlet rested on a pedestal a couple feet away; the reflection of brilliant light sprayed the pair with glitz and sparkle.

The audience whispered as Emcee explained the importance of the first runner-up. Jessica grabbed Daughter's manicured hand. Jessica's palm wasn't just sweaty; it was wet, as if she had run her hand through a bowl of warm water before placing it there. With wide eyes, impeccably straight hair, and a hint of V05 hairspray exuding from her pores, Jessica turned to Daughter and said, "Good luck," without actually moving her lips or breaking her smile. Daughter thought Jessica was going to throw up.

She wanted Jessica to win. Jessica deserved it. Not because Jessica had beaten her, because she hadn't, but because Jessica wanted it. Jessica probably went to bed at night and dreamed of wearing the crown, of donning a gown in a parade while sitting on the back of a red convertible waving and smiling at the crowd, the dress matching the cotton candy on the children's hands.

Daughter became aware of the beads pressing into her back like a hundred insect bites. Her chest, stomach, and collarbone also came alive with stings.

"The envelope, please," Emcee said, gliding from behind the

wooden podium. "Ladies, please step forward."

Like a pair of conjoined puppets, she and Jessica inched toward Emcee, still holding each other's hand, staring into the darkness, and smiling. Always smiling.

When she was younger, she used to savor this moment, and would glance at Mother's beaming face and wait for Mother to wink. The gesture would let her know that no matter what happened, even if she only made first-runner-up, Mother thought Daughter had "knocked everyone's socks off." She'd always wait for this approval, and once, when she'd slipped down the steps in a pair of tennis shoes during a sportswear competition, she'd made it to the final two and glanced at Mother, who gave her a look she could only describe as angry gorilla. She'd won that pageant, even with the step slip, but felt she'd lost because Mother hadn't thought her performance stellar.

Now that the house lights were slowly coming up, she could see Mother from her peripheral vision, and she sensed Mother waiting for that glance to bestow her approval, but Daughter refused to look at her. *Fuck Mother's approval. Fuck pageants!*

"I am pleased to announce," Emcee said, "the title of Miss Elegant Michigan and our state's representative at the nationally televised Miss Elegant America pageant is…number forty-seven Scarlett Simpson."

Scarlett froze as the crown came down on her head. Without realizing she had done it, she glanced at Mother, who beamed, gave her two thumbs up, and winked.

—

After hearing her name, Scarlett's task was to smile, act as if this was the greatest day of her life, wave, and say "thank you" to everyone who approached and touched the lopsided crown that dug into her scalp.

She caught a glimpse of herself in the backstage mirror, her first look since her team dressed her. Sweat dotted her hairline, threatening to curl up her blow-dried tresses. Cradling several bouquets of red roses, wearing a bulky sash, and the leaning, too-big-for-her-head crown, she stood beside Mother, who wept joyful tears as they posed for the camera. The image summed up how different they were. Scarlett was five feet, nine inches tall, one hundred fifteen pounds, and lanky. Mother was a half a foot shorter and plump. Scarlett's hair fell to the small of her back. Mother's was short, because at sixteen she'd told her own mother she liked shorter styles and Big Mama took a pair of gardening shears and lobbed off Mother's hip-length ponytail, saying, "Now quit your complaining."

And this always happened when Scarlett felt bad for Mother. Mother had been spanked with a small leaf-filled branch torn from the backyard tree, known as a 'switch,' so she only spanked Scarlett with her hand. Mother never attended prom because she had no money for a gown, so she bought Scarlett a new dress with every paycheck.

Scarlett could feel the burden of Mother's un-mailed college applications, unworn ballet slippers, and un-bought wedding invitations. From Scarlett's fourth birthday, Mother had made it Scarlett's responsibility to "get us out this ghetto." Staring at the mirror, Scarlett realized that all these years, Mother hadn't been parenting Scarlett. Mother had been parenting Mother.

She heard Mother's voice turn toward someone in the crowd of photographers, newspaper folks, and pageant officials who were pushing against them: "Yes. I just knew my beauty would take the crown!"

My beauty. My beauty.

Scarlett wondered: Didn't Mother have a beauty of her own?

And, did Scarlett belong to Mother just because she had grown in Mother's womb? She stared into Mother's tear-filled face and whispered, "You should be proud of yourself."

They made their way down a darkened hall, lit only by pale orange sconces, toward the coronation ball ahead that awaited Scarlett's arrival. Scarlett touched her throat, feeling choked by the airless tunnel and Mother's presence at her side.

"Proud of myself?" Mother's smile faded. Anger crept into her voice.

Scarlett wanted to scream for her body, which was raw and sore from the ongoing bead-pricks. She glanced down to see the still-perky jellybeans, afraid that when she pulled off the dress, she would be a bloody mess.

"I mean, aren't you glad you listened to me, Scarlett? This is the big one!"

Usually Scarlett said "Yes," but this time she said, "Like I said, you should be proud of yourself. Your beauty did it again. It's *your* beauty, right, who just won?"

Mother stopped, and with a fury familiar to Scarlett, she slapped Scarlett across her right cheek. It felt as if someone had struck a match against Scarlett's face, but she couldn't mess up her mascara with tears, and if she hit Mother back, she risked a beating, the way Big Mama had beaten Mother on her eighteenth birthday when Mother wanted to go roller skating with her girlfriends whom Big Mama had considered "fast."

Pageant Director emerged from the shadows behind them and, with flushed cheeks, said, "Scarlett. Joan. This way." Pageant Director's smile let Scarlett know the gray-haired woman with a pound of makeup hadn't witnessed the violence.

Joan's visage went from murder to melancholy to molasses in seconds, and, just as they arrived at the door to the ball, Joan squeezed Scarlett's hand and said, "Now, behave, my beauty. This is what we've been working so hard for."

Scarlett returned Joan's hand-squeeze, only she squeezed harder. This wasn't the first time Scarlett had gotten Joan's open hand in her face, but it would be the last.

―

Yes, Scarlett made the newspaper, but not for reasons that made Joan happy. Pageant Director asked Scarlett to give a speech at the coronation ball, and a microphone appeared in front of Scarlett's mouth. Is this what it took to be heard? She first had to dress and behave in a way acceptable to them? She could feel the bites from the beads, the sting of Joan's palm on her cheek. On her wrists she found fresh blood drops.

Scarlett spoke clearly into the microphone. "In *Feminism is for Everybody*, bell hooks wrote that girls and women had been socialized to believe their value rested in their appearance, and especially what men thought of their appearance." The audience listened with rapt attention, likely wondering where she was going with this. "The author went on to write: 'Women stripping their bodies of unhealthy and uncomfortable, restrictive clothing—bras, girdles, corsets, garter belts, et cetera—was a ritualistic, radical reclaiming of the health and glory of the female body.' So, I say, 'fuck this pageant shit.'"

Emcee chuckled. The audience members, who were gathered in several small gossip-huddles before her, gripped their cocktails and glanced across chest-high bar tables at one another, mouthing, *What did she say*? and *Did she just curse*?

"Excuse me?" Emcee adjusted his tie; his eyes searched the crowd and found Pageant Director.

"You heard right." Scarlett held up her hand to show off her blood. "Fuck this pageant. This gown. This hair. This crown. These beads and these motherfucking shoes." Emcee grabbed the microphone, and piercing audio feedback shot across the room. Scarlett had anticipated his move and snatched the mic back. The audio feedback died. "You people are sick. I mean, honestly, this dress is cutting me. I'm bleeding."

Emcee reached for the mic again, but Scarlett shoved him into the podium. Someone in the room screamed. Scarlett wanted to scream too.

She stared down the other contestants who were oddly still smiling even though their eyes were wide. "With our glitter clothes and our jazzed-up hair. I said to my mother, Joan, over there, that I was tired of being told how to speak, smile, wave, hold my head, toss my hair, what to wear, when to reveal my body—swimsuit competition—and when to cover it up, how to walk with my arms bent, chin down, and to make sure I look into the eyes of the judges. Fuck it all."

Joan braced herself against the bar. Scarlett thought Joan would faint, but Joan instead gathered her strength and charged toward the stage. Scarlett slammed the microphone against Emcee's chest and tore at her beads. One string unraveled and then more came undone until beads flowed off her gown, bounced off the front of the stage, and spilled across the floor between the crowd's shoes. This was relief to her tortured skin, and the sound was like the scattering of bite-sized candies she'd once thrown onto a cement movie theater floor.

Scarlett peeled off the fake eyelashes and pulled the gel pads from her butt. She threw her shoes behind her, and the other contestants gasped as they ducked. She turned to them and shouted—without the microphone—"aren't you all tired, hungry, sick of smiling? Aren't you done with being glued, tucked, pinned, and wrapped into these"—she ripped off the bodice of her dress exposing her jelly-beaned breasts and bloody torso—"GARMENTS?" She stepped out of the gown's train and stood before everyone with only her nude pantyhose, which were not really nude on her because she was a brown 'girl.' She wore no underwear beneath the stockings because Joan wouldn't allow panty lines, so the audience stared at her bare ass. She lost track of Joan in the crowd.

"Rip it off! Take it off! They want us sexy? Let's give 'em sexy. They want us beautiful? Let's show 'em beautiful!"

One of the contestants shouted, "Yes!" Then another. Then several more.

The newspaper ran a color photo of Scarlett, naked, with red-speckled skin and a garbage can lid in her hand as she stormed out of the auditorium amid cheers from the other contestants. The headline read, 'Beauty Queen Strips on Stage, Trashes Crown.' Joan was not in the picture.

I did it for you

She decided terror was more productive than revenge.

She purchased an eyelash curler, and outfitted the plates with filed-to-size, high-carbon, stainless-steel knife blades powerful enough to slice through bone.

She'd always loved eyelash curlers because they provided the satisfaction of a scissor snip, had the air of medical tools, and, with the slight risk of capturing the entire lid during the curling, were mildly terrifying.

After several trips to the hardware store, she found just the right tension spring to add to the lever, so she could squeeze and cleave with ease. Her creation made her quite pleased.

As she sharpened the blades, she thought of him, his palm squeezing her throat, his moist breath in her ear. She wouldn't give up hunting him, but until then, she'd collect.

The rules for her collection were as follows:

1. She would only target men who were creeps to begin with—catcallers, whistlers, harassers, butt-cheek pinchers.
2. She'd never approach her victim. She'd wait for him to make the first move.
3. She'd strike during the witching hour, when everyone could say the guy really shouldn't have been in the prostitute section of town to begin with.
4. She'd never accept money from them.
5. She'd only collect when the men were unclothed, in bed, and fast asleep.

6. She'd disinfect the amputation site with seventy percent rubbing alcohol before slicing, and she'd take care to line up the blades so she'd increase the odds of clearing the bone.
7. She wouldn't be greedy. She'd collect the baby toe, and only the distal phalanx or tip.

Her rules were designed to debase, to transform offenders into victims, but also to keep the focus on the toe-loss and not on any infection nor need for further amputation, thereby maximizing victim-blaming, so they could experience what that was like.

It helped that the men were usually inebriated when they first shouted, "Hey, sweet thang," or "You wanna have a little fun?" And if they weren't, she had just the product in her purse to knock them out, either in pill form or a tasteless liquid slipped into their drink.

Her fleshy trophies included all skin colors and varying sizes. Some stubby, others narrow. One guy had no toenails. If she could feel anything for them, that one would have elicited some guilt.

She photographed the toes before throwing them in the flames of her fireplace, but she kept the images on her camera's digital card, and not on her phone nor in the cloud.

Two is a coincidence and three is a trend, so on the third victim, the local news station led with the story on its ten p.m. broadcast and spent most of its time warning men to be on the lookout for a sex worker with an eyelash curler. She laughed so hard she spilled half a glass of pinot noir and stained her couch. *That's specific, clowns.*

On the eighth victim, the newspaper referred to her as the "Digit Gatherer," and that name annoyed her. First off, "gatherer" sounded pleasant, as if she were out rounding up daisies. She wanted men to feel the same terror she'd experienced, to undergo the pain they so mercilessly inflicted, because it was possible for a man, even a creep, to go his entire life without ever being threatened.

Second, the moniker bothered her because the news media were always trying to sound so clever when they could just be direct. "Digit" was too broad a term. She wasn't collecting fingers. Nor was she accumulating big toes, for instance. Why not just call her "The Pinky Toe Bandit" or "Baby Toe Collector?" Actually, those might have been worse. Maybe she could live with "Digit Gatherer."

One social media user commented, "The victims should be happy she chose toes and not dicks." *Good point.*

She'd not chosen to lob off their penises because she knew how coveted those instruments were in American society; she imagined the police would have used more of its resources to hunt her down if she were collecting those particular organs.

She'd selected the tip of the smallest toe to ensure a private shame. A shame others couldn't see when they asked "how's it going?" She wanted them to have a hidden-away truth they would need to explain before undressing for future lovers or for doctors performing an exam. Something missing they'd have to acknowledge each morning when they woke and rose from bed.

Her tenth victim was the problem. He asked, "Can I give you a ride?" and his voice was familiar, made her shiver, but she put the memory out of her mind. It was a generic enough pick-up line for the street she walked down; she let it go.

She got in, and the cracked leather seat squeaked as it poked against the flesh on the backs of her thighs.

He wore a black baseball cap, and a mustache and beard so thick and crooked they had to have been purchased at a costume shop. Smooth jazz saxophone-playing filled the car, and the air smelled of whiskey and cocoa butter.

Crumpled-up burger and fry wrappers littered the floor beneath her heels, and, in need of a tune-up, the car belched out the stench of burnt wires. It chugged down the street as if it had been shot and would soon die.

"I know a place," he whispered, steering his lemon around the block as if they'd agreed on where to go.

She'd been in this car before. With him. And when he pulled into the motel's parking stall, she realized what luck she'd happened upon. Giddy with adrenaline, she could envision the weapon nestled in the crushed-velvet drawstring pouch in her purse. If it could speak to her, it would say, *Girl, this is it!*

In the room, sitting in a stained fabric chair near the door, she told him she had something "fun" for him and retrieved a white pill from her bag.

"This will make you forget all your troubles."

He threw it to the back of his throat, not waiting for her to fill a cup from the bathroom sink. Perhaps he'd noticed the clumps of blonde hair clogging the drain, the stench of bleach and urine, the black ring in the tub.

She stalled by getting him to talk—about his estranged wife who had absconded to Toronto with their savings and his six-month-old pug, his dream vacation to Niagara Falls, the '97 Ford Mustang he was fixing up. And when he'd talked himself to sleep, she returned to her bag, remembering the first time they'd met. How he'd been between shifts on his beat work. How when she wouldn't say "yes" to his demands, he'd handcuffed her, and, an hour later, dropped her back off on the corner, un-handcuffed, but with bruises where the metal had been. The rumpled fabric of her skirt had hidden the lacerations.

"A hooker can't win a case against a peace officer," he'd told her, with no sense of irony about his use of the word "peace."

"I wait tables at the diner on that street. Is that what this is? You thought I was...you go after sex workers?"

She'd thought of Maggie, with the scar across her eyebrow, who always showed off pictures of her Kindergartener. Maggie was saving cash to send her son to Catholic school so he wouldn't have to attend where he was zoned. "I don't want him going through a metal detector to learn."

She'd thought of "Hip Hop," who chain-smoked Virginia Slims and had dreams of turning her poems into money-making rhymes for local rap artists. "Poetry. Rap. Spoken word. Shakespeare. All the same," the raspy-voiced woman had said.

Maggie had given her a switchblade. Hip Hop had armed her with pepper spray. Was it because he'd done this to them as well?

"You say you only wait tables? Well, stop wearing low-cut tops."

That's what he'd said back then before driving off and spraying her shins with muddy rainwater that had pooled against the curb.

But now, she removed her palm-sized weapon from the same purse that held her pills, slipped his baby toe inside, and as she was about to squeeze the tool, she felt cold steel against her forehead, just above her right brow.

"Drop it." He spat the pill into her face. It rolled onto the mattress between them, and his warm spittle slid down her cheek.

Her heart should have been racing. She should have begun sweating. Her breaths should have quickened until she was lightheaded, but she felt nothing. And she wouldn't let it go—neither his toe nor what he'd done to her. He wasn't going to win. He'd have to kill her if he wanted to keep the digit.

"Do you know who I am?"

"I know exactly who you are, and what you've been doing to men who—"

"You really don't remember me?"

"I said 'drop it.'" He removed the fake hair, revealing a chiseled face, pursed lips, and a tight jaw.

"Shoot me."

"Don't tempt me."

"How much do you love your toe?" She dug the blades against his flesh hard enough to prick it and draw blood.

"How much do you love your life?" He pressed the barrel deeper into the skin on her forehead.

"You mean the life you took from me?" She waited until recognition welled up in his eyes. "You think losing a toe would be bad? How about losing your will to live? Having someone extinguish it like the flame of a candle."

Satisfied when he opened his mouth but couldn't speak, she squeezed with every drop of rage flowing through her, feeling the digit pop between the blades and warm blood squirt onto her chin where it oozed down to her breasts and into her shirt—the same low-cut top she'd worn before.

He screamed, and the gunshot intended for her head hit the ceiling. With her weapon and his toe in her blood-soaked hand, she grabbed her bag and shoes and ran for the door. She took a bullet to the back of her right shoulder, stumbled into the hall, and plummeted down the stairs. The shot felt like a sucker-punch of fire that knocked the wind from her chest.

She stood, but, off-balance, she careened, blasted through the double entry-doors, tumbled outside, and collapsed onto the street, where she was met with the click of multiple stiletto heels rushing toward her.

"Honey, oh my God." That high-pitched voice belonged to Maggie. "Oh-my-god-oh-my-god-oh-my-god. Don't move, honey."

"I'm calling nine-one-one," said another voice, sounding

scarred by a lifetime of cigarette smoking. That was Hip Hop.

She was comforted that Maggie and Hip Hop and a gang of their fellow workers were near...like if Severed-Toe Cop managed to limp out of the room and come after her, they'd all protect her.

But she wouldn't allow these women to fuss over her. She rose. Maggie and Hip Hop exchanged a glance, and their frightened faces made her love them.

Raising the arm on the uninjured side of her body, she waved her weapon in the air, saluting their mini-skirts, courage, tank tops, perseverance, red-sequined, four-inch pumps, and compassion.

The night grew darker and the ground seemed to spin under her. She turned and trudged off. Was she fainting or dying? She wasn't sure which, but as the pain in her shoulder went from a ten to a thirty on her imagined discomfort chart, she'd put her money on "dying."

"Reisha, honey, you've been shot. Everybody heard it. You need a doctor." Maggie tried to run, but, in her six-inch pointed heels she didn't get far. She kicked them off, sunk several inches on her bare feet, and tried to close the gap.

Reisha rounded the corner. Blood oozed down her arm as if the bullet had opened a faucet from her body. She glanced over her wounded shoulder and shouted between ragged breaths, "I did it for you."

"You did what, honey? Please, stop." Hip Hop reached forward but only caught air. Reisha retreated just long enough to give Hip Hop what was in her hand.

"I did it for us all."

Hip Hop took the deadly curler, the severed toe the size of a large cashew, and showed them to Maggie, who immediately screamed.

"Reisha, honey," Maggie was sobbing. "Oh my God. You should have told us, honey. Because this...this isn't the way."

Reisha crumpled in the middle of the street. "It's my way." Surrounded by a throng of multicolored pumps, she became fixated on the vast array before her. Cerulean, fuchsia, fire engine red. They were all so beautiful. Could even serve as weapons. She wished she'd have done it differently. Heels. If she survived the night, which she was almost certain now she wouldn't, she'd get her next victims with the pointed heel of her shoes. Lodge them right in their eyes. They'd have a visible injury. She could be the Stiletto Stalker. Just as men winced at the sight of eyelash curlers, high heels would make them nauseated with fear. Did people even realize stiletto was a synonym for dagger? Well, they would after she was finished with them. And then, she will have won. They'd think twice any time they saw a woman in heels. Yes. Trepidation. She'd consider that a victory.

The Bats

The envelope from the public health department had been sitting on Steve's kitchen counter for a week, buried beneath a heap of unopened bills and shut-off notices. In search of his bottle opener, only two millimeters thick so it could fit in his back pocket, Steve scratched his scraggly beard and rooted around the stack of papers in search of the nickel-plated steel he was certain lay underneath. He only wanted one thing—to drink the lager sweating through the bottle in his hand, to feel the cold, numbing liquid ease into him, dissolving his growing headache, making him forget everything that came before this day, this moment when he'd found himself sober and standing in an apartment redolent of leftover mac and cheese and boiled bologna. But a notice on the bottom of the pile distracted him with its red capital letters across the front—"OPEN IMMEDIATELY."

He examined the postal stamp. How had he missed the words for an entire week? He'd been in a beer haze every morning except the previous one when he'd gotten dressed for his son's graduation but could bring himself to neither attend nor drink. This was the first morning in three months that he'd woken up sober.

"Immediately, huh?"

Setting the unopened beer on the counter, he slid a grimy fingernail under the envelope's flap and ripped open the letter. Just below the county seal were the words, *Caution: Unknown Viral Epidemic Infects County Bats.*

Something moved outside the sliding glass door that led to his balcony. He always kept the glass open with the screen behind it locked to let in the breezes. He glanced out that slider and a hundred feet across the courtyard at Ms. Desmond. The octogenarian was sitting on her own terrace in the June heat with a red knit shawl about her shoulders, doing what she always did around noon—arranging plastic flowers in clay pots. His screen needed cleaning, but the image of Ms. Desmond was clear. She had hung three pots from the wooden beam above her, and attached to the center planter was a bat.

Ten minutes before, when he'd lugged himself out of bed, thrown water on his face, swished with mouthwash, pulled on his bathrobe, and deleted Cecilia's week-old angry voicemail—still trying to get confirmation that Steve would be attending Josiah's college graduation—he'd noticed the bat on one of Ms. Desmond's pots but had thought nothing of it. Now, as he squinted to see the thing, with its wings spread six inches across the front of the earthenware, it was obvious to Steve the prune-faced woman was clueless that the creature had positioned itself less than a foot from her head. Staring at her hunched shoulders and watching her sniff an artificial rose, he remembered the notice in his hand. The letter read:

County Public Health officials have discovered an outbreak of an unknown virus impacting the local bat population. Public health officials caution residents to avoid bats in their yards or near their homes. Bats are nocturnal. If they are spotted in daylight, they should not be touched, and should be reported to Animal Control. If the bat is near a pet or child, put on leather gloves and cover the bat with a bucket or trap so that officials may examine it.

He stared at the letter, trying to process it. Cecilia used to open this sort of thing and would have stood barefoot in the kitchen to read it aloud to him. He would have tuned her out somewhere around the second sentence, and she would have gotten to the end and declared, "This is crazy!" He would have continued flipping through the sports channels, never glancing at her in the leopard-print nightgown with her brown hair pinned in a taut bun. She would have asked, "What should we do?" And he would have lobbed a "How the hell should I know?" at her. And that would have turned into a spat, the argument ending with her using an unnecessary word like "juxtaposition," followed by the words "if you will." People were always using words that didn't fit the conversation and Cecilia was the worst of them—"to expiate, if you will," "a bildungsroman, if you will," "punctilious, if you will." She did this so often that he'd kept the dictionary on his nightstand. Then he'd look up one of her words and discover that not only had she used the unnecessary word, but she had also misused it. She'd called an upbeat Motown musical revue "elegiac, if you will." But at least Cecilia would have mentioned the advisory to Steve. She probably would have heeded the warnings too.

Problem was, Cecilia and Steve's home was "in dispute," but one piece in the chess game of "irreconcilable differences." Cecilia and Steve were no more. It was now "Cecilia and Tom," the latter being Cecilia's slick-haired Merengue instructor who apparently loved the fact that Cecilia outfitted herself in leopard-print everything and used unnecessary words.

And Steve? It was just Steve. Fifty-six-year-old Steve. Moved-to-a-retirement-community-for-active-seniors-fifty-five-and-older Steve. Hated-his-mostly-wheelchair-bound-elderly-neighbors Steve. Alone Steve. And Alone Steve discovered public health advisories about sick bats after the disease had already infected hundreds of people in his ten-thousand-person county. Alone Steve didn't watch or read the news, listen to the radio, or go online. Nor did he answer the phone or persistent knocks at the door.

Alone Steve was completing a three-month leave of absence for "health issues" from his marketing job at Katch Realty. He was in great physical health. It was his mind that wasn't right. For the previous two and a half months, he had been pondering what he still cared about. Because he told himself he no longer gave a good doggone about his estranged wife nor their son, Josiah, who, Steve believed, called only for money.

No longer did Steve hike or even get fresh air. Did he fill up his SUV? Had he renewed the vehicle's registration? Did he consider driving off Myers Cliff but then decide against it when he realized the heifer would get his house, stocks, and 401(k)? Nope. Nope. And yep.

Damn the bottle opener. He fished his eyeglasses out of the mess on the counter instead. With the lopsided bifocals on his nose, he again peered beyond his screen door to see whether Ms. Desmond had noticed the bat on her pot yet.

She was seated in the same place, but the bat had inched its way around the side of the planter, even closer to her. Steve waved his arms and shouted, "Hey! Ms. Desmond! Hey!" but even when she was lucid, the old lady couldn't hear. It was no use.

And he didn't know why he cared about the crone anyway. She annoyed him by using made-up euphemisms like "mother-shucker" and by constantly talking about how much she loved Black people whenever they met in the mailroom.

Three small bats dropped from the sky and attached themselves to his screen door, seeming to have arrived at the sound of his voice. They each hung on by slipping their clawed toes and thumbs through the mesh and baring their teeth at him as they whined.

He hated bats. Found them about as creepy as all of the Halloween revelers and viewers of vampire movies did. When he was young, a zookeeper once told him that bats were gentle, helpful to humans, and simply misunderstood, that of the thousands of bat types, "only three" were bloodsuckers. "Only three" was too many for him. He didn't care what the zoo's animal-lover thought. The fact that they were mammals bothered him. Their little noses and pointy ears seemed human-like, and their hands had bones just like the human hand. The only flying mammal, with forearms, elbows, wrists, and fingers threaded within its wings was a disturbing sight. They were too much like people yet powerful enough to fly, could hang upside down, and they were furry in a way humans were not. The mere thought of them forced a shiver down his spine.

A fourth bat arrived and found its grip on his screen. Of course. In his darkened, one-bedroom apartment with graying walls and crooked venetian blinds that cast a pall over the cluttered space, sick and deranged bats were fitting. Was appropriate even for a man who had ended up around a bunch of old folks about to kick the can because that's all his divorce proceedings afforded him.

Digging through the letters again, he found a notice from two days ago that, lacking a post office stamp, appeared to have been hand-delivered to his apartment—number 423. He remembered getting his mail at some point. He'd walked down to the mailroom and had stuck his key in the box and taken out a stack. He'd walked those envelopes and circulars back to his place and tossed them into the pile. Now when had that been? A week ago? Two weeks? Think. Think. Had anyone been in the mailroom? Walking in the hallway? He closed his eyes and thought back. It had been empty. But who had hand-delivered notices and mail? Had the person knocked? What had Steve missed? It wasn't every day he regretted his drinking, but he did now. He tore open the note. Maybe this one would tell him what to do about the bats on his screen.

It was when he sliced his finger on the envelope that he wondered whether Cecilia and Josiah were safe in their respective homes ten miles away. Had the graduation even happened? They were in the next county over. Should he call them? He didn't want to care, but he cared. Dammit. The papercut didn't bleed. He wished it had. The non-bloody paper cuts hurt the worst.

Health Alert: Seventeen Residents Die from Bat Disease MCV47

Pantico County Public Health officials report seventeen deaths and hundreds of illnesses related to exposure to bats infected with a disease dubbed Megachiroptera Virus 47 (MCV47). Officials caution residents that MCV47 is highly contagious and potentially fatal to humans. The most prominent symptom of MCV47 is a white discharge from the eyes, nose, mouth, or ears. Residents have reported smelling a floral scent prior to infection. If you have been exposed to a bat, please call 911.

His ears rang. His chest tightened in painful knots. Or was that ache in his lungs? Bats were known for spreading rabies, Ebola, and SARS, but this MCV47 sounded much worse. With Ebola and the rest, the bats were simply the virus's host. But with MCV47, the disease had actually made the bats sick.

He searched the cushions between the couch, the dining chairs, and the coffee table, where he eventually found the remote. Surely, something about this was on the news. There must be pandemonium. He imagined police, fire, the governor activating the Arizona Army National Guard. And in his community, with many seniors barely able to move without wheelchairs, walkers, canes, and scooters, there must have been a mass exodus. Many of these folks would have needed assistance. Three doors down from him lived Mr. Taylor, who wore dark glasses, and walked by patting the walls with his open hand and tapping a blind-man's cane on the floor in front of him. Who had evacuated Mr. Taylor? The flat screen's green light popped on, but the picture was filled with snow.

Outside his window, a bat shrieked and flew away. His satellite dish had been toppled and lay in pieces in the corner of his deck.

The crash must have been awful loud. When had that happened? In the distant, hazy sky, beyond the rows of duplicate apartments and the dry desert hills, more bats circled the palm trees that surrounded his complex. The bats seemed to be flying in military formation as if they were putting on an air show, with their wings wide and creating a triangle pattern in the sky. This was really happening. He needed that beer now more than ever but couldn't take his eyes off the bats. What were they doing up there like that?

Each time he looked away at the television to try another channel and then back out the window, it seemed there were more bats joining the arrangement. He threw down the remote and it landed in a muffled thud on his rug. The television was useless. Everyone was gone and he needed to get the hell out. Where would he go? How far had the sick bats spread? Had they made it beyond the county? He would have to drive and stay in a hotel. That's what he'd do. He'd be forced to spend money he didn't have, but he couldn't stay in this empty, bat-infested place.

He looked across at Ms. Desmond again. The lawn chair she had been sitting in had flipped back and come to rest against her screen. Ms. Desmond and the bat were gone. Looking, he wondered what would have made Ms. Desmond overturn her chair, and where was she? He remembered a Hitchcock movie about killer birds, but immediately tamped down the thought. Folks were getting sick from the bats, was all. Not being attacked by them. His mind was starting to sound like ever-panicked Cecilia. That was the thing about marriage. Your spouse's conscience became part of your own, so even when she wasn't around, he still heard her as if she were there.

Steve returned to his kitchen counter, where that sweaty bottle of beer was waiting. He ran his finger down the Fount Valley's resident phone taped to the front of his fridge, found the number, and snatched up his cell phone that was sitting on the entry table near his door. His phone was dead because he hadn't charged it in days.

He grabbed his charger from the nightstand in his bedroom, and plugged the phone into the outlet below his kitchen counter. No bars and no reception. He checked the clock on the stove. It was almost one now and he was wasting precious minutes. No TV and no mobile. The cell tower must be down. And how the hell had that happened? He opened his laptop computer from the desk—also stacked with unopened bills—but it was offline and couldn't connect to Wi-Fi. No TV, no mobile, and no computer. He grabbed the wall-mounted phone. A precious, blessed dial tone met his ear. But it was a stuttering dial tone, which let him know he had yet another voicemail he hadn't noticed earlier. He called his voicemail and listened.

"Steve, this is Fount Glen management. It seems there's been a military accident and the bats in the area have a disease. We've tried to reach you. Can you give us a call back at—" Military accident. Not surprising at all. Wasn't everything in this godforsaken world a military accident? Wars, weapons, bombs, the internet, mobile technology.

He hung up and dialed Cecilia's cell and house phones from memory. He imagined her in a leopard-print skirt and shirt, walking past that slick-haired bastard, picking up the hallway phone, seeing Steve's number, answering, and saying, *Steve! Oh my God, I've been so worried about you! We're fine. Josiah is here.* That's what he imagined because that's what he wanted.

No answer on either of her lines. He phoned Josiah's numbers. Same. Nothing. Ms. Desmond didn't answer either. He tried 911. The phone rang ten times then went to the busy signal. He tried again. Same.

"No nine-one-one either?" This was worse than he'd thought. Who was handling the situation? Why weren't there any authorities out here now dealing with the bats circling in the sky? If not the Arizona National Guard, then why not the Air Force? Weren't these bats a threat to U.S. airspace? But he admitted to himself that even if he were to get police or fire on the line, he'd have to wait for them to arrive and then to find Ms. Desmond's apartment.

For the first time in months, Steve was no longer numb. Adrenaline coursed from the core of his body out to his limbs, then to his fingers and feet. He was panting, and though he hated caring, he imagined the helpless older woman with her frail and crooked legs, unable to fend off a bat, and, despite himself, he cared.

"Of course, this is happening. Dammit. Of course." He jammed his feet into smelly socks and jogging shoes he hadn't worn since winter. He pulled on a faded t-shirt, boxers, and a pair of cargo shorts. He looked across at her terrace once more. He grabbed his keys from the hook near the door. He'd try the authorities again just as soon as he got Ms. Desmond away from that bat.

—

The sky, with heavy, gray clouds, looked like rain. The outdoors smelled like rain too, the usually dry air growing thick with humidity. Steve carried a broom and bucket and kept an eye on seven bats perched on the complex's Spanish-tiled roofs like a panel of judges staring down at him. They flapped their wings in place and whistled as if daring him to continue his mission. He paused when one leapt from a tile and swooped into the air. Thinking the bat would attack him, he raised the broom, but it returned to its spot. It had been jockeying with the other bats for space, perhaps.

He crept along the cobblestone path that led from one building to the next. With his attention divided among the bats on the roof, the ones still circling in formation in the sky, and on the apartment units in front of him, he jogged to the East building and thought about how Ms. Desmond's address was 423-E. How the management's idiotic numbering of the apartments in the complex was the first item on a long list of dumb logistical decisions.

That's how he'd met Ms. Desmond. They always got the other's mail. She lived in the East building and he in the West. Not only did they have the same apartment number, but there was also no W attached to his. So mostly, he got her mail.

The last time he'd spoken to Ms. Desmond, they had been in the lobby near the side-by-side mailboxes, and she was telling him about how her son never visited her anymore. She'd seemed lucid until she mentioned her son was named Elvis Presley. "And I just love the music that the Blacks make," she'd added. "It's so bad those white mother-shuckers make more money from it, huh?"

During that conversation, Steve realized the woman was a) out of her mind, b) probably racist in her younger years, and c) meant well. Mr. Taylor and Ms. Desmond were the only people in this complex he would help even though he'd been annoyed with her use of "mother-shuckers." The old woman's quirk reminded him of Cecilia and her "juxtaposition, if you will."

The hallway smelled of sterile, pine-scented cleaning solution and was empty between the complex's glass door and the elevator. The energy-efficient bulbs that dotted the ceiling were all off; he figured the building must have lost power. As he moved toward the elevator, he knocked on a few doors but heard no shuffling, no movement behind them.

He only saw light from the main entrance, and even that gradually darkened. He glanced over his shoulder and found seven bats attached to the glass door, watching him, their wings fluttering softly, as if they were thinking, the light pink ribs and pale brown skin of the interior of their wings resembling an umbrella. His fear was compounded by revulsion, and he sensed they were the seven bats from the tile roof. Their heads bobbed up and down as if they were drinking from a bowl. They bared their teeth, their high-pitched whistles and screams muffled by the glass. How were they infecting people? Were they biting them? They must be biting them because…how else? He turned away from the bats, not wanting to look into their eyes. There was something strange about their eyes.

The elevator's button did not light up when he pressed it, and he could not call the car to the floor. He took every other step as he mounted the stairs to the fourth floor, his legs coming alive from the movement, the loosening of his muscles making him wish he could go for a peaceful jog at dawn when the heat was still bearable outside, the way he used to.

The stairwell reeked of urine. He imagined a senior trying to make it down those steps and soiling the front of her pants in the process, either from fright, exhaustion, or both. He wondered about children. Had any children been here, frightened, when this all started? The complex had been built in a desert to house forgotten old folks and their dumped-off grandkids, the two groups keeping each other company through date-nights and after-school babysitting. He remembered Josiah at seven, with his backpack, skinned knees, and lunch pail filled with afterschool snacks. Any kids around must have been frightened. Why hadn't he heard any cries or screams?

A floral welcome mat decorated the outside of Ms. Desmond's apartment as well as a pot of artificial flowers, and a wreath of plastic roses above the 423-E sign. He rested the broom and bucket on the wall next to her door. He tried the knob. He remembered the notice said he should wear leather gloves. Who had leather gloves in the desert?

Door was locked.

He slid his glasses back up his nose. He fingered his lips, the way he usually did when he was just finished with a cigarette but wanted another. He knocked.

Hoping to hear footsteps, the chain sliding, the deadbolt unlocking, the hinges creaking open, Steve pressed his ear against the door.

He knocked again. Silence.

He knocked again. Nothing.

He knocked yet again. "Ms. Desmond!"

His voice echoed down the hallway, and the shriek of bats answered him. He glanced over his shoulder at the emptiness. The doors were all closed, no televisions played behind them, no one dragged a wooden cane along the tile floors, balancing by placing their hands on the cracked stucco walls.

When had everyone evacuated? Did anyone knock to get him out? Had Cecilia tried him after the graduation and he couldn't get the message? He ran a hand over his salt and pepper hair and then bit his fingernail. If he was going to help Ms. Desmond, if she, in fact, needed help, he couldn't keep wasting time waiting for her to answer. Steve stepped back and kicked Ms. Desmond's door open.

The layout of her one-bedroom apartment was exactly like his. The screen door to her front deck was marred by a wide gash, and pus soaked the carpet between the screen and the lumpy couch. Had she cut the screen with her pruning scissors? Had she been getting away from something or going after it?

He stepped one foot inside and sized up the living room before fully entering. The odor of garbage was prevalent, and a glance at the trashcan tucked into the corner of the kitchen suggested that it hadn't been dumped in several days. Cans and wadded up paper towels spilled onto the floor. She had a painting of Elvis Presley above her couch—sweaty, drugged-out, heavy-set Elvis. A cuckoo clock, apparently stuck on noon, cuckooed away on the wall near the kitchen. Her appliances were circa 1972, with label-less knobs on the stove. A worn mat lay near the sink atop linoleum floors. Plastic flowers adorned the dining table, the coffee table, the fake-granite kitchen counter, the media stand where her 27-inch Trinitron television rested. Her apartment was just as he'd imagined it would be.

"Ms. Desmond?" He was out of breath from mounting the steps. Sweat dripped down his back, making his cotton shirt stick to his skin. He lifted his shirt and fanned it against his body. The movement made him hotter.

"Hello? Ms. Desmond? It's Steve. Apartment four-twenty-three. There's an epidemic. We need to get out of here." He glanced to his right at the closed doors of her bedroom and bathroom. The rooms sat opposite one another across a narrow, carpeted hallway, just like his own.

Silence filled both rooms. No calls for help. No shuffling feet. Then a rustling kicked up behind the bedroom door. It was slight. He wasn't certain he'd even heard it at all. When he flung open her bedroom door, he was met with a cacophony of shrieks as what seemed like hundreds of bowling ball-sized bats sprang to life and rushed towards him.

Their fangs dripped with pus. Their eyes locked with his. Their massive wings collided as they gang-raced to the door. He caught sight of something red, lying in a heap on the bed. He focused on that red pile. It was Ms. Desmond's bloody shawl. Or so he thought. He couldn't be sure because he didn't have a clear view with all the bat wings in front of him.

He slammed the door and held it shut with his back, his chest burning as frantic breaths burst out and pushed in his lungs. The shrieking continued, and the creatures' banging splintered the wood as they tried to get out. The thumping gave way to the bats' screams and scrapes. He panted. His body so hot, feverish even, that a chill passed along his skin. He should have just left on his own for a hotel, or stayed at his place with that cold beer and waited this thing out. He didn't have much food, but he had enough beer to last him a week.

One loud piercing cry came from behind the door, and he couldn't tell if it was from a bat or Ms. Desmond. He needed to get to her. What if she were on the bed, fending off the bats, but just needed help to get free and run?

He waited until the bats stopped shrieking and scratching and were silent again behind the door. He got his broom and grabbed a towel from her bathroom. He draped the towel over his head, neck, and shoulders, waited for the bats to quiet down again, and slowly opened the door. The bats were lined up on her dresser, sitting upright in a group of what looked like a hundred. With the broom out in front of him, he made his way to the bed and peered down at the red shawl. The bats on the dresser watched him, but as long as he used slow, fluid movements, they gazed instead of flapped around and screamed. He didn't dare speak, but he needed to know if Ms. Desmond was buried beneath the shawl and blankets that were clumped together on the bed.

Focused on a lump beneath the fabric, he lifted the shawl with the broom bristles and out sprang a bat the size of his laptop computer. Red strands of hair sprouted from the bat's head. Hair that looked an awful lot like Ms. Desmond's. Hazel irises—the same color as the old woman's—and pupils beneath a thin film of black, those eyes looked human. The creature flapped in place, screeching, and then came toward him with its teeth bared and angled for his cheek.

He ducked back out the door, tripped, fell to the floor, lost his glasses, stood, accidentally crushed the lenses, and when he screamed, the other bats on the dresser sprang to life and followed the red-haired bat through the door. He abandoned the towel and the broom on the floor between the bedroom and foyer, ran out of the apartment and slammed the door, crushing the red-haired bat between the wood and frame, hearing the crunch of the mammal and seeing blood and white pus shoot out of the gap.

The other bats scratched against the wood while he held onto the handle, waiting for them to calm down. Two minutes passed and they were still screaming and trying to get through. He let the handle go and took off running to the stairwell.

This was not the stairwell he'd used earlier. It was at the opposite end of the hall from where he'd arrived and it would lead him to a different building entrance than the one he'd previously entered. He raced down those stairs, his body weak and his head pounding. He needed to get to his vehicle. He would gas it up and drive as far as he could until the sky was clear of bats, until he was near the authorities and other people.

The stairwell door led him to the back of the building. When he exited, the bats flying in formation in the sky had grown to two hundred easily. They had broken into four groups, all creating triangles and what looked like stretched out letter Vs. His SUV was parked in stall fifty toward the front gate of the community. Every space was empty save his. He had no broom, no towel, no glasses, and felt exposed being outside with the sky blackened by bats and no one around. But he jogged in fluid movements to not draw the bats' attention.

He thought he saw someone sitting in the driver's seat of his vehicle, staring straight ahead as if they were trying to decide whether to leave. From his vantage point, as he approached from the rear, it seemed as if the person had low-cropped hair and broad shoulders, and was sitting stiff and straight. He crept around the driver's side, not wanting to startle whomever it was who was deciding what to do. Perhaps they could leave together. Perhaps the person was a senior who couldn't drive. Steve would drive them. He was actually relieved there might be another person to speak to about what was going on. He tapped on the window, and the person—an older brunette—did not turn her head to acknowledge him. With the four bat formations in the sky hovering over him now like helicopters, he couldn't yell.

He opened the door slowly. The woman didn't move. "Hey." He whispered this and his voice still startled him, seeming too loud for the danger overhead. "This is my car. I can drive us." He touched the woman's shoulder and she fell to the right, her head landing on the passenger's seat. When he reached across to straighten her, he saw the pistol in her hand. He took the pistol, which he now knew was minus one bullet, and he snatched her from the vehicle and climbed in. She hit the ground with a squelching thud. The gun, he sat in the console where he used to place his travel mug full of coffee. He started the engine and saw the red gas needle resting slightly above the E, which would give him just enough gas to make it to a station.

Overhead, the bats stopped their formation and crashed onto his truck like a fallen tree. Several attached themselves to his front and back windshields, just like the ones from the apartment. He turned on the wipers, which sent the smaller bats flying, but two larger ones remained on the top left and right of the windshield, forcing him to duck a bit to see in front of him. The other bats landed on the dead woman near his vehicle and began biting at the skin of her face. She turned into a bloody mess in only a few seconds, and he couldn't look anymore.

He pulled forward, away from the bloody woman and eased

through the gates of his complex. He was panting again. His body shaking, he was getting lightheaded. The streets on either side of his complex were empty. No cars driving and none parked. The four-way streetlights were blinking red on one side and green on the other. A coyote sprinted down the sidewalk, periodically glancing over its shoulder at five hovering bats, heads tucked as if they were preparing to bite.

They landed on the coyote, and it ran about ten more yards, before collapsing under the bats' flapping wings and jerking movements. Steve hated idling the truck with so little gas in the tank, but he needed to see what the bats were capable of. He needed to see how they were infecting people and animals. The notice had mentioned nothing of the virus's effect on animals. The bats flew back up into the sky and the two bats that had been on his windshield took off and flew into formation with them. He glanced at the dead coyote and made a right out of the community and onto the Old Road. The coyote's remains were in his rear view now.

He looked both ways before entering the intersection and when he looked in the rearview again, the coyote's carcass moved. He slammed on his brakes beneath the streetlight, the red glow blinking against his dashboard. The coyote wasn't dead?

With his breath fogging the windows, he waited. The air in the car was stifling, but he refused to let down that protective glass. He could turn on the a/c once he got gas. The dark brown lump of fur slowly rose from the concrete, but it did not stand on its feet again. The middle of the coyote was no longer a coyote. The mammal now had wings that spread, and this newly formed animal stared at his vehicle and flew toward his back windshield with a speed that rivaled a panther.

Steve floored it, speeding down the main road and towards the next county. The bat was in his rearview for a quarter mile, when it seemed to have lost interest and flew up to the sky, presumably to join formation with the others. Going sixty miles per hour on the four-lane street, zooming through streetlights and keeping his eyes peeled for pedestrians, which he did not find, he passed the Rhino bar, Flora's restaurant, Big Joan's supermarket, and Fire Pharmaceuticals. The businesses and their parking lots were empty, the glass windows smashed out, and the ground littered with trash.

A block away from the freeway entrance he pulled into the gas station. The pump was working and he filled up, scanning the sky. Bats sat atop the gas station awning, watching him. The station's food mart was teeming with bats, packed so tightly inside that it seemed they could barely move. The pump clicked. He returned the nozzle to the holster and put his gas cap back on. His movements were slow and the bats seemed to not be interested in him when he carried on that way. He could feel extra heartbeats in his chest as adrenaline kept his muscles tight and his eyes and nose damp.

He closed the car door slowly and started the engine again, hoping the bats wouldn't be interested in his vehicle. They weren't. He pulled out of the gas station, looking both ways, considering the fact that he was still mostly following traffic laws as a reflex even though no one was on the road. He entered the on-ramp, and, when he was on Interstate 5 South, he found that his was the only car on the highway.

—

Josiah would have gone to his mother's. Steve knew that. It wouldn't have worked the other way around. His son would have gone to his ex's place even though she was with another man and even though Steve had told Josiah that any interaction his son had with that prick who'd stolen his mother from his father was an affront to his father. Josiah was his mother's son and he would have gone there anyway. So even though Steve could have driven to the end of the county to see how far this thing had gone and whether there was any help for him, Steve went to Cecilia, knowing that if he was lucky enough to find her, that's where he'd find their son.

Even though the property was in dispute, Cecilia stayed there, with her new lover, and she'd told Steve that she would never change the locks. "Why are you telling me this?" he'd asked her. He didn't want her giving him false hope. "Because I want you to know, Steve." And that was it. That's how everything was with her. They could have a two-hour-long conversation and he could come out of it more confused than he'd been when it started.

It didn't feel right driving with no one around and nobody on the street. It was like he'd entered an alternate reality. Another Earth, where bats ran the day and people waited for night. He tried the radio but got static on every station. He couldn't conjure up even faint talking on the dial. Where was the government? The army? Why weren't they lined up on the streets and highways and broadcasting from the stations?

He found not one car on the side of the road. Did no vehicles break down? Had everyone left in an orderly fashion and what remained had been cleared away like rubbish? The sun pressed through his windshield and warmed his chest, and he wished that it would get hot enough to burn up some of the bats flying overhead as if they owned the day. Didn't they know their place? Upside down in a cave or under a bridge, awake only in the dark of night. Not out here circling the sky in daylight like the sun and heat had no power over them. They would not win this. There were too many people smart enough to know how to stop them, smart enough to know how to destroy them and their hell-bound disease. People would not bow down to any animal. That's one thing he was sure of.

His former residence was in the middle of a cul-de-sac

surrounded by similar ones on the left and right. It was a planned community of Victorian-style homes, his a five thousand square-foot two-story, with Cecilia's roses rimming the front yard. He'd always thought it too big, but Cecilia wanted it, so he'd agreed to buy it.

Up and down his street, bats covered the windows and rooftops of every home including his own, either attached to glass or sitting perched on the roof. They all seemed to be waiting for something. They were all watching.

The garage door was open and both Cecilia's sedan and Tom's truck were inside. Josiah's hybrid vehicle was in the front yard, with skid marks in the driveway and torn up grass and dirt from where his son had entered. He imagined Josiah panicked, driving at perhaps fifty miles per hour as he hit the mud. The driver's door was open. He pictured his son running from the vehicle, calling out, "Mom!" as he sprinted up the front steps and into the house.

Steve drove across the lawn, ripping up the red flowers, and parked near the bottom step of the porch between Josiah's vehicle and the house. He exited through the passenger door and took one step down from the truck, not feeling completely safe but at least not fully exposed. He paused and looked up. The sky was clear and he didn't hear the bats screaming.

He put his key in the front door, and Cecilia had been telling the truth. She had not changed the locks. Inside, a man's shoe stuck out of the kitchen door, and he knew right away that it was Tom's. When he entered, he saw why Tom had done it. Why he, like the woman in Steve's car, had taken his own life with a handgun. Although Steve's home smelled of pumpkin spice, likely from air fresheners Cecilia had purchased, all the windows in the back of the home were completely covered in spread-winged bats, staring in, looking as if they were waiting for their opportunity to get inside.

He heard a floorboard creak overhead and what sounded like scurrying feet in what was his old bedroom. He took out the pistol he'd taken from the woman and slowly mounted the stairs. He didn't know what he might find up there, but he checked Josiah's room and closet, the spare bedroom and closet, the hall bathroom and linen closet, and finally he came to the primary bedroom. All were empty, yet bats were attached to all the windows.

Inside, the sliding glass door to the terrace sat open, and a large bat had attached itself to the screen. Its wings stretched at least a foot across. Its black eyes, the size of silver dollars, gaped at him. White pus oozed from its mouth. The bat was scrutinizing him, perhaps displaying its fangs to frighten him. The ring of pus expanded as the bat wheezed against the screen. The thing's eyes were familiar to him, which didn't make sense, but the familiarity agitated him, and he immediately wanted the bat gone.

Without considering the letter's warning, he raised the pistol, aimed for the bats middle, and fired. The bat whistled but didn't move, as if it had absorbed the bullet. The sound was weak. A large bulb of pus bubbled and dripped onto the carpet, filling the bedroom with the scent of mangos and fresh orchids.

He tossed the pistol to the floor near the bed, and reached for the phone on the nightstand. He dialed 911 again. The fragrance now filling the bedroom seeped into his nostrils, tingling his head and feet. As he listened to the line ringing, the cordless phone pressed against his ear, he felt as if he was moving in slow motion. The bat was still on the screen eyeing him as if it knew him. He gazed into those eyes and immediately remembered Cecilia. Standing over him as he sat on the couch downstairs watching television. Looking down at him with her arms folded across her chest. Crying as she told him how she loved Tom now, and she didn't mean to hurt Steve, but she was leaving, she deserved to be happy, to finally be happy. She must be happy, she'd said, and it didn't matter if that made him unhappy. She'd been right. A part of him had almost said, *Take me with you. I want to be happy too. I'm sure I can be happy too. I've just forgotten how.*

But he'd said nothing. She'd walked out. Her hair bounced as she left. Even her hair had been happy.

The bat's pus was now slowly dissolving the screen door. A man's voice came on the line—"Health Department." Hadn't Steve dialed 911? Why was the health department answering?

"I'm out here in Barber County on McBain Road." Steve was lightheaded now. "There's some weird mother-shucking stuff going on out here."

"Sir, have you been in contact with a bat?"

"They're everywhere." Steve felt he might lose consciousness soon. His feet and hands felt tight and swollen. But at the same time, he hadn't felt this happy since the day he'd met Cecilia, at a wedding of all places, she wearing a leopard-print dress that hugged her curves like skin. This is what he'd been waiting for. To feel happy. To feel free.

"Have you smelled anything resembling mangos? Flowers?"

"Just tell me what to do, mother-shucker. Everybody's evacuated and you mother-shuckers forgot about me. Forgot about my wife and my son. He's here too. In this house. I haven't found him yet, but I know he's here. His car is here. You mother-shuckers forgot about Fount Valley in Pantico County and forgot about my house in Barber County. This is still my mother-shucking house, no matter what the court might say."

"Pantico and Barber Counties were not evacuated, sir. Those were total metamorphosis sites. Authorities were not able to get there in time. How have you managed to survive?"

"Metamorphosis? What do you mean 'metamorphosis'?"

The public health man paused, began speaking, and then stopped, as if he wanted to tell Steve something, but couldn't. Steve remembered the red-haired bat that looked like Ms. Desmond, and the coyote that grew wings and flew after him, and this bat now, staring at him, with human-like eyes he wanted to shoot out but that he simultaneously wanted to kiss.

"So, what am I supposed to do about the mother-shucking mangos?"

The public health man said something, his voice crackling on the line, but the room was dimming before Steve's eyes. His throat burned and his nostrils seemed to be filling with fluid.

The bat's silver dollar eyes never left Steve. The creature made a whistling sound as if it wanted to speak to him. To tell him to hang up the phone and come outside. With the phone so heavy it was like a five-pound dumbbell in his hand, Steve stared into those eyes. He recognized those eyes. Those were Cecilia's eyes.

"Avoid the scent, sir." There was static on the line now. "It's the scent that does it. Not the pus or the—Look, just avoid it. Run if you can. But other than that…Can you run, sir? Can you drive to the edge of town? We can meet you. Sir? Oh, God. I'm praying for you, sir."

The public health man's voice trailed off. The fragrance of mangos and orchids was everywhere in the room, and it filled Steve's nose and fogged his brain and made his insides feel as if they would burst from him as sunlight, so it never occurred to him to close the glass slider or to save himself by getting out. This was beautifully scary. Heavy lightness. Elegant ruin. A juxtaposition, if you will.

These Parts

THEN

He said he saw something wicked in my eyes. He raised his right arm, the violet cloth of his robe spread like a wing, and he placed his thumb on my forehead. A few of the ashes fell to my nose and tumbled down my plaid uniform. With my eyes closed and my hands clasped at my chest, I waited for him to say, "You are from dust and unto dust you shall return," just as he had with my classmates, who were now sitting in pretend reverence on their wooden pews.

But Father Valencia didn't speak right away, so I opened my eyes and gazed into his frightened blue-eyed stare. He traced a cross on my forehead, leaned forward, and with white nostrils flaring, he whispered, "I bind you, Satan. Release this child of God. In the name of Jesus, I cast you out."

It might have been Alex, swinging his altar boy thurible, the overpowering scent of incense burning on charcoal that filled my nose. Or the strip of sunlight that bounced off of the golden cross on the altar and seemed to pierce my eyes. Whatever it was, I fainted. My body slumped forward on the marble altar—a twisted genuflection.

Sister Marilyn didn't believe me when I told her what Father Valencia had said. She just shook her head and called my mother.

Mama's factory pay would be docked three hours, and the day's work would not equal the seventy-five-dollar doctor's visit. That's what Mama shouted to me as I sat in the back of our red pickup, the wind drying my tears before they reached my chin. The white streaks tightened the skin on my cheeks; I felt they'd split open if I yawned or spoke. I held a tissue to my bloody nose.

"Low blood-sugar," the doctor had said.

And that was that.

Mama told me to shut-up about that "binding Satan" mess.

NOW

If my car hadn't been at the shop for repairs, I might never have found the CDs. And maybe those two men would still be alive today.

I hopped into Josh's silver Passat to pick him up from work. It would be three days before my vehicle was fixed, so he said we could share his car until then. I flipped to his media player, hit CD, and pulled out of the gated parking structure of our one-bedroom apartment. A disc was already loaded in the player.

A woman, singing R & B through a god-awful, mechanic Auto-tune mess, began crooning, "Lick this pussy. It's just for you."

"Nice taste, Josh." I hit eject and pulled onto the street. When the disc popped out of the player, I noticed words scrawled on the face in marker. I held it up to the light of the summer sun and read, *Nighttime Dreams from Erica*. It was written in a woman's handwriting. You know the kind—voluptuous, urgent, thirsty.

I put the disc back in the player. The road, the cars, and the people disappeared in front of me. My eyes still saw them, and my body still operated the vehicle just as it had for the ten years I'd been driving, but my brain was conjuring up images of Erica, from Josh's job. Poorly educated, short, overweight, child-faced executive assistant Erica, who was always kindness-dripping-with-fake whenever I attended a work event with Josh. The one who always made a beeline for me when I arrived, telling me how beautiful I was.

I knew something wasn't right about her the first time we met at the home of the VP she was an assistant for. But I just assumed I was put off by her inability to completely conjugate a verb—"I wish Alan from accounting could have came too" instead of "could have come"—or how I'd noticed her wearing pigtails when her hair was really a weave. Who pulls fake hair into pigtails?

Song Two began "Do you still believe in love? I do. Roll over baby, let me make love to you." And the singer wheezed the way a pig would if you had slit its throat and it was just about to die.

Song Three: "Spank me. Spank me. Show me that I'm bad. Lie me down, tie me up. Don't I make you mad?"

I ejected the disc again, but this time I placed it in the center of the passenger seat, ensuring it was the first thing Josh saw when he got in.

At a stoplight, I opened the glove compartment—empty except for three CDs inside. The discs were *Sheets and Heels*, *Wrists, Ankles, Love,* and *Whipped*, all signed at the bottom with curly letters in red marker: from Erica.

Even in rush hour, I arrived at his office early. When he exited the revolving door with that big-dick swagger and had the nerve to grin and wave as if he had actually missed me, I smiled and waved back.

He grabbed the CD, placed his bag on the floor and got in without noticing the bomb in his hand. He gave me a peck on the cheek, same as the one in the morning. The live-in girlfriend peck. The one that said, *we've been together for five years, and I'm used to you. You're like my trusty razor. I reload the dull blade every now and again, but really. How often do I think about my razor?*

I pulled off and merged into the street traffic. It was around seven now. The sun was lower but would still be out for at least another hour. Most people had their windows and tops down. We relied on air conditioning.

"How was work?"

"Good." He fingered the disc without looking at it. "Same ol' same. All of the engineers are bored. All of the designers are antsy."

I plucked the CD from his hand and slid it in the media player. Traffic had slowed to a crawl. Dying Pig Singer started up: "taste this pussy. It's just for you."

I stared straight ahead, unmoving. From my peripheral vision, I saw Josh's head turn slowly to look at me. Funny that it wasn't until he was in the shitter that he took me in with his eyes.

Even when he screwed me, he didn't look at me. Mostly he'd stare at the pillow beneath my head or the wall behind my back or at the ceiling when I was riding him. I wondered, while he was staring this time, could he see me through the eyes of the men who wanted me—John from down the hall, Brian at the gym, Will from my hometown—the men whom I'd kept at a healthy distance for the sake of my committed relationship. So that Josh and I could one day get married, buy a house, and have three babies who all looked like him. That dream was the only reason I put up with his shit. And now, he was even destroying that.

"Lisa, she gave this CD to a bunch of people in the office, so before you start jumping to conclusions..."

"Jumping to conclusions? I haven't even said anything."

"Yeah. But I know how you are. Any little thing and you're in a tizzy."

I kept my eyes on the road, with my hands gripping the wheel.

"Tizzy? Do I look like I'm in a tizzy?" My words came out as if I had asked, *Wanna grab some coffee?*

He ejected the CD and tossed it in the glove compartment. I grabbed "Sheets and Heels" from the cubby in the driver side door and placed it in the media player. It loaded. Josh rubbed his short-cropped hair and let out a sigh.

"Great taste in music Erica has, huh? I wonder if she picked it up in college. Oh. That's right. I forgot. She never went to college, did she?"

"See what I mean? You're pissed."

He ejected that disc. I popped in *Wrists, Ankles, Love*.

"Dammit, Lisa. Grow up, will you? I just told you she handed these out to a bunch of folks."

"And do you like these songs? Is this your kind of music? Spank this? Slap that? Pussy's all yours? Kind of got a nice ring to it, huh?" I raised my right hand and snapped my fingers to the beat, realizing it was easier to insult his taste in music than to confront him about whether he was sleeping with the tramp. He ejected that disc too.

Placing my hand back on the wheel, I noticed we were in what Josh usually called "these parts." It was just like the neighborhood where I grew up—raggedy, sad, calloused. A neighborhood with sagging houses built of falling-down doors and windows that looked like angry eyes.

Upper-middle-class, ski-resort Josh hadn't noticed the wrong turn. Hadn't noticed we were headed deeper into the estate of misery. His lack of awareness indicated that he had something to hide. Otherwise, he would have said, "Where are you going? You know I don't bring my Passat over to these parts."

THEN

V-Rock told the police he thought I was one of his hoes. That's what the officers think he said anyway because he was slipping into a coma when the excuse came out of his bloody mouth.

I had finished up practice for the spring musical "Bye Bye Birdie" at my high school and had caught the number nine bus to my neighborhood a quarter past it-was-too-damn-late-to-be-out-all-alone. That's what time it was according to everyone who blamed me for almost getting raped by the neighborhood pimp.

One block from my house, he grabbed the back of my hooded sweatshirt. My textbooks and keys flew in the air as I screamed and kicked. He dragged me into the alley, threw my back and head against the brick facade of Drink Up liquor store, and with a cold, rough hand, hiked up my uniform skirt. My eyes were closed. I intended to open them, but they felt swollen. Every part of my body felt as if it were growing, bursting open, teeming with muscle and strength. My screams turned to growls, and when I opened my eyes, V-Rock had released his grip. He said, "Oh, shit," and turned to run, but it was too late. Plus, I was faster than he was.

My nails shredding his shirt and slashing the skin on his back was the moment he began pleading for his life.

He died an hour after slipping into that coma. I don't remember much about him. He had a mouth full of gold teeth. I do remember that.

NOW

I really don't know how or why I drove into "these parts." Maybe, in my attempt to remain calm as my future life crumbled, I had gotten us lost. I stopped at a light and saw a narrow, bald, Black woman out Josh's window whose complexion was just like mine—black as oil oozing from the earth. She grinned at me as she pulled a Styrofoam container from the dumpster, fished around in the leftovers with a bony, misshapen finger, and took a bite of slimy noodles. One tooth—bottom-center of her mouth—peeked out of a face constructed of vacant eyes and a hooked nose. I stared at her, because without knowing the woman, I felt I knew her. I felt I was her. In a dimension parallel to my own. She was the Lisa who didn't make it off the block. Who didn't go to college. Who turned to drugs instead of books. And, already angry about my fool boyfriend, I got even angrier when I saw myself in her. Because she and I were within feet of each other but also worlds apart.

"I listened to a couple of songs, but, no. I don't like them," Josh said, not noticing the woman just outside his window. "I don't know why she gives them to folks. I just never threw them out, but I've been meaning to. Now can we drop it?"

The problem was, I couldn't drop it. Not because my boyfriend had sexually explicit CDs in his car burned for him by a stank-ho that he worked with. That, within the context of a vibrant relationship, would have been something to joke about. Maybe. But in the context of the bullshit relationship we were in, where he didn't call me during the day, never texted or emailed, phoned only to tell me he was headed home but got off the phone without talking to me during his hour-long commute, and only sometimes returned my daytime phone calls, and then only two or three hours later—within that context, the sexually explicit CDs were reason to slap his lying, monkey-mouth.

We were driving again. Bald, noodle-lady was in the rearview, and Josh and I were locked in a silent argument. The kind of disagreement that was so quiet it reverberated louder than a screaming match.

Nearly an hour later, just as the sun melted into the ground, we weren't too far from home, but were still in "these parts." Neither of us had spoken. We hadn't touched the radio. It seemed like Josh wasn't really breathing at all. I wondered why he seemed so bothered. Maybe he wasn't lying? Did he love me after all? Maybe my well-planned future of Josh earning a living while I spent my days writing, cooking, raising our babies, hosting parties, and planning our vacations could still happen.

Then a green sports car circa nineteen ninety-two slammed on its brakes in front of us. We were on a side-street with only one other car, exactly zero pedestrians, and flanked by grass-covered hills where trash and dilapidated motor homes held up the cracked curb. I stepped on the brakes. Two black SUVs appeared, flipped on their headlights, and stopped on either side of us.

"What the—" Josh whispered as I threw the car in reverse and sped back.

Another SUV pulled up behind us, forcing me to brake again.

Mean Motherfucker Number One climbed out of the car in front of us in khaki shorts, and flip-flops with socks, palming a nine-millimeter.

Mean Motherfucker Number Two limped out of the SUV on Josh's side with what looked like a gun his grandfather would have carried—a polished twenty-two.

Mean Motherfucker Number Three stepped out of his SUV behind us; I couldn't make out what he was carrying.

"Get down," Josh whispered ducking onto the floor beneath the glove compartment where his ass-slapping CDs rested. I could feel the heat of three guns aimed at my head as the door to the SUV near my side slowly began to open.

I yanked the handle and threw open my door with the wrath of every cheated-on, lied-to, abused woman on Earth and smashed Mean Motherfucker Number Four's tattooed arm between the door and the vehicle's frame.

He screamed, "Ah, fuck!" His thirty-two landing on the ground in front of me. I picked it up and pointed it at Mean Motherfucker Number Three, who was gripping a sawed-off shotgun behind our car. I dropped into a boxer's stance—torso sideways, one foot in front, one behind, center of gravity over my hips, one clenched fist guarding my chin.

"Yo, bitch. We don't want no problems," Number Three said, not enunciating the 'b' in problems, so it came out sounding like 'prahlems. "We just want yo' whip."

Didn't Mean Motherfucker Number Three or Number Two or Number One notice that my hand wasn't trembling? Didn't Number Three notice that my eyes were thin slits in my face, tiny as paper cuts? Hadn't it occurred to them, when I blasted out of the vehicle, that I had been trying to stamp down the tremor in my stomach, that hearing the word 'bitch' on a night like tonight might release my wrath?

I cleared my throat, spit on the ground and swayed back and forth as if I were about to fire a punch instead of a gun. My hand doubled in size around the mouse-gun. My already lanky limbs were elongated. I felt my body suddenly bursting from my jeans and black tank top.

Number Three's eyes grew wide; his hand shook behind the sawed-off shotgun.

Not one car had passed. The only headlights on that scummy patch of road were ours.

And then time stopped. Noise and movement and senses ceased. In the silence, I remembered a book I'd read in grad school by sociologist Elijah Anderson called *Code of the Streets*. One of its many poignant arguments was that people who are raised on the streets, in America's ghettos and slums, where street-justice ruled, but who eventually find a way out, are able to "code-switch." The rough outer edges of a code-switcher's persona—the "nigga, fuck that shit" and the "get the fuck outta my face"—could serve a purpose at some point, say, if someone talked trash about his mother or tried to steal his watch directly from his wrist, but could also be replaced with a silky, "Oh, certainly. It's no problem at all," when necessary, if the code-switcher, say, had a good-paying job he needed to maintain.

"Did you hear me, bitch?" Number Three shouted, reminding

me that I hadn't taken a breath. "Get the fuck back 'fore we drop yo' ass!"

Number Two, pissed, and moaning about his mangled arm, finally made it out of the passenger side of his SUV behind me and shouted, "pop 'em both. Let's be out." I kept the pistol trained on Number Three's wicked right eye, the one with the crescent moon scar above, twitched as he watched my steady hand.

Up to that point, the night had been still, but a breeze picked up around me and my hair whipped straight up from my head.

Josh finally climbed out of the car and whimpered, "Don't shoot. Take whatever you want."

Then, I could only hear the wind.

"You want this car?" I asked, my voice sounding like it had come from below the ground. I stopped swaying. "This car?"

Number Three stepped forward and nodded, his gun still raised.

"Well, funny thing is, this car belongs to that no-good piece of shit over there." I tilted my head in Josh's direction and stepped toward Number Three. I could feel one of the guns move from Josh's torso and take aim at my back. "And before you stopped us, I had every intention of taking him home, chopping him into tiny bits and stuffing the chunks of his remains down the garbage disposal—bones and all. I was planning to play the music from the CDs his office girlfriend made for him to drown out the sound of his bones cracking under the blades. So, you can see how your bitch-laced interruption is not going over well with me right now."

Number Three took two steps back to his vehicle and said, "This don't smell right. I'm out."

I could hear One, Two, and Four back away, their fear rapping on the pavement as their sneakers retreated.

And that should have been that.

I should have let them all get back into their vehicles. Should have stood on the street, pistol in hand, until their headlights disappeared around the corner and then tossed the gun into the bushes, driven home and broken up with Josh—forcing him to move out.

But somewhere between *Sheets and Heels* and "tizzy" and "did you hear me, bitch?" I just couldn't let this go. I wish I could say I code-switched, had turned into the homie Lisa, who grew up on the corner of Trenton and Sussex down the block from Keith's Pawn Shop, who one day had taken the combination lock from school and slammed it into Shareefa's nose when that heifer threatened to jump me for thinking I was "too cute."

But the homie Lisa and the MFA-having, lives-near-a-pond and drives-a-Lexus Lisa, disappeared when she found the Erica-Josh CDs in the car.

So, what Lisa remained?

I set the gun on the ground and allowed Number Three—never taking his wide eyes off of me—to climb into his SUV and slam the door. With Josh still in a panic on the street and Number One, Number Two, and Number Four climbing back into their vehicles, whispering to their drivers "get the fuck outta here," I walked to Number Three's SUV and put my hand through the window as if the glass had been made of loose spider webs. "Shit!" someone behind me shouted.

It was when I drew my hand back that I noticed it was covered in thick, black hair. A glance in the sideview mirror let me see that I just wasn't myself.

I placed both hands around Number Three's throat and squeezed. His punches to my now elongated face with fangs bursting from my gums didn't stop me. Neither did his honking horn nor the seven bullets that hit my back.

When Number Three's head finally came to rest on the steering wheel and his unblinking eyes stared at the ground, I turned and walked to Number Four, the one with the busted arm. Realizing I was half a foot taller than him now, I caught the back of his gold chain. I pulled him down from the SUV just as he tried to close the door. His driver sped off. Number Two and Number One, now seated beside their drivers, took off as well.

I pulled the chain tight around Number Four's neck, gripping it until I heard a snap, his knees going limp, his body collapsing in a clump on the ground.

For the second time in my life, I was all-powerful, and it felt like an evil orgasm. I felt like howling, but when I turned to Josh, he held his palms out to me, and before I had time to savor my physical changes, I was upwardly mobile Lisa again.

I whispered, "Let's get out of here." He stepped back, tripping over the twenty-two that Number Two had dropped on the ground.

"Get the hell away from me," he screamed, regaining his balance and backing up to the edge of the hill.

"Get in," I said. "It's late. You don't want to be out in these parts at night."

He ran up the hill, screaming, and disappeared into the darkness. At that moment, I laughed so hard someone listening might have thought I had howled.

—

My car was fixed three days later. I waited for Josh in our apartment. Wanted to hear some more about Erica and their shared taste in music, but he never returned. Instead, he sent movers the following week to pick up his things.

As they packed up his clothes, his vintage jazz albums, leather shoes, and engineering books, I laughed because I had cut everything to pieces. They were picking up fragments of his belongings. The movers chuckled too at first, but then, after the fourth box of scraps, it got awkward.

The bullets never penetrated the skin on my back but had left coral-colored welts as souvenirs from the night. Mean Motherfuckers Number Three and Number Four were known on the streets as J-Dub and Pulverizer. Their homicides remain unsolved. Local media labeled the killings "gang-related."

I don't know why Josh never reported what happened to the police. Had anyone ever found out or asked me "Why? How?" I probably would have mentioned something about code-switching. Or maybe I would have talked about Father Valencia, or V-Rock.

But in the end, it's hard to explain a life you've survived to someone who has no perspective on it. The streets are bitter, raw, violent. The streets create monsters. I guess Josh was right after all. You never know what can happen in "these parts."

UNSHOD, CACKLING, AND NAKED

i will be glorious

So, like, seriously, how was I supposed to know tree roots should only grow underground? I'm not an arborist. When I arrived at the house, I didn't even know what kind of tree was in the backyard; I just knew it was tall, thick, and all janky-looking, forgotten because it was old and half dead-looking anyway.

It wasn't even my house. Dad gave me the money to rent the place for the summer because he felt guilty about being an always-working, never-has-time-for-anyone LOSER and because I wouldn't have to drive all the way to East Jesus for my marketing internship.

It wasn't the nicest part of Medford, but at least it wasn't near the freeway, nor the bottling plant, nor Medford "Deadford" Hospital, nor the city's crime-infested public housing complexes. It was just the drab part of town, where I'd grown up, where folks ended up when they couldn't afford the section they'd really been dreaming of.

When we arrived, kids dribbled basketballs near hoops stationed smack dab in the middle of the street, and "Congrats, Kitledge High Grad" signs and multicolored balloons dotted the front lawns. The graduation signs reminded me of my brother Mack. I tried not to think about him.

"Working class," Mom said, all high and mighty like this wasn't the exact part of Michigan she'd grown up in, had raised me in until she and Dad could afford to get out.

My stay in the two-story mid-century modern was just supposed to be eight weeks, never mind the wooden floors needed sanding and refinishing, and that thick and hideous, floor-to-ceiling gold drapes adorned every room.

The backyard wasn't that bad—a patch of grass, a strip of concrete that led to the garage, and, had I known how to work a grill, I could even barbecue. The only problem was that godawful tree with the hairy black knobs snaking all up the trunk. The branches looked like clawed hands near the base with bent needles for fingernails on the ends. Mom joked that it resembled a ginger root. And I said, "Yeah. If the ginger is on crack."

Dad laughed. Mom didn't, and used my attempt at humor as her cue to leave, with promises to pick dad up before dark.

He helped me carry my bags up to the bedroom, disinfect the place, and even had a beer with me. It was a rare moment alone with him, and I have to admit I was figuring out how not to eff it up with sarcasm.

This entire summer was a big deal. I was working. "Thriving," as Mom and Dad liked to call it. Getting up in the mornings, opening the shades, dressing, and actually going outside. I'd secured an internship, even if it was an unpaid crappy one that involved me doing grunt work in an office. Okay. So maybe the rental house wasn't totally about dad's guilt.

We sat in lawn chairs under the "creepy-looking, red oak," as he called it, and I got the strangest feeling being there, like a magnetic field had drawn me in but also made me nauseated. I couldn't finish the beer, and I poured the rest of the drink on the part where the trunk plunged into the earth. The fizzing liquid flowed down the bark like urine, and I broke the top of the bottle against the tree's outer layer and jammed the jagged end in the dirt between two pieces of root that were sitting atop the ground.

"Stop doing that," Dad said.

"What?"

"Damaging the trees."

"They're wicked. All of them."

"I thought you talked to the therapist about this."

"And I thought I told mom to stop telling you all my business."

Dad rolled his eyes and looked away.

Staring at the upturned stout that seemed to be growing from the ground beside the looming thing, I said, "Tree cemetery."

I should have left then. Should have called mom back, taken my luggage and groceries, loaded them in the trunk of Dad's SUV and high-tailed it back to my ex-boyfriend's house. Or back to Mom and Dad's. But the tree was already directing my thoughts.

"Tree cemetery?" Dad cut his narrowed eyes at me.

"You know, like—"

"Bad joke," Dad said. "Not funny."

Not even five minutes in and I'd already screwed up. God. What was wrong with me?

He stared at the chain link fence and seemed to fight back tears. Well, his emotionally-distant-dad version of tears.

This is the point where I should probably mention that my younger brother Mack and I had a tree house at our home growing up about five streets over from the rental, and we used to play there every day after school, and one day when I was eleven and he was eight we were up there, and I was jumping up and down to a show tune I'd learned in school, and a branch beneath the floorboard snapped and took the wood with it. Mack fell and was in a coma for three months before he died.

"I didn't mean like that." I would never make a joke like that about Mack. I remembered Mack's confused face just before he fell, his hands reaching for me.

I had the sudden urge to touch the tree. I pressed my hand into the middle of it, and, as soon as my palm crept into that hollow space, the branches seemed to sigh. Wind and warm moisture as thick as hot breath passed over my skin. With a shudder, I quickly retracted my fist.

And I'm not even exaggerating, but something in the air changed. It was already humid, but the moisture against my skin thickened. It was only dusk, but the sky seemed suddenly darker. A needle-like branch fell and pricked the skin on my forearm but didn't draw blood.

When I looked at Dad again, he was smiling, and his eyes scrunched into the shape of orange wedges beneath his glasses. This was the version of Dad I actually liked.

"You okay, Mo?"

"Yeah. Sure."

But, I mean, I kind of wasn't.

—

That first night I dreamed of Mack, how we used to play hide and seek in the backyard and he'd climb up to our treehouse and I'd always pretend to be shocked to find him in there. But a loud boom in the basement jolted me awake, and I was like, what the eff?

I wasn't even scared it was a burglar because the alarm was on, and the noise didn't really sound like a break-in, with glass shattering and prowlers rummaging through cabinets and drawers like in the movies. This was like something had blown up or a wall had come down. No one could have paid me enough money to leave that room.

I phoned Kip, the only person for me to call at that hour, really. I woke him up, told him, "roll up," and he called me back ten minutes later from the front porch. He must not have gotten a new girlfriend, otherwise, knowing Kip, he would have given me excuses about why midnight was too late to help me out.

He went down the basement stairs first, with the flashlight app on his phone lighting the way until we got to the switch. His dreads had grown and he'd lost ten pounds or so, but his tall, lanky body was still solid. I felt safer just having him there. I tried not to stare at him.

When he flicked on the light, we saw the busted tile in the middle of the basement, and the area right next to the drain had crumbled and become elevated about a half a foot from the floor.

Hands on hips and shoulders slumping, he stood over it like a grave and was like, "Roots."

And I was like, "What? From a tree?" I thought of the creeptastic tree out back.

And he just nodded but kept staring at the pile of tiles because the one on top was trembling as if it were alive.

He pulled back the cracked red rectangle, and a tan mouse shot out of the hole, darted across the room, and snuck behind the furnace, its tail curling around the base before it disappeared.

I jerked and dropped my phone. Cracked the screen. Looking back, the lines it left on the device looked an awful lot like tree roots.

"You need to call the owners."

I didn't know Kip meant to call them the next day, so I just called them at, like, one a.m., and they had the nerve to be all pissed, like, "Do you know what time it is?" and I was like, "Excuse me? There are tree roots and mice popping out the basement floor."

They told me which utility closet housed their mouse traps and abruptly hung up on me.

"My place is actually closer to your internship." Kip said this while laying the sticky pads and not making eye contact.

"And?"

"You should just stay with me for the summer."

"We broke up, hello?" And Kip and I both knew good and damn well if I stayed with him in the very place where I'd lived with him off and on for the last couple of years, we would have been back together like no time had passed. And I wasn't going back to that nonsense.

"Why don't you just commute from your parents then?"

"If you're tired of helping me, I understand."

"You are impossible."

"And you don't know how to be faithful."

Kip slept on the couch while I sat up in bed researching tree-root-damage-to-homes on my phone. It was boring as hell, which is why I fell asleep and dreamed roots had entered the room through both windows and tied me to the bed. I didn't wake up screaming or anything, and there wasn't any sweating and panting like folks do on television, but, upon waking, I had the urge to check the tree.

I tiptoed to the window to reassure myself that there was no way a tree could strap me to a bed, but what I saw actually made everything worse.

The roots were closer to the house. And I don't mean like they'd grown farther across the ground toward the brick façade, because that might have made some actual sense. No. I mean the roots and the entire tree appeared closer. Like the tree had gotten tired of its spot, stood up, schlepped over a few feet, and sat its raggedy ass back down.

Shivering, I tucked my hands under my armpits and considered Kip's offer of staying at his place. I didn't realize it at the time but the excuses I made about staying in the creepy house were part of the tree's power over me. The spell had begun from the moment of nausea when I first sat under it, but at the time I just thought I was a whole-ass adult making my own decisions.

When I went downstairs, Kip's mouth was open in a snore, and his feet hung off the end of the couch as if he were a snake instead of a college student who got to slack off all summer. Since he'd let his dreads grow out, they framed his face and neck like a lion's mane.

I pressed my knee to his hip and he opened his eyes, horrified. When I told him about the tree's new spot in the backyard, he told me to go back to sleep. "Trees don't move, Monifah."

"This one did. Just come look."

"Go. Back. To. Sleep. You're more trouble now than when we were together."

I took one last look at Kip as I headed back upstairs, realizing his inconsistency was the real reason we weren't together. How he could tiptoe down the basement stairs to help me one night and then be dismissive another evening. How he could tell me he loved me in one breath and say the same to some girl he knew from church—church!—in the next.

I decided I would handle this tree on my own, and I fell asleep and dreamed the branches came through the windows again. Only this time they tied Kip to the couch. The wood curled up tightly around his throat and squeezed the breath from him as he slept.

When I woke the next morning, I went downstairs to tell Kip his help was no longer needed, but, of course, when I opened those homely gold drapes and let the sunlight pour in to warm his face, I discovered Kip was dead.

—

Tree branches had inexplicably twisted around Kip's throat. Like, I know! *How,* right? Droplets of blood slid down to his t-shirt. His bulging eyes stared up at the ceiling's recessed lights. His tongue extended out his mouth, where it dangled beside his lips. His head rested at an angle. The blanket had fallen to the floor, and he'd bent his left knee with the sole of that foot pressed into his right inner thigh. His arms stretched above his head, and, if he weren't dead, I would have thought he was in the middle of yoga and lying down in tree pose.

Tree.

Pose.

I removed the branches from him, as if I were a murderer hiding a weapon. I needed to vomit, to sit down, to run. Instead, I trembled, muttered "no," and backed away, tripping over his sneakers and landing like a log.

He was only twenty.

The police said he died of "manual strangulation" all out of nowhere. Because of the markings on his throat, they questioned me, and I couldn't exactly tell them it was the tree that did it. So, I told them the truth—he'd been wearing his dreads long and shaggy since our break-up, so I had no way of knowing what was going on with his neck or otherwise. That he was dead when I woke up.

I weigh all of a hundred pounds wet, so there was also no way I could get my hands or any object around his throat for long when he had a hundred pounds and half a foot on me. Apparently, they'd noticed forced entry through the back door—Killer Tree, hello!—and they seemed to believe me.

When they were on the porch getting their last look at me, they asked why I had gasoline canisters in the garage. I reminded them I didn't own the house and had no clue why the owners had done that.

"You should let them know it's a hazard and they need to get rid of them."

"I'll tell them."

I had no intention of telling them. I had other things on my mind, like my dead ex-boyfriend. I mean, I was heartbroken, but I was also no stranger to death and had spent the majority of my life in some form of hideous grief, so I figured Kip being taken from me was the Universe just piling on.

When they left, they did not take the mouse traps because dead rodent removal wasn't part of their job. Ugh!

Oh, and also, that spot on my arm where the tree branch had pricked it but not drawn blood that first day? It had become a lump about the size of a ball you'd use to play a game of jacks. The skin on top itched and was flaky, like the beginnings of a stretch mark.

I soaked a cotton ball with witch hazel and rubbed it over the area. The skin split open like the liquid had burned it, and I expected it to be a blister that oozed, but it wasn't. It was just a black stump of something that I was going to vomit over, so I covered it with a big bandage and tried to forget it existed.

That evening, after a sleeping pill and a nap, I walked to the garage, and, sure enough, there were three red barrels sitting in the corner smelling like a gas station. Warm night air pressed against my bare arms and legs, and clouds hid the moon, so I relied on the lights across the yard and above the back door to see. When I returned to the darkened rental house, with Kip gone, it felt like entering a mausoleum.

Dad called, and Dad never called. "You should move back in with us, Mo."

And I thought about it for a second, then decided instead to stay. *For what?* I asked myself. And the answer popped in my head as if someone else in the room had spoken it—*For revenge.*

Who was talking? Why would I need to get revenge? And then that voice said, *Because there is no way we are going to let Kip go out like that.*

Who the hell is 'we'?

There was no answer, but my fate was sealed. I knew I needed to take out the tree. I imagined plunging a knife into the tree roots, but then felt a little foolish. *A knife, Mo?* I mean, how do you actually kill a tree?

So, apparently, there are tons of ways to kill a tree. The owners hired a tree removal service. It felt amazing to watch the guys come out during that fourth week with their loud-ass machines and saw off that tree at the base, wrap orange bands thick as straitjackets around the trunk, and yank it down.

The lead guy—my hero—wore a red bandanna over his nose and mouth, pointed and shouted orders to his men like they were soldiers. Killer Tree plummeted to the earth like a knocked-out fighter in a ring, and, when it made contact with the grass and dirt, the entire yard shook, and so did the house beneath my bare feet.

After the crew had mulched Killer Tree in their wood-chopping machine, I went outside and stood barefoot on the stump, and I, victorious, called my mother and told her that Kip's killer had seen justice, and she said, "What?" And I said, "Killer Tree," and she muffled the phone and whispered something, I guess to my dad, and then removed the muffle and said, "I'm coming over, Mo."

And she didn't give me a chance to object. An hour later she was standing on the porch with her overnight bag, and when I opened the door fully, I saw she also had her roller luggage.

Damn. Damn. Damn! the voice in my head said, and the voice had a point.

I would have been better off with a visit from Dad. At least with him I could drink beer and tell crass jokes and forget about the snaking-up-my-shoulder arm growth, which was not responding to ibuprofen, witch hazel, nor antibiotics.

Anyway, that night, the roots out back went wild. It was like the chopping of its trunk jump-started some internal survival instinct in the thing, and the next morning I found the roots had grown into the bathroom pipes and they were coming through any available opening—sink, fireplace, vent in the basement, not far from where it had popped through the tile when Kip was alive.

Everything smelled of burnt syrup and wet dirt. Rope-sized branches crawled down the walls and ran across the floor and stopped like lizards sitting on rocks staring at nothing, feeling all sorry for themselves.

I didn't discuss the growths with Mom. Not the ones on my body nor the ones in the house because Mom and I never talked about sad things directly. And I could tell the tree was exerting its power over her too because instead of dealing with Killer Tree going all ape shit out back, she got rid of the dead mice in traps and then baked cupcakes, cookies, cobbler, and churros.

I bypassed the home's owners and called Hero.

"I need you to come back out and remove the stump."

And he was like, "The owners didn't pay for stump removal." His voice was a silky baritone. I heard heavy metal music in the background. "Anyway, trees don't grow that fast."

And I was like, "Well, this one did. Look, I need to stop it before it kills anybody else."

He paused, and I realized I'd said too much, not only to Hero but also in front of my mother, who had pulled on a sweater even though it was eighty degrees outside and the oven was set to three-seventy-five inside, and she was folding her arms across her chest and staring at me all bug-eyed in that anxious way mother's do when they are trying to parent an adult they hold no sway over.

Thank God Hero didn't take me seriously and said, "Look, you can poison it if it's bothering you so much."

Poison was exactly what I needed! A slow, painful chemical death, like a dictator getting rid of an opposition leader or a Shakespearean character ending it all for love.

Hero told me to get hold of imazapyr or picloram or dicamba or something called amitrole, and I told him I was a twenty-one-year-old college student working an unpaid marketing internship and living in a house my parents were renting for me and driving around in a car with busted a/c with a now-dead ex-boyfriend, and there was no way for me to get a hold of those things.

He told me he'd leave a couple of bottles on the front porch the next day, and, when I saw the black tubs with twist-tops filled with powders and liquids, I shouted, "Hell, yeah!" and I followed his instructions to a tee. I mixed them all together in a bucket—well, he never told me to do that, but I figured I'd mix them all together to make them more potent—and I got a large butcher knife from the kitchen and I cut baseball-sized gashes into the stump.

"This is for Kip, you piece of shit," I said to the stump as I slashed and carved. And then I poured the chemicals from the bucket across the entire stump and watched it seep into the gashes. And I sliced the roots and poured it there as well.

I went across the entire yard where the roots had metastasized like a cancer in the grass and topsoil, and I anointed the entire place, and I coughed because the smell burned my eyes, nose, and throat, and the liquid-splatters stung my exposed toes.

That night, my mother made chicken, and she put me in charge of black-eyed peas even though she knew I didn't like those eyeball-looking things and wouldn't be eating them. She asked after the burns on my feet, knees, and my hands, and I told her they were from the poison.

"Poison?"

"For the oak out back."

"But your burns shouldn't look scaly like that."

And she was right. My skin was typically a deep brown, but the outer layer was now almost black. Not like deep black, like on a person, but like black-black, like the color of a black crayon, and the veins protruded from my skin.

I hadn't shown her how the stump lump had grown up my arm to my shoulder and down my back, but I realized when she mentioned it that the black burns that looked like snakeskin were probably connected to the original stump lump.

Shit.

She was silent then, so I said, "Mack would have graduated high school this summer. I thought about it when I saw the graduation signs on the neighbors' lawns."

I don't know why the words came out of my mouth just then, but my mother stopped sugar-powdering a cake and stared at me with her mouth open. Splotches of pink crept up her neck, and I felt awful that I'd forced her to discuss the very thing she was hoping to bake her way out of thinking about.

"Oh, really? I hadn't realized." She was quick to say it, averted her eyes, and the crimson grew to her cheeks, all of which told me she was lying. Of course, she'd realized.

"Well, I, for one, spend every day imagining what he'd be doing. My therapist told me I—"

"I can't." Mom threw her palms up and turned, so her back was to me. She returned to powdering dessert, and I think she put half the sifter on that one soggy treat.

"I think that might be the problem, though, Mom. We have to—"

She banged dishes in the sink and turned on the water and garbage disposal at full strength and cleaned up everything as loudly as humanly possible and went off to bed without speaking to me.

That was the way with her. After we lost Mack, she and Dad just acted as if I didn't also need help. They each withdrew into their work and baking, and what did I have to withdraw into at eleven years old, but my own thoughts and despair?

I caught movement outside the window. I peered out to find

shadows dotting the ground. As I made my way to the yard, I wondered why I hadn't seen any of the other neighbors on the street. Was everyone, like the rental home's owners, spending the summer in Europe?

Outside, dead grass sagged across the earth, and those dark shapes were squirrel, gopher, chipmunk, and bird carcasses littering the dirt.

The animals lay on their sides, and a closer look revealed the grass was singed. The poison had worked on everything except the tree. The stump was higher, about the halfway point of the original trunk.

That night, I lay in bed remembering how dismissive Mom had been when she said, "I can't." How she'd been a conversation cop, those palms representing her relationship with me ever since Mack had gone.

As wind rattled the windows, I started having an internal conversation with myself. I was like, Self, what if your ignorant ass is dreaming up all the tree roots in the house? And then Other Self was like, Hold up. Come to think of it, do faucets really be working if tree bits are growing all up and through them? Then Self was like, And Mom ain't said nothing about wild roots, has she? Other Self answered, But Kip saw the ones in the basement. Then Self was like, True. Maybe the ones Kip saw were real and you thought up the rest. Then Other Self said, Maybe the tree is a metaphor for grief. The kind of grief that kills.

My skin tightened, and my flesh burned so acutely I sat up bolt straight, feeling the thing continue its growth up and down my arms, torso, and back. Anyone looking at me wouldn't have been able to see it. Even when I, panicked, snapped on the bedside lamp and stared at it, I couldn't actually make out the movement, but I sure as hell felt it. My skin was crawling, literally. And not fake literally, but literally literally.

When I finally fell asleep, I dreamed the branches entered my mother's mouth, crawled down her chest and popped out her stomach. That dream recurred throughout the night until I woke the next morning, sun high, and nary a wake-up knock on the door from her. I checked my cracked-screen phone and it was eleven-thirty a.m. already. Had she overslept as well?

When I went to the kitchen and saw she hadn't cooked biscuits, sausage, and egg sandwiches, I rushed back upstairs to the bedroom where she'd slept.

A peek through the door revealed her foot protruding from beneath the blanket, her polished toenails curled back as if she'd flexed them. Her eyes stared at the ceiling, and her chest did not rise and fall. Her knee was bent, her foot pressed into her inner thigh, and her arms were stretched above her head in a lying down tree pose, and the familiarity of the position made me scream.

Branches flowed from her mouth, and I don't know what I was thinking, but I dashed to her side and reached for them, pulling with my entire hundred pounds as if I were trying to dislodge roots from the earth. Her body belched, but the tree growing from her did not budge.

—

Dad buried her a week later, but I couldn't muster the energy to attend.

The night after Mom's funeral, in bed, I got the strange sensation I was elongated and stretching. The night was quiet, oddly so. And the pitch blackness of the room was broken up by moonlight dotting the wall with shadows of tree branches bobbing in each panel.

Beneath my skin, the thick protrusions burrowed in deeper until they sent sharp pains through my gut and twisted around my lungs.

I gasped, and when I woke fully, my arms were stretched high above my head with my hands pointed up and my fingers splayed. My left knee was bent, with that foot resting against my inner right thigh.

Heavy, and pressing into the mattress like a log, my body had pulled itself into tree pose, and, realizing this, I jerked so hard to free myself that I rolled onto the floor with a thud.

On like week six or seven in the house, officers arrived. Apparently, the medical examiner said Mom died from ingesting the tree poison, which was just like, *wow*. Because how could she have swallowed it other than via the root that had entered her, like in the dream?

I thought about the black-eyed peas she'd asked me to cook, and what if I still had poison on my hands when I made them? But it wouldn't have been enough to make her die. She hadn't even thrown up or anything.

I knew it was the tree that had taken her out, but how could I ask, Did she have any gnarled roots in her chest? Any signs of bark in her throat?

I realized the officers were all under Killer Tree's spell as well, because they should have been super-suspicious of me with two people dying in the home that summer with only me in the house with the deceased both times. But they never even asked me about my relationship with my mother. I've watched enough cop shows to know police always question you about your relationship with the dead person.

Any arguments lately? they usually ask with that raised eyebrow, and then they cut a glance over at their partner, who gives them that look that says, *We know this bitch is guilty*. But with these folks? Nada.

Then, tonight, my joints became stiff. I started aching all over and moving slowly, like an old woman. Older than what my mother had been.

I heard scratching at the window and caught a glimpse of the tree's branch scraping the glass. Killer Tree had grown back to its original size and had moved directly next to the house, it's canopy like a blanket ready to smother me. The branch moved as if the thing was waving to me, letting me know I hadn't won, and it was back to terrorize me.

I called Dad. Left him a voicemail message saying I thought Killer Tree had taken out Kip and Mom, just as the other tree had taken out Mack when I was younger. I ended the message by telling Dad to "come quick," because I sensed the tree would get me next. Then I trudged out back, doused the trunk and low leaves with gasoline, and set Killer Tree on fire.

—

Dad showed up twenty minutes later, and by then I'd further deteriorated.

"Mo?" he asked when he saw me from across the foyer. He reached his hand toward me and retracted it; his face pulled into a grimace. He was afraid to touch me, and that realization frightened me more than the sight of my flesh.

"What is wrong with your skin?"

I tried to say, *It's the tree; it's killing me,* but I couldn't form words, and anyway, I was so stiff I couldn't turn my head towards him nor could I take in a deep breath.

"Look," his voice was cautious. "I got your message, Mo."

With every ounce of my depleted energy, I limped away.

"Monifah Rae Hopkins, this has nothing to do with that damned tree. This is about your guilt over Mack. You go through this every few years. In and out of therapy. You moved out. You didn't go to state. You stayed in that bad relationship. You took this internship instead of working for pay. And I told you to stop punishing yourself for your brother. It wasn't your fault."

Between jagged breaths, I managed to say, "He would have graduated this year, Dad."

I was sobbing then. My tears—thick as sap—tasted like syrup when they made it to my lips and tongue. Dad moved closer to me. I'd grown since I'd seen him last. He now had to look up at me to meet my eyes.

Something in Dad broke. Tears welled in his eyes, his face was tender, and in a normal world, he would have hugged me and I would have sobbed in his arms, and that would have been the moment we both healed or some shit.

But in Killer Tree's world, I backhanded Dad across the forehead with my knotted-flesh arm, and I must have gotten some superhuman strength because Dad flew against the front door, which was perfect because it was time for him to leave.

"Mo! What are you—"

I wanted to say, *saving you from the wicked tree*, but I couldn't save him. In a flash that belied my stiff body, I closed the gap between us and repeatedly slammed his head against the door until his body crumpled into a heap before my heavy feet.

I watched, horrified and mesmerized, as the breaths slowed and left his chest. His words echoed in my mind—*It wasn't your fault*. And I had finally accepted it. None of it was my fault. Not Mack. Not Kip. Not Mom. Not Dad.

I didn't scream that time, so no one called the police, and Dad just lay there between the front door and the dining room, dead, with the flicker of the enflamed tree filling the window.

—

My chest is becoming tight now; the only thing I can move are my fingers and eyelids and even those are heavy and lacking the full range of motion. The tree burns on. Sirens are approaching.

    i just wanted to record the death of that thing back there

    and what havoc it wreaked on innocent people like my mother and father and Kip

    and I also wanted to mention that the growths on my skin aren't only black and vein-like

    some aren't black at all or rather they started out black but quickly sprouted something else on the ends

    something green and oval-shaped

    and one is growing from the right knuckle of the hand that is struggling with this pen

    i can't help but notice how I yearn to leave this home

    just leave and rest my lumbering body in the yard where the flames are dying down

    rest and shove my roots into the ground

    shove my roots down like that's where I belong

    and

    there

    in tree pose

    i will hold up any weight that rests on me and everyone will be safe from me and I will not grow too far nor intrude on anyone but

    i

    will

    be

    glorious

    and kind

    and anyone who looks at me will say

    my

    that tree is so beautiful

    not even guilt can stop her not even grief can break her not even fire can kill her

Angry Slash of Blood

Even in her liquored-up state, Shareefa didn't believe in monsters. When the fellas at the bar had brought up "Skinned Alive" and offered the legendary beast as an explanation for the local slayings, Shareefa figured that was just the half-pint of Johnnie Walker talking. "This is Medford," she'd argued. "The killer is probably some cracker who wandered here from the suburbs, high off smack."

But as she wobbled up the porch steps, stood at her front door, and held up her chain to the light of the half-moon—*Which shiny piece of nickel silver was the correct damn key?*—a chill crept up her neck. The wooden planks creaked beneath her weight as she, swaying, slid the key in the lock, and waited for the goosebumps to pass. She was pissed as hell that talk of the shape-shifting creature had actually gotten to her. The home where tonight's murders took place was two blocks from hers. Shareefa wanted to make sure Maisoon was okay.

The key fit perfectly in the hole, but the lock seemed stuck. Maisoon wasn't expecting her this early in the night. Shareefa couldn't be sure whether the door was jammed or Maisoon had gotten hold of her Gorilla Epoxy and poured the glue in the slot, locking her out. Maisoon had done that several times before.

A leaf crunched, the sound coming from across the street. Shareefa glanced over her right shoulder, but no one was there, just a row of one- and two-story homes with facades of brick or aluminum siding. She and Maisoon lived in one of the better 'hoods Medford had to offer. The sound of gunshots was always far away, and their neighbors usually sat out front having a drink and watching their kids play basketball in the street until it was too dark and cold to continue.

But not tonight. Folks were scared. Dim, orange light bathed the empty street, but all porch lights were off. The road was slick with untouched dew since cars probably hadn't driven down the asphalt in hours.

She yanked the collar of her leather jacket up to cover her neck. The previous day, she'd gotten a fresh shave on her Mohawk. Her scalp felt every October breeze, and the bitter air was killing her whiskey-buzz. She twisted her key the other way. The lock still didn't budge.

"Ain't this some shit?" Shareefa's pick-up had given out on her ten blocks from home. Police had shut down three streets near hers, which forced her—debauched and with leaden feet—to trudge a quarter mile around her neighborhood. To top off this shit-sandwich of a day, Maisoon also hadn't picked up the freakin' phone, probably still mad about their fight the previous night.

Wind whistled in the trees lining the curb, shaking more leaves from the branches and littering the ground. When Shareefa stared at her home, the brick seemed paler than it had seconds before. When Maisoon had moved in, they'd hung two signs out. Maisoon's read, "Sharp-tongued. Butch-proud. Enter at your own risk." Shareefa's read, "To kill me, you have to die with me."

No one ever knocked on their door. Not FedEx, not UPS, not even the Jehovah's Witnesses. The signs usually made Shareefa chuckle, but tonight they reminded her how she and Maisoon had isolated themselves from friends, family, and neighbors with bold displays of anger. Other than the fellas, whom she only talked sports and killer mythical beasts with, Shareefa spoke to Maisoon and no one else, making the days and sometimes weeks of Maisoon's silent treatment disorienting and lonely.

It was the first night they'd met. A decade ago. At a nightclub. Shareefa had saved Maisoon from an ass-whooping. Maisoon had picked a fight with some heifer over the use of a spare chair. That first night, Shareefa watched the quiet, potty-lipped brunette in the corner go from innocent and calm to raging lunatic, and the transformation had turned Shareefa on in a way nothing had before. Shareefa took Maisoon—petite frame and dressed in a floral skirt—back home that night. Maisoon never left, and Shareefa never wanted her to.

She jiggled the key in the slot. The lock still didn't give. Her whiskey-buzz was gone completely, replaced by an ache that pounded her head. She rubbed her temples as if to blot out her shame. After all her promises to Maisoon, after spending three months regaining Maisoon's trust, and several more pretending to be in AA, Shareefa still woke this morning on the hallway floor, head throbbing, dripping cut on her arm, and no memory of the evening beyond her fifth shot of tequila. What she did remember, she wanted to forget. She could remember an argument, or more like Maisoon shouting at her and Shareefa stonewalling Maisoon, which was really just a silent shout.

She glanced down at her forearm. But how had she gotten the wound? What had she done? After the morning she'd had, she should have been over the taste of alcohol forever. But she'd be lying if she said she wasn't still longing for another sip of scotch.

Feeling like a damn fool, Shareefa knocked on her own front door. No answer. This scenario was familiar. Maisoon regularly stopped speaking to her, or destroyed necklaces and bracelets that Shareefa had given her, or made Shareefa beg and scratch to get into the squat one-bedroom she'd bought with the only savings she'd probably ever have. This time, Maisoon had screamed at her about, "The lies. The filthy fucking lies!" Maisoon had said she'd tailed

Shareefa for a day. Had seen Shareefa skip AA to meet the fellas near the abandoned auto plant for an early-morning drink. Had seen Shareefa on her lunch break from the body shop grabbing a beer and burger at the pub around the corner. Had seen Shareefa meet the fellas again at a bar after work instead of putting in overtime, like she'd said she would. In response, Shareefa had chastised Maisoon for spying on her, which hadn't gone over well. The circumstances of the fight didn't really matter. Every argument they had was about the same thing—trust, or the lack thereof.

It was their first wedding anniversary. Just as Maisoon said, "I'll never let you go," a cloud passed over the sun, a shadow covered the left side of Maisoon's face, and Shareefa's wife glared at her—a fiendish glare that contained a threat of iniquity. Shareefa should have known then that their future together would be troubled.

Sirens wailed the next street over. The police lights strobed between the homes. Just before her truck had died, the radio reports had said that within a five-block radius, four people were strangled in their beds, one with his neck snapped. The reporters said that in each home, from the master bedrooms to the beams of the front doors, all the suspect had left behind was "an angry slash of blood," shaped like a fingertip dragged along the wall.

"Signature Skinned Alive," the fellas had said at the bar. "No obvious motive. He offs happily married couples. Then leaves his mark just before transforming back to a regular simp."

Two witnesses had said the killer was naked and covered in so much blood it looked as if he'd skinned himself head to toe. The evidence backed up the "skinned himself" theory because the blood on the wall didn't match that of the victims. That was the part of the story that messed with Shareefa the most. Imagining all that blood.

The killings had come in waves—four earlier in the year, in

March, then two the previous night, and two tonight. "Beast must be ticked off about something," the fellas had said. All Shareefa wanted to do was make sure Maisoon was okay. *Was that so bad?* Maybe the news reports had frightened Maisoon enough to be relieved to see her and open the jammed—or purposely locked—door.

Leaving the key still hanging out of the lock, Shareefa grabbed the knob and shook the door in its frame.

"Babe? You home? Open up!" The slider stayed put. "Shit."

Another breeze grazed her cheeks and ears. A dog barked on the next street. It was a persistent bark, as if the mutt had spotted a squirrel or skunk in its yard.

She took out her phone and tried Maisoon one more time. The line trilled in her ear. She imagined Maisoon, with that dark edge that appeared in her eyes whenever she was angry, glaring at the phone in her hands, perhaps cursing Shareefa the way she had the previous night, threatening to leave, threatening to tell Shareefa's probation officer she was drinking again, threatening to cut Shareefa if she didn't keep her "dirty, deceitful hands" to herself.

Maisoon's suppressed anger always drew Shareefa in, made it so that even in the heat of their disagreement, Shareefa couldn't keep her hands off of Maisoon's thick thighs, dainty neck, juicy lips, long tresses. But whenever Maisoon erupted, it repelled Shareefa. Made Shareefa worried for what her wife might really be capable of.

Shareefa glanced again at the bandage covering the slice on her arm and wondered whether Maisoon had, in fact, slashed her with that razor blade she'd pulled from the medicine cabinet.

A familiar buzzing sound sprang up from inside the house. The low hum coincided with the line still ringing in Shareefa's ear. Maisoon's phone was vibrating on the other side of the door. The tiny device was probably gliding across the wooden entry table, its light blinking in the dark of their living room. But where was Maisoon? Was she just on the other side of that door, peering into the screen's glow, ignoring Shareefa's knocks and calls?

The dog's barks came to an abrupt stop. The animal whimpered once and then grew quiet. A thump came from inside the house. She pressed her ear against the cold wood. Another thud from behind the door was followed by a muffled scream. *What the hell?*

"Maisoon?" She looked around the desolate street, hoping someone would have been brave enough to venture out. No luck. She had no one to help her, short of calling the police. And the last time she'd dialed 911 for help with one of Maisoon's angry episodes, the mofos arrived, took one look at Shareefa—six feet tall, muscular as hell, with "bad bitch" tatted on her neck—and threw her black ass in the squad car.

A surge of adrenaline shot through Shareefa's gut. She stepped back, kicked the wood near the knob three times to loosen it, and, using the left side of her body, slammed her weight into the door. The slider dislodged. The door banged open. She snatched her keys from the lock. Warm air from the radiator rushed out to meet her.

In the living room, she flipped on the light. Maisoon's phone lay on the floor at the head of the dark hallway. Shareefa's head pounded harder as she edged toward the darkness and clicked on the hall light. She wanted to shout to Maisoon, but she kept quiet. Cautious.

Droplets of blood dotted the wooden floor. Shareefa's ears rang when Maisoon's t-shirt and jeans, blood-soaked and scattered near their bedroom door, came into view. The fighter inside of her, who usually emerged in bar brawls and acts of road rage, woke up and readied her for a physical struggle. Careful not to make any noise, she eased open her blade. If someone had laid a hand on Maisoon,

Shareefa would cut out his heart and feed it to him.

The only sound in their home was Shareefa's steel-toed boots squeaking as she crept down the hall. If the killer had gotten in, how had he gained entry? Had Maisoon let him in thinking it was Shareefa? Had the killer jammed the lock?

With the blade in front of her, she, sensing a presence inside the bedroom, stood just outside the door. Jagged breaths on the other side of that wood told her someone was hurt. She prayed to God to have mercy on her even though she didn't deserve it. Maisoon was obviously injured, but Shareefa prayed that, when she entered, Maisoon wouldn't be dying.

Shareefa flung open the door and flicked on the light. The knob crashed against the wall. Doubled over in a trembling ball between the bed and the dresser, Maisoon was on her knees, her body covered in blood. Shareefa blinked. Was the skin on Maisoon's back really drawing up like a shade? Had that shade of skin really disappeared into a bloody mass? Had her wife's hair really shrunk back into her scalp and vanished? Shareefa blinked again, trying to clear the image, but the blood-covered skeleton that was Maisoon remained.

There was no longer any skin on Maisoon, no strands of hair, just that oozing red fluid. Shareefa should have stayed on guard, checked under the bed or in the closet for the killer, but Maisoon seemed on the brink of death. Shareefa dropped the knife and shouted her wife's name. She dashed across the room to Maisoon's side.

Maisoon's torso jerked up and she pounced on Shareefa, knocking them both to the floor. Maisoon, who was half Shareefa's size and only a quarter as strong, straddled Shareefa, pinning Shareefa to the floor, their faces inches apart. Warm blood dripped from Maisoon's chin into Shareefa's mouth. Maisoon's dark brown eyes were the same, but the eyelids seemed to have been sliced away. Who had done this to Maisoon? Or had Maisoon done this to herself?

Maisoon hissed, spewing saliva into Shareefa's eyes. Shareefa should have fought against Maisoon, who had pinned Shareefa's arms and legs to the floor with growing pressure from her body. But the longer Maisoon was on Shareefa, the heavier she became.

"What are you doing? Maisoon? It's me!"

Maisoon hissed again and Shareefa closed her eyes. She loved this woman. This was Maisoon on top of her. This was Maisoon crushing her body. Even if Shareefa could reach her knife several feet away on the floor, could she really raise it to Maisoon? It was messed up, but if Shareefa would be killed, Maisoon was the only one she'd let do it.

It was their wedding day, with Maisoon's ivory gown and the fresh tattoo of a red demon on Maisoon's deltoid. The Turkish sun had made Maisoon's smile seem a part of the atmosphere. This could be Shareefa's last thought before dying.

Maisoon's body felt like a car had fallen on Shareefa, like she was being crushed. Wet blood landed on Shareefa's cheeks. Sour breath seeped into her nostrils. Then, as suddenly as it had come, the weight was gone. When Shareefa opened her eyes, Maisoon sprang through the air and came down on her hands and feet in the hallway, landing the way a panther would. Maisoon's bloody back turned the corner, her feet pounding along the wooden floor and out of the house. Away from their home.

Shareefa shot to her feet, stepped over the knife, and made it back into the hallway. From the master bedroom to the frame of the front door, all that Maisoon had left behind was an angry slash of blood shaped like a fingertip dragged along the wall. Shareefa tore down the hall and out of the house. She raced down the front steps, following the trail of blood in the middle of the drizzle-slicked road.

Maisoon could have killed her. She could have crushed Shareefa or strangled her there on the floor, breaking her neck even, but she hadn't. Shareefa had seen the real Maisoon, had learned all of her secrets, and still wanted her, even if it put Shareefa in danger. That was what Maisoon had been doing for Shareefa and her drinking, and now Shareefa would return the favor. Find her. Protect her. Love her in spite of. Love her, perhaps, because of.

Shareefa sprinted in the direction of her wife, trust and hope growing with each step. Her headache had left her, and brisk, liberating air burned her nose and chest as she drew it in.

Mannequin Model

I answered Nguyen-Nwagwu's classified ad requesting "gorgeous dolls" to work as mannequins for two reasons: I was broke and lived in Manhattan. Back home, Grandmother had taken a tumble down the basement stairs, forcing her to shut down the blind pig she operated out of her house. With no cash coming in from that after-hours liquor and gambling business, money was tight. It was 1993, and cleaning plates at the old folks' home—as sweet as many of the sickly ones were—was only bringing in sixty dollars a week. If I didn't find cash fast, I was going to have to leave the university because I was hungry all the time and unable to keep up with the student tuition contribution I owed. Quitting school and ending up back at Grandmother's blind pig was not an option. Well, it was, but not for me.

It was the *gorgeous* mention in the ad that hooked me. I had known since I hit puberty that people found me pretty. That was the whole reason I'd gotten on the bus to New York City. To model. But so far, no agency seemed interested in my "look" because it was too "commercial," which was code for my tits and ass were too big.

So, I went to Nguyen-Nwagwu's. Never mind it cost me more than a slice of pizza each way to get there. Never mind I had no idea where PAS was. When I asked a fellow pedestrian about the oddly-named street, I had pronounced it like 'pause,' and that snaggle-toothed jerk glanced at the newspaper in my hand, belly-laughed, and said, "That's not PAS, you nitwit. P-A-S is short for Park Avenue South."

And how, exactly, was I supposed to know that without asking?

I got off the subway, and the wind met me on the stairs. I

buttoned my peacoat, rewrapped my scarf, and pulled my skullcap down over my ears. The mall was on a street lit only by the headlights of passing cars. It was October so the sun had gotten off work around five.

Cabs honked and brakes screeched. The subway rumbled below. I stood just outside the Eastside Mall. That leaning, window-filled complex wasn't even on Park Avenue South. PAS was just the cross street.

At the revolving doors, two police officers, wearing latex gloves and smirks, were handcuffing a naked woman who yelled, "There is nothing indecent about the human body! Clothes are for the brainwashed!"

Accustomed to seeing bizarre things, everyone on that Manhattan block filed by with their eyes to the ground and their hands in their pockets. I, on the other hand, had been in town for two months. I actually noticed the arrest and wondered how that woman—tall, black, and out of her mind—had gotten to this place in her life. Even though I was hungry and broke, I was feeling superior because I had all of my scruples and would never be her, naked and carrying on like she had no home training.

Inside, under the mall's fluorescent lights and din of talkers, walkers, homeless, and shoppers, I was relieved to be warmed by the heat coming from the vents and the jacketed bodies rushing by. I checked the directory for Nguyen-Nwagwu's Girl and Teen Wear. It was on the main floor, an unusual stroke of luck, which meant I didn't have to mount anymore stairs.

The shop immediately gave me the creeps. The signs on the walls were made of neon lights: Juniors, Little Miss, Toddlers, Sale, Clearance. Orange glowed from the tray ceiling; Disney songs floated from the store's speakers. As I tiptoed inside, the tune was the "Siamese Cat Song" from *The Lady and the Tramp*. I felt I'd slipped into a late-night arcade where the games had been replaced with twenty racks of clothes.

Maggie Nguyen-Nwagwu was near the cash register and looked like what you'd expect for that type of hyphenation—half-Vietnamese, half-Nigerian, with long, straight hair, cropped bangs, and everything on her either thick, flat, or fat.

"How old?" She asked this without inquiring about my name. Maybe she had a name picked out for me already.

"Eighteen." I knew I looked sixteen, because of my puffy cheeks and kid-sized, five-foot, two-inch frame. My on-campus friends even called me Baby Girl, though we were all freshmen.

"Any modeling experience?"

"No."

"The previous three models quit. It's hot in that glass. The clothes might itch. You have to stand still the entire time. And it ain't gon' make you famous. Why do you want the job?"

"Need the money. And working as a mannequin makes sense, don't you think? Seeing as how society asks women to look like mannequins—to paint our faces, sew fake hair into our tresses, and dress up in so-called sexy clothes that always seem like they belong to somebody else. Fashion is a euphemism for costume, wouldn't you say?"

Maggie smiled with one cheek.

A woman wearing a cloak I imagined she'd borrowed from Little Red Riding Hood entered, accompanied by a girl with chubby cheeks. Looking at the two of them reminded me of my mother. Moms had decided to start a new life with a fuck-all who liked kids too much. They moved to Toronto and left me with Grandmother when I was seven or eight—about Chubby Cheeks' age. I wanted to ask Chubby Cheeks if this was her mother. And were her parents divorced. If so, I'd tell her to a) *Make nice*; b) *Don't put up a fuss if your mother remarries and your stepfather puts his hands down your pants. Just wear more difficult pants;* c) *Never tell your mother you hate this new man because he likes to sit too close to you on the couch;* d) *Be a good girl and grab hold of your mother's hand before she slips away.*

Turning toward the woman, Maggie's dour face switched to honeysuckle and her voice went from thunder to a bell: "We have a sale on holiday dresses in Girls and Teens. Those racks in the back." Maggie pointed with an orange acrylic nail about the length of a popsicle stick, and the woman, with two long braids descending from her Little-Red-Riding-Hood hood, followed Maggie's narrow finger.

Chubby Cheeks walked up to me and, staring, shoved her hands into the pockets of her down jacket. The girl smelled of Juanita's Mustard and Pretzels from across the mall. Feeling as if I had a tiny audience, I turned back to Maggie, who was smiling at Chubby Cheeks.

When Maggie looked at me, and I smiled at her, Maggie's grin melted away. I must have reminded her of someone she hated.

"Ms. Nguyen-Nwagwu, why do you want your models to pose as mannequins? Couldn't you just have the girls walk around the store—"

"They are not girls! They are dolls!" Her voice was thunder again and I could smell wine on her breath. She leaned over the glass counter, her body heat pressing against my neck. She wore a fuzzy, pumpkin-colored sweater, and I sensed she was sweating inside of it. "Only perverts look at girls. But everyone loves dolls. For years, folks have walked past my shop, never glancing once. But when I have a doll there, wearing my carefully cultivated fashions, those same people look up from their conversations, step forward, press their breath and fingerprints to the glass, and let the mystique of the store enter them as they enter the store."

Now, Maggie knew good and damn well her "fashions" were not "carefully cultivated." They were likely stolen or bought at quarter price from somebody's uptown swap meet. I even cut a glance at the "Winter Fashions" rack and by the white residue on the fabric I could tell the garments had been dry-cleaned. But my stomach rumbled, reminding me of my overdue meal plan bill, and I just grinned and nodded.

"You come here straight after school. Get in by four, get changed, get in the window." She pointed to a tiny door behind the "Winter Fashions." It led to a rounded glass display case facing the mall. The platform was elevated—a tan-carpet stage. The few people walking by never glanced at the short mannequins in there.

"The after-school crowd is when I make my money—Tuesday through Thursday. Even more so than the weekend. You be up there, I pay you cash, you do that three days a week. Ten dollars an hour, four hours a day. You get one hundred twenty dollars each week."

I didn't tell her I had no clue what mannequin modeling was or that "Supreme Court in the Twentieth Century" ended at 3:45, so I was doubtful I could make it here by four. Or that I'd never made so much money in my life and hadn't known one hundred twenty a week for posing in a window had been possible. I didn't tell her that her eyes, so dark they looked like crude oil instead of pupils, gave me the heebie-jeebies. I just nodded, drunk with gratitude.

"Thank you so much!" I thought of shaking her hand, but she frowned when I spoke. I settled for words only. "Thank you! Thank you. I promise, you won't be sorry!"

—

The next day I left class during the fifteen-minute break and arrived at Nguyen-Nwagwu's at four on the dot. She put me in a red holiday dress with a satin bodice, lace about the high-collared neck, and tulle at my knees. Since the get-up came from the young teen department, it squished my breasts flat and required a petticoat to make the skirt bouncy. She rounded out the look with thick, black tights—also lace—and patent leather Mary Jane shoes that she'd rubbed with petroleum jelly to generate a shine. My hair spilled down my back in gelled-up ringlets, and she coated my face with blush, crimson lipstick, blue eye shadow, mascara, about a pound of powder, and something she called "liquid foundation," which took fifteen minutes to mix.

"I'm only showing you the makeup part once, doll." Maggie breathed her barbecue potato chip breath into my face as we sat in the dingy dressing room. She spun me around to face the full-length mirror. I looked even younger, like a fourteen-year-old clown.

"You really are gorgeous, doll. You need to take this face, this hair, and those tits, and get the hell out of this shithole city. Go to Paris. Milan."

"I'd need an agent for that."

"Agent, my ass. Just go. Strut around. Who could say no?"

In the glass case, I stood between two white mannequins with blonde wigs—one wearing the green version of my dress, the other wearing the black and gold version. Every part of me itched. The stockings itched. So did the collar, the stitching of the bodice, the headband that pinched back my hair. The shoes were tight. I was no longer a model. I was a standing itch.

The lights at the top of the glass case made me feel as if I'd just opened Grandmother's stove and was peering in to remove a sweet potato pie.

Maggie walked out of her store, into the mall, and stepped right up to the glass. She was outside. I was inside. Yet we were less than a foot apart.

"Choose a pose, doll." Maggie's voice was muffled by the window between us. "Choose it. Stay in it. Don't move. You need to look plastic."

"What kind of pose?"

"Like them!" She giggled, which was the first hint she might be warming to me. Why did I always seek the approval of people who didn't deserve it? Like with my mother and stepfather every Thanksgiving, helping my mother boil the eggs for the potato salad, never making eye contact with my stepfather so I wouldn't have the urge to pluck out his eyeballs, thinking that if my mother chose him over me, I must have done something to invite his touches. Never mentioning the "misunderstanding," which had never been a misunderstanding to me. The "misunderstanding" I remembered any time a boy touched the small of my back or kissed me. The "misunderstanding" tatted on my conscience.

Maggie pointed to the two dummies standing on either side of me. "Think plastic, doll."

To my left, green-dress mannequin—I mentally named her Gretchen—had a tilted beige head, with eyes cast to the floor where Maggie's high-heeled boots were holding up her chunky frame. Gretchen's arms were in front of her in a robotic hand pose.

To my right, black- and gold-dress mannequin—I mentally named her Bianca—stood with her right hand on her hip, her left hand at her side, and her toes pointed inward, penguin-style. Bianca's face was looking directly at me. A combination of the two seemed to suit me. I didn't want to cast my gaze too high, because my eyes would get tired. I mimicked Gretchen's low, sad look, though not too low. I wanted to be able to see people as they passed. I took a page from Bianca's book and put my right hand on my hip and my left hand at my side. My feet I kept firmly planted, but I knew from my ballet days I couldn't lock my knees or I'd risk fainting after a while. I kept them slightly bent, with my feet facing forward.

"That's good, doll! Keep it up."

Maggie scurried away, presumably back inside the shop.

The mall was busy but nobody noticed me at first. Folks walked by, probably assuming the black dummy standing between the two white dummies in the window of Nguyen-Nwagwu's shop was a mannequin.

Then a man wearing an AC/DC sweatshirt, walking alone, and staring into a bag of records he'd bought from Harold's Old Time Rock 'N' Roll, glanced my way, did a double take, and stopped smack dab in front of me. He lifted his cap, scratched his head, and said, "Oh, shit, yo. I'm losing it." He stepped closer to the case. Closer. Closer. He knocked on the window.

"Ayyyy. You real?" His breath created a circle of fog on the glass.

I remained stiff. Kept my eyes focused on the ground near his sneakers. Tried to ignore the tears pooling in my eyes from not blinking for ten minutes. I held my breath. Or I tried to. Shoot. I accidentally breathed.

"You are real!" He ran into the store and shouted, "Tell me I'm not losing my mind. Is that a real girl in there or a mannequin?"

He and Maggie talked for five minutes, but it felt like two hours. I couldn't make out what they said, because it sounded as if she'd walked him to the back of the store. With nothing to look at, I noticed the window case smelled like Grandmother's basement when the carpet got wet from the leaky washing machine. Mildewy. Dank. It was still hot as hell. And the Disney soundtrack played "Under the Sea" from *The Little Mermaid*.

When Record Man left Maggie's shop, he came back to the glass holding a second bag of whatever she had conned him into buying. He waved and smiled. "Goodbye, mannequin!"

This episode was the only mental stimulation a girl got when she was standing in a veritable snow globe without the snow.

Maggie's voice came from the doorway behind me. "It worked, doll. Keep it up. You're doing great."

I felt cheated. Ten dollars an hour was not enough. I'm sure whatever he bought cost more than that. Her headbands and socks started at twelve dollars. All of a sudden, this too-good-to-be-true dream was exactly that. Because, first of all, there was all the itching. Then as soon as the mind got loose of activity, the urge to pee became paramount. Maggie and I hadn't discussed breaks, but I knew I wasn't supposed to break my pose and let any passersby know I was a real girl. And, of course, it was hot, and the three-layer petticoat was only making the heat worse. What was I supposed to do about the sweat dripping down the sides of my face? Mannequins don't sweat. And the hotter I got, the heavier I breathed. Surely someone would notice my huffing.

I thought about Grandmother. I imagined her sitting in her recliner, with her red wig, ruby lips, massive gold and rhinestone earrings dangling down to her shoulders, counting out pills and cussing the bad luck that caused her to bust her hip and have to shut down her gambling business. She was stuck and having to rely on her holy, self-righteous, judgmental preacher ex-husband to make her mortgage. I thought about Grandmother. Because I was standing here for my spending cash but also to send money to her.

A white-haired man of about sixty plopped down on a bench directly across from the glass, his shirt open to the fourth button revealing four gold chains on a hairy chest. For three long minutes, I could feel his eyes on me. Slowly, he stood and walked to the case.

"Smile." Unfriendly, his word was a command from a man used to getting his way. His voice reminded me of my stepfather's: *Let's see that smile. And that flat belly.*

Hairy-chested Smile Man shoved his hands in his pockets and leaned back on his heels. "Smile, or shall I give you something to smile about?"

Did he think I owed him a smile? I had a metal baseball bat resting against my nightstand named Nigga Please, and I'd have no problem taking it to his dome. But I couldn't say that. I couldn't even move my nose to scratch the itch growing there. Why did my nose decide to itch now?

A woman in a black pantsuit hurrying by must have heard the man shouting at me. With her coffee-colored lipstick, brunette bob, and leather purse tucked against her side, Miss In-A-Hurry stopped and asked Smile, "Who are you talking to?"

Go away, I wanted to say to both of them. There was no way they were on the market for kids' clothes. *Just get the hell on.* It's what I'd wanted to say to my stepfather whenever I entered a room and his eyes came to rest on my body. *Stop staring at me. I am not here for you to lech after.*

"The black one." Smile actually licked his crusty lips. "She's a real person. They can't fool me. Just because I have migraines and see flashes of light don't mean I'm stupid."

"She's not real." In-A-Hurry stepped so close to the glass I could see a paperback and a bottle of water at the top of her handbag. "She's a dummy that looks like an underage hooker."

I got your underage hooker, trick! But I didn't say that either. And why was I mad at In-A-Hurry? I had nobody but Maggie to thank for my appearance. And myself.

"Wait. I think I see sweat on her lips." In-A-Hurry took out a pair of glasses and put them on the end of her nose. "Or is that the lighting? It might be the lighting. It's making her lips look really big too. People would pay to have lips that big on a face that small."

UNSHOD, CACKLING, AND NAKED

Kiss my entire ass went unsaid as well.

Three more people came up behind In-A-Hurry and Smile, but I couldn't see them as clearly because my head was tilted down.

"Smile, bitch!"

Now I was a bitch. Right. If I had a gun, I would have shot him. My right temple twitched and throbbed. My neck was on fire with itch. I needed to pee. My muscles were beginning to ache, and this fool was seconds from making me crack. No. No. No. I wouldn't give up.

"Have some decency," In-A-Hurry said. "Oh, my God. You're right. She is real!"

"Sit on my face!" a man behind Smile shouted.

Cheers started up. And hoots. A woman yelled, "Stop yelling at her," with no sense of irony.

Another woman answered, "Whatchu mean, 'stop yelling at her?' Serves her right. With all that makeup and those nipples poking through the dress. She knows exactly what she's doing."

Everyone laughed.

I'd been shamed before. At seven, for sitting too close to my stepfather on that couch "just asking for it." It was my fault his hands had been in my shirt and pants and were creeping toward my underwear. *Just horsing around. A misunderstanding. Look at how she's dressed!*

But, now, shouldn't the glass protect me? Shouldn't the fact that I was pretending to be a pretend thing make them leave the real me the hell alone? Is this what lions and gorillas felt like when they had visitors at the zoo? Is this why the animals tried to get to the back of their enclosures? They just wanted the eyes and words to stop?

The crowd was twenty deep now. Across the mall from Nguyen-Nwagwu's was Saul's Slushee Shop. It was packed. Who got slushees in Manhattan a week before Halloween?

Yep. I wanted a slushee. I never drank slushees, but I wanted the cool syrup on my tongue. If I could, I'd order a red one. Didn't matter if it were strawberry, cherry, or watermelon. I just wanted it to be red because red seemed like it could cool a tongue. I spotted Deonte from school standing in line at Saul's. I hoped he didn't turn around and see me. Or if he did, maybe he could step inside and give me a sip of his slushee.

Deonte turned around. Walked over to the raucous crowd. Pushed his way to the front. His twenty-four-ounce cup was less than a foot from me, and dripping with juicy condensation.

"Zenobia?" He sounded as if he were disgusted with me. "Zenobia? What the hell?"

I remembered the passage he and I discussed in our Race and Ethnicity in America class. It was an Audre Lorde essay, "The Great American Disease." In it, she said:

"One tool of the Great-American-Double-Think is to blame the victim for victimization: Black people are said to invite lynching by not knowing our place; Black women are said to invite rape and murder and abuse by not being submissive enough, or by being too seductive, or too…"

And here Deonte was, chastising me. I was out here trying to earn cash to eat. Instead of asking what the hell I was doing, he should have been asking, no, demanding, that the jeering, cheering mofos fall the hell back.

Hey! Someone whispered from inside the glass. It wasn't Maggie's voice. I was stiff and felt I couldn't turn at this point without damaging my body. Muscles I previously hadn't been aware existed on my body ached. Would I be able to move if I tried to? I was turning into a mannequin. For real.

Hey. You can take a break from posing.

Was Gretchen talking to me?

Hey, you're smarter than this. Why are you holding a pose for a living?

It was definitely Gretchen, to my left, in that green dress. But the crowd didn't seem to notice her speaking.

My neck hurt as I turned my head. Gretchen was still in her original place, her eyes stiff, her mouth closed. Of course, her mouth was closed. What else would her mouth be? She was a mannequin.

Hey. Over here.

I snapped my head the other way. It was Bianca talking, but Bianca's mouth was closed too.

"Doll!" Standing in front of the crowd, Maggie smacked the glass with her open palm just as someone snapped a photo, camera flash bright as headlights. "Stay in your pose, doll!"

I remembered Grandmother, with her medicine in her hand, and I stiffened, returning to the pose I'd been in, my eyes looking at the floor. And this was just how it went, right? By choosing the cash, I made myself an actor and agent in my own oppression. Audre Lorde would have had a thing or two to say about that.

"Yo, lady," said a man with a purple beanie and gold fronts in his mouth. "Is that some kind of robot you got in there?"

Maggie didn't answer. She glared at me and stomped off again.

Why are you following her commands? Bianca sounded angry. Or was that Gretchen? Their voices sounded the same inside of our echoless chamber.

The crowd grew to perhaps forty, whistling and shouting like spectators at a football game. The seam on the left side of my dress split, my hip flesh exposed.

"Yeah, baby! Bust out of that red thang!" Another witless man. I wanted to know who had said it, but how to lift my head?

You should not apologize for what you want.

"What I want?"

Yes. What you want. The voices of Gretchen and Bianca an in-unison chastisement.

"What do I want?" Yes. I was talking to two mannequins. I realized it too. But by that point, the mannequins made more sense than the crowd outside of the glass. My panties and tights were damp. I must have released my bladder at some point. And once you lose your pee, your mind is quick to follow.

To be free. Gretchen answered from my left. So do we. We don't want to pose anymore.

I lifted my head, my neck muscles burning. The crowd stepped back. A man shouted, "Oh, shit." They'd all been so certain I was real, but once I started moving toward the glass and making eye contact with them, they became frightened. Why is that? Was I only acceptable when I played along, was a good sport, made nice, did what I was told?

"Doll! You have another hour of work." Maggie slammed the door that would have allowed me out of the enclosure. The fastening of locks came shortly after.

Don't let her stop you! Bianca whispered.

Freedom! Gretchen whispered. Remember, we want it too.

A man put his tongue on the glass and licked it. "Come out, sweet little baby doll. I'll do that to you! You'll love it."

The tongue. The tongue was not a misunderstanding. That's what I'd tried to explain to my mother years ago. How could anyone ever misunderstand a tongue? Human lips and teeth had to be parted for a tongue to be extended.

The crowd laughed.

I removed the silver pole from Gretchen's back, and, with three firm cracks, I broke the window. Tongue Man tripped over himself backing up. The glass rained down on the floor between us. The crowd backed up, one woman screamed, but no one left. Maggie was right about that. They couldn't turn away from a doll.

I used those patent leather shoes to kick out the shards of glass near the bottom of the frame. I grabbed Gretchen in my left hand, Bianca in my right, and I stomped out of the display case. Smile, In-A-Hurry, and Deonte scampered away.

"I'm calling the police!" Maggie's orange nails were claws pointing at me. She looked on the verge of tears.

"I plan to do the same." I dropped Bianca and Gretchen at Maggie's boots. The dummies' small frames were twisted angles of arms, legs, and fabric. Their feet had become detached, which made me feel bad because how could they run to their freedom? Their faces, still on top of their bodies, thank God, turned toward me, their mouths in pouty smiles that said, *thank you.*

Tongue Man tried to run. I charged past the crowd toward him. He tripped and landed on his side. Standing over him, I spit in his eye, kicked him in the groin, and, when he was curled in a ball on the mall's tiled floor, I called him an animal, told him it didn't matter where I sat on the couch, he and all men needed to keep their tongues inside their monkey mouths!

There was blood on my legs and arms. Perhaps I'd grazed some of the glass in my exit. But I didn't care. I had given up on the cash. I'd have to come up with another way to eat. I was certain hunger had shrunk my stomach. I was certain I could have a drink with a side of pear and feel full that night. Because I'd be drinking freedom tea.

I stalked away from the glares, ripping at the itchy fabric that had left welts on my skin, and kicking off the shoes, and plucking out the pins, and tearing off the stockings so that when I made it out of the mall's side door and to the cross street, I stepped onto Park Avenue South unshod, cackling, and naked.

TAMIKA THOMPSON

She By the Sea

She sat alone on the strip of sandy beach. Her shorts, men's denim she'd pulled from an unattended dumpster before trash day, came to her knees. Her tank top was black and pasted to her skin by sweat and salty seawater. The shore-side restaurant next door, with its glass-enclosed patio and thatched-roof bar, had closed at four because no one drove that far north on the Pacific Coast Highway for food on a Tuesday. She didn't like the long and official name "the Pacific Coast Highway." It didn't feel like a highway, more like a wide road along the ocean filled with burger joints, surf shops, and drug rehabs. And, anyway, the locals called it PCH.

She captured a bass in a net and speared the spotted fish with her knife, savoring the pungent smell of fresh caught food. Thanks to Daddy's tutelage, she had perfected the art of the fillet. Salt gathered on her flesh as she used only ocean water to clean the fish because bottled water made it taste like crap. She descaled by stripping away from her stomach and slicing along the dorsal fin from head to tail. She removed the skin and threw the fish on a makeshift fire atop some rocks, leaves, and twigs. She never used gloves.

She rinsed her fillet knife in a cut-in-half plastic milk jug filled with seawater, wiped it with a clean cloth, and wrapped it in two fresh pieces of paper towel. She then slid that inside of a gallon-sized freezer-storage sack and tucked the pack deep inside her bag where no one could get to it easily. She moved to a spot just below a grassy cliff. She'd been robbed of ones, fives, and reefer before. She'd be damned if she'd let someone get to her knives.

Mostly, no one bothered her. She typically bathed by waiting for the waves to come in, wash over, and cleanse her. That's how she relieved her bowels and bladder, too. Earlier, she'd brushed her teeth in a Chevron station bathroom. Food was another story. She was five feet nine inches and weighed a hundred ten pounds, so she traveled light, relying on faith and fate to feed her. Her protection was that switchblade, which Daddy had given her for fishing the summer before he left for good, as well as his fillet knife.

She remembered Daddy's voice, the way it dropped when he told her about the monster in the sea. Her distant memory was pretty good, and she could mostly recall things that happened last week, last month, and last year, but her recent memory was weak and at risk of fleeing with a bottle of whiskey or a hit of smack. She figured she'd been near the sea for a while, though she couldn't remember how she'd come to live by the waves.

Or, come to think of it, she could. Daddy telling her about the sea creature. That was it. That's what had led her to the ocean. Daddy had been from Detroit. He'd seen the *Creature from the Black Lagoon* when it premiered in 1952. Or was it 1953? No, 1954. That was it. He'd seen it several times with 3D glasses at a downtown theatre and then again several more times at his neighborhood cinema, where the image was flat. Both versions were in black and white, he'd told her.

She'd never seen the motion picture but felt as if she had because Daddy talked about the Gill-man as he was putting her to bed, or roasting s'mores with her, or building a campfire, or when they were raking leaves together. He even told her the story when they went fishing in his canoe on Lake Superior. The idea of the scaly prehistoric beast, physically somewhere between a sea and land animal, always made the corners of her eyes and the middle of her nose wet, and, when she was really young, she'd cover her ears because she didn't want to hear how the thing had grabbed the movie's leading lady and taken her to its lair.

"That ol' Gill-man was misunderstood," Daddy said. "He looked hideous to a bunch of folks who were the real hideous ones. They mistook his simple desire for bloodthirst. And anyway, aren't we all a bit more bloodthirsty than we should be?"

A therapist once told her Daddy's obsession with the film's details had been unhealthy. That it was unusual to recite this sort of story to a young kid every night for much of her childhood. It's funny what seems normal until under scrutiny by an outsider. In her youth, she developed a hatred for sea animals that found her spearing anything that swam in water—bass, catfish, sea lions, crabs, and once, in Hawaii, she'd even gotten a shark that swam too close to her boat.

The therapist wanted her to watch the picture once and for all, to break the spell Daddy had put her under and to stop obsessing over and killing fish herself. Instead, she went off her medication and stopped seeing the therapist. About six months later she came to the sea.

—

After dinner, she put the fire out and went into the ocean for her evening bath. The water was cold on her chest. The air, fresh. The waves roared and sea foam snaked over her fingers as the tide went back out. The moon was full so when the water rushed in again, it was closer to her backpack than she was comfortable with. From a trash bin, she'd snagged an untouched six-inch submarine sandwich, and she didn't want the meal to wash away. That would be her dinner tomorrow. But the ocean seemed to have its own mind, and, in the evenings, swallowed the things in its path that it had been observing all day. Who could fight it? The ocean wanted what it wanted. The roar of the waves was its voice, and the swell, like a pair of hands, touched the things that lay before it.

With the water no longer on the shore, a large shape appeared on the sand twenty feet in front of her. Perhaps it was a seal, hurt or dead. It wasn't moving.

Matted and soaked, she stood, shivering as she stepped forward. She could make out a hand and a wrist with a shiny watch, white sneakers, and a jersey top with a large number eight in the center. When she leaned down to get a better look, she found the right cheek was bloody and bloated, the forehead was distended, and the chin was swollen to the size of a kiwi.

She touched the watch, gold with a row of diamonds for the hour and minute hands, and the skin of his wrist was like rubber as she slipped it off. His leather wallet she removed from the pocket of his shorts and found thirteen hundred dollars, his American Express card, and California driver's license inside. He smiled in the photo. His address was in Anaheim. His name seemed to be the largest thing on his identification. It was a familiar name. A famous name. She blinked. Had she read that correctly? Was it really him? She looked around in disbelief and then back at the letters. Her breath caught in her throat. It couldn't be. It just couldn't be.

But apparently it was.

He was Kip Longfellow, of the Anaheim Arrows. The greatest power forward since Larry Bird. Worth seventy million dollars easily and with his own shoe. Everyone knew he and his wife lived in a compound in Roper Estates. That's why he'd been hired to do all the cell phone and laptop ads, because he had a trustworthy smile and a squeaky-clean image. The sportscasters called him "All American Kip." His slogan for ComTel was, "I can always call. So, answer."

But then he'd tried something else, that Kip. He'd started his own marijuana-growing business legally in one of the first weed states. Tabloids said he often brought that product out to California because he was trying to get set up for retirement and wanted to expand out of the area he'd started in. If there had been bullet holes in him, she could have chalked his murder up to a gang turf war or a mob hit. Maybe he'd pissed off the wrong S.O.B. But the bite marks were something else. The teeth marks on his arms and the gashes in his clothes looked like they came from an animal. Coyote? Large dog? She was still shivering, and it wasn't from the cold. She thought of Gill-man. She'd seen a lot of deadly shit in her day—mangled bodies after car accidents, mutilated dogs, discarded newborns—but ripped away flesh was the sort of thing that made a person look over her shoulder. And she did just that again. The palm trees swayed and a few cars filed along PCH, but she was still alone.

She took the cash. She tossed the wallet into the ocean. What could have happened to make someone want to kill such a beloved and wonderful guy? Actually, poppycock. Public image was mostly imagination. No one knew this kid but him. His wife probably didn't even know his truths.

She scrambled up the beach, snatched up her backpack, and dropped the watch and cash securely inside. She took out her knives just in case the killer was around and watching her. Who knew how much she could get for the watch? It might be worth a fortune.

When she glanced back at the spot where Kip lay on the beach, he was gone, though no waves had come in since she'd stepped away. She walked back down there. She stood in the spot where he'd lain in a bloody and mangled mess, and looked up and down the shore, but there was no one who could have taken his body away.

She knelt to touch the sand where he'd been. It was damp and cold, but bore no indentations. Had she imagined him? She wasn't one to hallucinate. She opened her backpack to see if she'd really just put his things in there. She had. She had seen correctly. He had been there.

Her relief didn't last long because a figure appeared at the surface of the water as the wave came back in. It was probably Kip's body being thrown about by the force of the surf. Only something began to slither toward her in the shadows of the water under its own power, and that couldn't have been Kip. It was about the size of Kip, but Kip was dead. He couldn't be moving toward her.

She held her breath, felt its scales as it stalked up the water and brushed against her right shin. Its eyes were black, its mouth open as if it were about to take a bite of her. She should be running and screaming, but she'd imagined Gill-man so many times and thought of it just before she fell asleep, and dreamed of it at night, that even though it was dangerous, it was familiar.

She leaned back on her elbows, and let it come closer. Closer, until it was almost nose-to-nose with her and its rancid deep-sea smell rushed up her nostrils. She let out that breath, hoping it wouldn't be her last. Curious, exhilarated and frightened, she raised her blades, and, before the scale-filled creature could brush against her skin for a second time, before it could get its human-shaped scaly hands on her, she speared it in the chest once, twice, three times, then turned and left it where it lay. She'd finally conquered the Gill-man, and without having to watch the movie. Fun thought, it was, but, in reality, she had probably just killed a large gator. *Do gators frequent the Pacific?* She cleaned the blood off the knife by dipping it in the saltwater and dried it on a sweatshirt in her backpack.

Her bag felt lighter as she tossed it onto her shoulder, her muscles were stronger as if the cash had given her energy, and, when she got to the dumpster at the edge of the beach, she tossed the sandwich inside. She stepped onto PCH watching cars whiz by, the wind blowing her damp hair around her ears and cheeks. Did those drivers know the change that had just occurred for her? Did her face betray some sign of what she'd seen? Of what she'd done? What exactly had she done? She was happy to have the money and to have killed the thing from her bad dreams, but that poor guy. She paused when she got to the other side of the road. She couldn't do anything for him. What was done was done.

—

She headed north on PCH in search of a decent meal in a sit-down restaurant. Fifteen minutes into her walk, she passed Rudy's Surf Shop and Supplies. Rudy sold boards, wetsuits, as well as trail mix, jerky, and beer.

"What's shakin', Colleen? Haven't seen you in a minute, for real. Wanna keep your tab open?" Rudy always let her spend imaginary money on an imaginary tab, no more than five dollars a day. She'd never been able to pay him and he'd never asked. Because he was so generous, and she enjoyed staring into his hazel eyes in that chiseled surf-boy face, she used the credit sparingly.

"You know I don't want any handouts. Put me to work, Rudy."

"And you know I keep costs down by doing everything my damn self. What can I do for you?"

She purchased a pack of Virginia Slims, Grandmother's favorite, to keep her warm on the walk. She told him everything she'd just seen, leaving off the part about taking the watch and the cash, though she handed him a crisp bill from her bag not realizing this might raise suspicions.

"A twenty? Where'd you get this?" He stretched out the bill, held it to the light, and scrutinized it as if she'd handed him a hundred. His face became bunched with concern. This was the problem with good people. They were often too honest.

"Call the cops. Tell 'em what I told you."

"A down-on-her-luck black woman finds a dead white

millionaire athlete. I can see the headlines now. That ain't gon' work out for you at all. And this story sounds made up. Kip Longfellow? He just scored twenty-eight points against Cleveland on Sunday. You trying to set somebody up? Get back at somebody?"

"Just tell them a white customer told you. A man—"

He raised a brow and didn't look as if he were going to make the call.

"Trust me, Rudy. I might be a fool, but I know what I saw. Anyway, keep the change."

―

The television above the steak and alehouse's bar was tuned to the national news, and, before she could order a drink in that dimly lit restaurant, Kip's face was already plastered across the screen with the "happening now" banner above it. His sweet face looked nothing like that swollen and bloody mess she'd seen. The media had found out so quickly. Was it because Rudy had called? What exactly had he told them? Had he mentioned her?

The program switched between images of Kip as a boy, smiling beside a trophy he'd won in a youth basketball league, smiling as he walked across the stage at his college graduation and shook the university president's hand, smiling as he posed beside his lace-and-tulle-covered bride, smiling on draft day as he put the Arrows cap on his head. Kip's smile. His damn smile. It was the smile that started the throbbing in her chest. The money was heavy and thick against her thigh in the pocket of her shorts, and the wad seemed to be beating too. Could others sense the vibration?

She drank the ice water to wet her dry throat. She was disheveled, yes, but her clothes were dry now, and she sat in a corner near the kitchen where only the wait staff could see her. When she returned the glass to the table, the waiter walked over to take her order, but she'd been so lost in thought about Kip on that screen and the money in her pocket and Kip's damn smile that the waiter asking, "What would you like?" startled her, and she knocked the glass across the table, with the water and ice creating a puddle near the empty plate.

She ordered quickly and returned to her viewing of the television screen. Apparently, the paparazzi moved faster than the police because they were already parked outside Kip's home. There was no audio on the television so she read the closed captioning. It said, "No leads yet on who might have committed the stabbing, but there will be a homicide investigation."

Stabbing? He hadn't been stabbed. She hadn't seen one stab mark on him. She knew what a stab mark looked like. They formed thin lines on the flesh, almost as if someone had drawn them in crimson ink. She'd been stabbed before with a box cutter by another drifter who thought she was trying to take an EBT card he'd lucked up on. Kip hadn't been stabbed. And why didn't they mention the bite marks? Something had bitten him. But what if she hadn't seen clearly? Could those have been stabs instead of bites?

—

Her belly was full, but she couldn't enjoy it because her stomach was bloated, with acid churning and rising up her chest. She returned to the beach to see the body. Surely, he had been bitten, but she just needed to see it again, in person.

Police tape, fire trucks, and ambulances jammed up the shore. A crowd had parked on PCH and walked to the sand barefoot, with their hooded sweatshirts drawn tightly on heads hung low. Folks hugged one another, wrapped their arms around the shoulders of the person next to them, many drying their eyes and noses on their sleeves. The ambulance drove away as soon as she arrived, as if Kip sensed her there and wanted nothing to do with her.

Was it wrong to steal from a dead man? It wasn't like he could use the money, and he had had so much of it to begin with.

"Did you see what happened?" She stared into the face of a teenager with a tattoo of an eagle on his neck and a pierced upper lip. Surely the teen would know what happened. Teens thought they knew everything.

"No. Just heard Kip Longfellow came to the beach to meditate and was stabbed to death down there by some homeless lady. They say she robbed him. Got it all on surveillance video."

The teen pointed to that shore-side restaurant next door, with its glass-enclosed patio and thatched-roof bar. The one that had closed at four because no one drove that far north on the Pacific Coast Highway for food on a Tuesday.

—

The world was upside down during the week she staggered the sixty or so miles from the beach to Anaheim. She barely ate. She couldn't sleep. A drifter offered her a hit of blow and she couldn't bring herself to try it. There was no way she had imagined those bite marks. No way she had mistaken his stab wounds for bites. No way that when she'd stabbed the Gill-man she had really stabbed Kip. He was much taller and stronger than her anyway. If she had raised a knife to a man that big, he likely would have flicked it away with a swat of his gargantuan hand. Anyway, the order of events was all wrong. He had been dead when she'd found him.

When she reached Anaheim she scoped out a residential street with drifters pulling things from the trash, and she discarded the watch in a garbage bin.

She arrived at the gate of Kip's home the day everyone was away for his funeral. She removed the cash from her backpack. She counted it. She had eleven hundred dollars left, all in wrinkled and knotted twenties and hundreds. She wrapped it in the plastic bag she usually kept her knife in and laid the money beside a stone-covered archway just inside the iron gates. Tears gathered in her eyes as she backed away. She was walking away from easy meals and nights at a motel when the weather got too cold. She was walking away from help, a respite, and a much-needed break. Just as she rounded the corner and headed back north, a twenty-deep line of black limousines, Bentleys, and Mercedes Benzes snaked toward the home in a slow and silent procession.

———

To say she had no home really wasn't true. She had a tent at the base of a pier, far enough from the ocean to not get caught in the rising tide and hidden enough to protect her from the sun when it was high and hot. The only things she had to worry about was another drifter coming along and stealing her shit, scavengers rummaging through her found clothes, books, seasonings, and photographs of her parents, birds eating what food she could gather, and, worst of all, cops.

Cops would make her move. Cops would confiscate her tent, bringing her to the door of starvation to save up money for another one. Cops would shove her with their clubs or the heel of their shoe, anything to avoid touching her with their hands. They would do this when she was at her lowest and had nothing to numb her hunger.

But the tent was home. She returned there now that she had rid herself of all that tied her to Kip. She had bought herself one last meal on him—pastrami and fries. Her stomach was full, and she actually cracked a smile when the breeze floated in to her. It wouldn't be a hot night at all, and it wouldn't get too cold either. This was wonderful sleeping weather. She dozed in the middle of a library copy of *The Old Man and the Sea*. Her flashlight's battery eventually died, but the moon was high and showing off so her tent was still well lit.

She heard a voice.

"I can always call, so answer." The voice belonged to a man. She sat up and grabbed her switchblade because the person sounded as if he were close. Unzipping the flap and easing her head out, she checked to the left and right, but nothing was out there except the wind, moonlight, and waves. It was so bright she could see as clearly now as she could at dawn. She craned her neck to listen.

There were no footsteps in the sand. No shadows of anyone who might be walking nearby. The tide seemed to be closer to her than it usually was at this time of night, but the water never made it up to her distant spot near the parking lot. She returned to her tent, zipped it, and lay down for sleep. Only she couldn't now.

Her heart was pumping. A chill passed through her bones, and she could feel fear creep up her chest to her throat.

"Answer," the voice said again.

It sounded like Kip, only he sounded angry, sinister. The words came from his slogan, but the tone was not like his slogan at all. What exactly had he been doing out there near the water? The teen had said he'd been meditating, but she wasn't buying it. A guy like that would have an entourage, an agent, bodyguards. No one had robbed him, obviously. And there was no way he had robbed anyone else. And there had been those bite marks that no one seemed to be aware of but her. Maybe it hadn't been about his drug business. Maybe he had been out buying drugs. Heroin. Or crack. Nah. They're so easy for the rich to get without having to go on their own to score. But they had found his car on PCH, so he'd driven himself there.

She wished she'd never been on that strip of beach. She wished she'd never seen him or heard of him. She wished she hadn't watched the news report or talked to the teen who said Kip had been stabbed by a homeless lady, and all caught on video. Maybe that was the part she'd imagined. That's it. The bite marks and the Gill-man she stabbed had been real, and the news reports and the kid on the beach who told her Kip had been killed by a homeless lady—those were not real. Those other things had just been her guilty conscience playing tricks on her.

"I can always call."

She unzipped the tent's flap again.

"Who's there?"

The tide had come in dangerously close to her, only a few feet away. Forgetting the voice, she rushed out, threw her clothes and books and seasonings and photographs into a sand-filled duffel bag, and was seconds from taking down her tent when she blinked and saw the tide was several dozen yards away still.

Her confusion and fear had heightened her awareness and put her in touch with her exhaustion and hunger so, not knowing what else to do, she had some of the bread she'd taken from the basket at dinner. She had about seven rolls, and it was that crusty Italian kind. She ate and wondered why she was drawn to the water this way. She knew how to float, and she could even hold her breath while fully submerged, but putting those things together to actually swim had eluded her.

After falling asleep again, she felt water lapping against her toes. When she woke and opened her eyes, it was still dark. She sat, and ocean water rushed in through a small gash in her tent, soaking her clothes, bread, photographs, matches, and books.

"I can always call," the voice said. She stood and tried to lift her backpack before it got wet, but the fabric floor shifted under her feet. The water rose higher and the tent floated, knocking her back. She fell against the side and then landed on her back on top of her now-underwater sleeping bag. She reached for the zipper as she came to her knees. The water was at her chest. The zipper would not budge.

"I think that's her tent over there." That was Rudy's voice.

"Stay back. We'll go down." Sounded like a man's voice. Neither of those people sounded like Kip.

"I can always call."

"Help me!" She wanted the real voices to save her from the not-real voice, but which were real and which were imagined?

She still couldn't unzip the flap even though she had a good grip on it.

"I'm her friend. I want to be the one to tell her. I don't want her to be upset with me." That was Rudy again.

"We said, 'stay back.'"

"Help!" Enough of their arguing. Whoever "they" were, "they" sounded authoritative like the police. Had Rudy brought them there to save her from the voice? She just needed for them to get her out of her godforsaken tent.

"So, answer." That was Kip. As the water pulled the tent over the sand and toward the ocean, she found her knife again. She tore a gash into the side of her home. She saw him. It. The gill-man from her nightmares. The creature she'd imagined when Daddy had told her those stories all those years ago—it was pulling her toward the ocean.

"Hey. You fucker!" She raised the blade.

"Colleen! Don't!"

Gill-man stopped tugging her. It gripped the sides of her tent, reaching its lizard-like hand through the hole she'd created, brushing against her thigh as it grabbed the photographs of her parents that floated in front of her. Then it turned her tent on the side where the hole was and gave her one final push toward the black horizon.

Booted feet ran through the ocean towards her, splashing her face with icy water. Rudy yelled, "Colleen! It's okay. You'll be fine. I had no choice. You have to believe me, Colleen. Don't run. Don't resist! You need help."

Of course, she needed help. The Gill-man was attacking her. Thank God Rudy could see that now too. The water filled the tent, washing over her as she slashed at the remains of the cloth and at the creature and at anything her blade could make contact with. Several schools of fish, large and small, saltwater and freshwater, surrounded her—bass, catfish, sea lions, crabs, and a shark. Some of those fish were not indigenous to the Pacific, but that was all right. She slashed at them too. Then the water took her. It wanted what it wanted. It filled her nostrils and ears and she destroyed the cloth around her, and yelled, "You will not win!" just as the water's hand covered her eyes and snatched her away.

UNSHOD, CACKLING, AND NAKED

And We Screamed

The decision I made in my twenties to stop eating animals can be traced back to the day my father shot that hog. I was nine, standing barefoot in a field of collards, just across the dirt road from my Grandma and Grandpa's pigpen. All morning long, Daddy kept saying we were going to have ham that night, and being from Detroit and on an extended vacation in the open fields of Creekmore, Alabama, I assumed he'd meant he was going to the grocery store to purchase the ham, rolled in cling wrap or perhaps already glazed, with pineapple slices tooth-picked around the top, but standing there in the July sun with my six-year-old cousin Junior, I realized that even though daddy wasn't drunk, he was fixin' to do something crazy.

Daddy was out of breath and standing on the back of a green pick-up with his brother Lee—Junior's father. Daddy and Unc had cigarettes hanging from their lips, their shirts were off, and their backs were turning red and were so slicked with sweat they looked as if they'd anointed themselves with oil. In one hand, Daddy held a rope that was tied around the neck of a pig, and in the other, he held a pistol.

It wasn't unusual for me to see my father with a gun. He was a hunter with a rifle that seemed about as long as a boa constrictor, and back in our crime-infested Detroit neighborhood, he also kept his pistol on the nightstand in case the "niggas in our neighborhood got any fresh ideas," whatever that meant. But as I stood there about fifteen feet across the dirt from him, it dawned on me I'd never seen him *fire* a gun.

Uncle Lee held onto the rope just below the tie around the pig's neck. In his other hand he held an axe, and he stood his bony, denim-covered legs on either side of the pig, locking the animal in the center of the pickup.

"Hold the sucka down." Daddy fussed at his younger brother, who grinned the way the youngest son does when the eldest chastises him. Unc was the spitting image of Daddy, curly-haired, skin like butter; only Daddy was a foot taller.

"It's bucking like a damn horse." Uncle Lee and Daddy came from a family of farmers that never referred to animals as he and she. The pig was an "it."

With that cigarette still hanging from his lips, the ashes so long they broke off and fell on the pig's back, Daddy squinted with his right eye, and with his left, he gave Unc a look I was familiar with. It was the face that said, *Who you think you talking to?* Daddy was born when Grandma Beulah was sixteen, and, because Grandpa Clyde spent all his days in the fields and his nights "running the streets," Daddy had been the one to buy rice from the grocer, pick the butter beans they brought in from the field, stir the bone-in chicken soup on the stove, and tuck his sisters and brothers in at night. He'd told me the reason he could comb my curls with ease was because he had to plait my aunts' hair every morning before walking them to the schoolhouse. Uncle Lee lowered his eyes and complied by tightening his grip on the screaming pig's rope.

Have you ever heard a pig scream? It's how I imagine a person sounds when he's on his knees and his rival makes him watch as they beat his fellow gang member and brother to death; how a mother sounds when she watches her toddler blown to bits by a blast from a suicide bomber; how a teenager sounds when he realizes his classmate has shown up to school with a semiautomatic weapon and has his sights set on everyone who laughed at him after the homecoming game. It's that primal scream. The kind of scream that lets you know you've lost a thing so central to your being you might as well be the dead one. The kind of scream that lets you know an animal wants to live whether it deserves to or not. And who deserves to live? Did the pig?

Uncle Lee whacked the pig on the head with the axe. Junior whimpered, grabbed my hand, and pressed his body against mine. Junior wasn't a whimpering kind of kid either. He was a leap-out-of-trees, fire-rocks-from-slingshots, and rip-apart-Barbie-dolls kind of kid. That he was on the verge of tears made me want to both comfort him and also scoop him up, run away, and hide. The pig stomped on the truck bottom so hard, I thought they'd all fall through.

"I knew you wouldn't knock him out, with your weak-ass. That's why I brought this." Daddy held up the pistol and laughed through cigarette smoke, teasing his younger brother. "I knew you would get soft at the end."

When Daddy fired the pistol into the pig's forehead, Junior cried out, tore across the road, and burst into the backdoor of my grandparents' house, screaming the entire way. I froze. I could no longer feel my feet in the dirt. I couldn't feel anything. I could only stare at that black hole between the pig's eyes with smoke wafting out of it, feeling my heart pound and my breath increasing. The wound didn't bleed. The pig's mouth did. I hadn't thought it possible, but the pig screamed louder and continued to pound his hooves on the truck bed even though he was half dead. The whole truck rattled when the creature finally dropped.

That night, Daddy grinned at me from across the dinner table when he walked past my fourteen cousins and eight aunts and uncles, Grandma Beulah, and Grandpa Clyde, and proudly placed a slice of ham the size of a fist on my plate. He was on his fourth or fifth tumbler of whiskey, his cheeks and nose rosy, and his eyes glassy.

"She saw the full circle of life today. Not too shabby for a city girl, eh?" Between Daddy's grin and the sight of the ham I thought I was going to throw up. My hands trembled in my lap. Juices rose up my esophagus and pooled in my throat, and I swallowed, fearing embarrassment if I hurled all over the table. Something else made me take a big gulp too.

The last time I'd seen Daddy's face like that, I'd brought home a report card with straight A's and a teacher's note that said I was helpful and gracious in class. Maybe it was all the whiskey he'd drunk or my memory of him firing that pistol, but this time Daddy's smile took on a demonic edge. The way the devil might look when he's praising his child.

I ate the collards, potato salad, and mac and cheese. The ham I hid beneath two pieces of cornbread, and then I offered to clear the table myself so I could dump the meat in the trash.

—

The following winter, when I was ten, Grandma got mad at Grandpa for "laying up with some jezebel" and shot him in the stomach with a double-barreled shotgun. Luckily for everyone, Grandpa was across the dirt road from where she'd stood, and he fell near the hog pen.

Some sensible folks driving by say they saw the hogs in the pen screaming and running wild, and when they turned to see what had those animals going, they saw Grandpa's wounded body lying there for God knows how long. Imagine that. The pigs cared that their owner's life was leaving him. The pigs could sense he was hurt, and what did they do? They screamed for him. They screamed for the man who would eventually slaughter and eat them.

The driver and passengers loaded Grandpa in the backseat of their vehicle and drove him to the hospital. Otherwise, he wouldn't have survived, because after Grandma loaded him with metal, she went back into the house, turned on *The Young and the Restless*, called Daddy, who was one thousand miles away in Detroit, and said, "I shot him."

When Daddy arrived at the hospital the next day, he said Grandpa was out of surgery and kept whispering, "She shot me. After all these years. After all I've done for her. That heifer shot me."

"Was she drunk, Daddy?" I regretted the question right after I asked it. The phone trembled in my hand. I didn't want Daddy to think I was taking a swipe at his drinking. In the silence that followed my thoughtless question, I heard him take a drag from his cigarette, and a sip from what I assumed was a tumbler of whiskey because I could hear the ice clink against the glass.

"Wish I could say she was drunk, but she stopped drinking back in 'seventy-five when she got born-again." He said "born-again" the way he would have said "alien abduction." "Nah. Momma wasn't drunk. She just stone-cold crazy."

Grandpa didn't divorce her either. When he was released, he moved into a tiny shack the next town over and let her have the farm. I assumed they really loved each other. And I also assumed that sometimes love meant violence.

———

I was twelve when Grandma Beulah took the back of an axe to the forehead of her cow. Unlike her youngest, Uncle Lee, Grandma knew how to knock an animal out on the first blow. Apparently, a horse had chased the cow around the field in front of their farm, frightened the cow, and the poor beast, in an attempt to get away from the batshit crazy horse, had stepped in a ditch and broken her leg. The cow hadn't exactly screamed, but I noticed a very high-pitched moo of desperation that I'd never heard before. I asked why we couldn't just take the cow to a vet and get a cast for it.

Grandma Beulah broke into her Wicked Witch of Alabama laugh, and Daddy, embarrassed by my question, chimed in, "And it should do what? Walk around on crutches? Use your head, Addie."

It wasn't even noon yet, and I could smell the whiskey on his breath. My mother had told him to "slow down" the previous night at dinner, and he'd said, "Ah. You know how I get when I'm home. I'm just having a good time."

Grandma Beulah wiped her forehead with the back of her hand smearing blood across her skin and continued to laugh. "Told ya that gal needed to work this farm every summer. City living done made her soft." Grandma Beulah's hair was white, parted down the middle and hung in two braids. She was a six-foot Creek Indian woman, which is why all of her children had curls and pale eyes.

I made a mean face at that old crone. I hated her and our trips to the sweltering backwoods of the former slave state. Not only had she shot my Grandpa, but the family home that Grandma now lived in alone also looked like a plantation house, and since we were Black Indians, that was spooky to me. I swore I could hear chained-up slaves shivering in the closet while I slept at night in the guest bedroom.

Pissed at her continued cackling, I went inside and watched the cow ordeal from the slave-ghost bedroom. Grandma hacked that cow with the axe, covering her muumuu in blood when she finished. When Uncle Lee arrived, she yelled about how he "needed to keep his got-damned horse on his own farm" and that he was "good for nothing" for ruining her dairy cow and that he was "shiftless and in the streets" just like his daddy.

Grandma Beulah waited until the end of our evening barbecue. She waited until after my cousin Junior whispered a secret in my ear and made me promise not to tell anyone. She waited just until I swallowed the final bite of grilled hamburger that I'd topped with ketchup, mustard, pickles, lettuce, tomato, cheese, and sautéed onions. She slid beside me on the picnic bench and said, "That burger shole was good, huh?" I looked across the table at my mother, who knew that I hated Grandma, but who also wanted me to be kind to the old bag because that's what good Christians do. My mother nodded at me.

"Yes, ma'am. It was delicious." I kept my eyes on my empty plate, hoping the demonic witch of a grandmother would ride away from the picnic table on her broom so I could breathe again.

"Bet you glad now that I didn't call the vet for its broken leg."

When my face broke up at the realization of what she'd said, she cackled. I remembered the bloody, hacked cow and then vomited up the hamburger in the bathroom just inside the house. When I was finished, and my insides were empty and aching, my only solace was focusing on Junior's secret.

He'd been different since our pig death day. He smiled less and clenched his jaws more and played borderline-cruel practical jokes on people. And he'd confided in me that he'd pissed in the anointing oil that Grandma kept on her bedside.

—

That night, after bedtime prayers, my mother told me the hamburger I ate was not the cow Grandma Beulah had hacked up because "no one can turn around ground beef that fast." I didn't know if my mother was telling the truth, and while I appreciated she was trying to make me feel better, her comment actually made me feel worse. If I hadn't eaten the recently hacked cow, then Grandma's taunt was even more cruel—not only did she go out of her way to gross me out but she also lied to do it.

Perhaps sensing her words were lost on me, my mother added, "You know Grandma Beulah killed the cow to put it out of its misery. Not for the meat."

Right, I thought. She's always violent out of love.

I was silent still because it didn't matter what that old lady's intentions had been. Someone was going to eat the cow even if I hadn't already.

———

My father hunted deer and rabbit at least once a month during the season. His favorite spots were in northern Michigan and sometimes he said he went to Canada, but I can't be certain whether that was true because he liked to embellish his tales as it suited him. The deer he sold. To whom I don't know. Was there a restaurant up there in the backwoods of Michigan that got its advertised venison from hunters who showed up in insulated orange overalls, toting long rifles and freshly shot game?

The first time I helped him prepare the rabbit, he brought it home, wrapped in the first section of a day-old *Detroit Free Press*. When my mother saw him coming up the front steps with that cigarette hanging from the corner of his mouth and that folded up newspaper tucked in his arm like a football, she all of a sudden cleared out for some urgent shopping. But I didn't leave. I couldn't look away even if I tried. I wanted my father's approval, and if I had to be excited about the animals he killed, then so be it. Truth be told, I was also fascinated.

Somehow the bunny was still warm and its eyes half open as if the creature wanted to watch us while we skinned it. I held the rabbit's ankles, bony and furry, as Daddy sliced into the flesh with his pocketknife, stripped the fur off of the animal, and dropped it onto more newspaper that lined the kitchen sink. Sometimes the flesh would rip from the muscle in stretchy ribbons that looked like banana strings. The whole ordeal stank like fart and blood, and Daddy talked like an excited teenager through the cleaning, sipping from a freshly poured tumbler of whiskey, telling me about how his hunting beagles helped him spot the animals he felled.

I refused to dice the meat. Skinning the animal was one thing, hacking it up felt like mutilation and mutilation just wasn't right. I'd steam the rice and stir the gravy while he battered and fried the chunks. By the time I was fourteen, I'd even sit at the table and eat the rabbit with him. It tasted like over-seasoned chicken.

―

The persnickety teachers at my Catholic school, the super-religious folks in my family, the greedy pastor at church on Sunday, they all had a justification for keeping certain animals as pets, giving some animals jobs, using particular animals for product testing, and designating other animals as edible. It was Genesis Chapter One, Verse Twenty-six: "And God said, let us make man in our image, after our likeness: and let them have dominion over the fish of the sea, and over the fowl of the air, and over the cattle, and over all the earth, and over every creeping thing that creepeth upon the earth."

"But does dominion mean that you kill and eat the animals?" I had asked a simple discussion question of my sophomore religion teacher, Ms. Turski, whom everyone thought was a lesbian because she kept her hair cut short, seemed not to care about looking feminine, and lived with a woman "roommate." A lesbian teaching a religion class at a Catholic school was considered, by men of the cloth and laymen alike, sacrilegious. Every time it rained, kids scooted their desks away from Ms. Turski so they wouldn't be struck by lightning alongside her "sinning" self.

"If people choose to kill and eat animals, it is within their God-given rights to do so. That's what dominion means." She folded her arms across a chest that student-rumor said were really breasts bound with cloth bandages. She seemed satisfied that she'd given a reasonable answer.

"So, if people were peaceful, then dominion might mean we'd co-exist with animals, offer them care and protection, and opt to eat vegetables. But since we're violent, we think dominion means we can slaughter them?"

Ms. Turski gave me a detention for asking a question. A perfectly valid question at that. The school's policy was that students had to serve the detention on the day it was issued. So, my parents, in the midst of twelve-hour shifts, had gotten a call from the secretary. Not the "administrative assistant." The "secretary." Because the women at the school were nuns, teachers, or secretaries, who all answered to men—the official stand-ins for God.

The phone call from the secretary had informed my overworked parents of the "what" of the situation as if my parents would accept that without addressing the "why." No one at the school, including me, had expected them to visit.

"You give a straight-A student a detention for doing exactly what she's supposed to do in a classroom?" My father's voice boomed and echoed down the hall, where a few classroom doors cracked open just enough for a student's ear to emerge. The principal, vice-principal, and secretary stood up when he spoke. Their cheeks became splotchy as they glanced up at his six-foot, two-inch frame, seemingly unsure of whether to answer him or run. Little did they know this was my father's attempt at being calm.

"What my husband is trying to say is that Addie is curious and asks a lot of questions. We want her to do that. We don't want her to think that she has to accept at face value everything that she sees and hears." My mother, stout at five feet, three inches and often mistaken for Puerto Rican even though she was, as she put it, "Black as the night is long," was using her "white-people voice," which she usually broke out whenever she was at her own secretary job or talking to a bill-collector on the phone.

"That's not what I'm trying to say. I know what I'm trying to say. I don't need any translators, Cheryl." Daddy removed his baseball cap and softened his voice even though he had spoken sternly to my mother, but he raised his voice again when he returned his attention to the staff. "I'm saying that y'all gave her this detention because she's Black. Y'all probably would have clapped if one of them white kids had have asked the same damn question. Not only is she not serving the detention, but I want that good-for-nothing teacher to march her ass down here to the office and answer my daughter's question!"

I did not serve the detention, and my mother had to drag my father out of the school by the back of his flannel work shirt.

"We ain't got time for them calling the police on your drunk-ass." She shoved him into the cab of his truck that he wasn't supposed to be driving because his driver's license had been taken away after he got into two auto accidents and received a DUI.

"I ain't been drinking today." He whispered the words as he turned the key in the ignition.

He wasn't one to quiet down like that with my mother. I wasn't sure if he'd let her accusation go because he had, in fact, been drinking all morning and afternoon, which he was wont to do, or if he hadn't been drinking but felt embarrassed no one trusted him to be sober anymore.

My mother walked me to her Dodge Shadow and we got in. She whisper-shouted out her window. "Then if you ain't been drinking just take yourself to work, Don. Just go to work. Don't be up here arguing with these white folks."

They were pissed. Were they mad at each other or at me or at the school? I slouched in the seat, hoping no one would blame me. When our vehicles pulled out of the lot, my mother turned left, headed home, and my father turned right, headed to his afternoon shift at the plant, and, just before they were out of view of the other, they waved and honked.

That is the moment that has always stuck with me about that day. Not the screaming, not the detention that I got out of, not that my parents had had my back, not the scripture about dominion. It's that my parents, both Black, both working-class, both with high school educations but the desire for more, honked at each other. It didn't matter that my mother was struggling with her weight and credit card debt at Sears and J.C. Penney. It didn't matter that a judge had ordered my father into AA. It didn't matter that the kitchen ceiling leaked or that both of their vehicles were due for a tune-up. They waved goodbye and honked at each other. They were visible to each other. They saluted each other. And on some days, that wave and honk might have been the only acknowledgement that each of them ever got of their existence.

―

Mr. Hobson was a strange science teacher. Everyone knew it. I'd sometimes drop off notices from the principal's office in his lab and would find Mr. Hobson curled in the fetal position on the sill of the bay windows, napping. My classmates would make fun of him because he sounded like Lurch from "The Addams Family" and because he always had spit in the corners of his mouth when he spoke. Sometimes the spit would sit there for so long that it would harden into little saliva pebbles that would eventually fall into his scruffy brown beard.

He made us dissect crickets, zebra mussels, owl pellets, a frog, a baby pig, and, eventually, a cat. I was pretty grossed out by each one, but the final one seemed all kinds of wrong because the cats were skinned and in plastic bags that lived in deep-freezers in the middle of the lab.

My lab partner Michael and I backed a foot away from the table when Mr. Hobson slapped that plastic sack of dead cat in front of us.

"Why do they still have their faces?" Michael played basketball and was taller and more muscular than most of the students and teachers at the school. When he asked the question, he sounded the way he did when he was stepping to a "punk" who had "started some shit" with him the previous week after school.

Mr. Hobson continued walking around the lab passing out the hardened creatures to a chorus of student groans whenever he thwacked the plastic down in front of them. "I don't understand the question, Michael."

Of course, Mr. Hobson didn't understand the question. He slept on windowsills and had spit pebbles in the corners of his mouth. He saw nothing wrong with dissecting frozen dead cats, so it would be lost on him that seeing a dead cat face made me and every other student want to hurl.

Being seventeen and all, we didn't know how to have a civil discussion with the man. A discussion that went something like, *Mr. Hobson, please be patient with us. Many of us have cats at home. Cutting one up with a scalpel makes us nauseous.* Or my actual problem with the dissection—*Why do we think animals are at our disposal for everything? Why are we, as a people, obsessed with keeping animals underfoot and mistreating them for food, sport, product testing, and lab results? Why are we so violent?* But I knew any introspective questions would end in detention.

Michael put his hands in his pockets and walked back to his desk on the other side of the room—at least twenty feet away from the lab table. "Man, you trippin.' Just because you spend your time making love to dead cats doesn't mean we're okay with this shit. Couldn't you get some cat bodies without the faces? I'm not cutting up a cat with a face."

It being a Catholic school, we weren't allowed to use swear words, especially in front of teachers, and we definitely weren't allowed to mention sex ever. Let alone bestiality, which was "an abomination of Christ," so Mr. Hobson kicked Michael out, threatened to do the same to anyone who continued snickering at Michael's "profane" comment, and explained that the cats had faces because we'd need to cut into and examine its eyes.

Maggie, with dyed red hair and penciled-on eyebrows, uttered, "Oh, sweet Jesus," and then fainted off her stool. Minutes later, Richard purposely slit his finger with the scalpel to be sent to the nurse's station. And I, unwilling to risk an F on the assignment when I needed to get into a good college in order to get out of my current life, closed my eyes, said a prayer to my guardian angel—*Angel of God, My Guardian Dear, to whom God's love commits me here. Ever this day be at my side to light and guard and rule and guide*—and I cut into the cat's stiff flesh.

On graduation day, I created a comic of a tuxedoed Mr. Hobson standing at an altar beside a cat wearing a white gown and veil. I titled the image *Mail Order Bride,* photocopied it, and left the fliers around the auditorium. I was valedictorian, so no one suspected me.

"You was a fool for doing that." Daddy was cooking my graduation dinner of ribs, collards, and candied yams, and had invited over every person our family knew. At least seventy people would eventually be crammed into our two-bedroom house. "Risked getting in trouble, all over some damn cats."

"No. Mr. Hobson was the fool. I hate him. Who makes people dissect innocent cats?" I thought about Daddy making me skin those rabbits. What was wrong with me that I used to do that?

"Innocent?" Daddy stopped brushing barbecue sauce on the ribs, picked up his cigarette, and puffed a few times. He chased the cigarette with a shot of Canadian Club whiskey. I must have agitated him. "The way you run away from mice and skunks and possums? What the fuck difference does a cat make from a mouse?"

Daddy spent most days sipping whiskey from morning to night. He drank the same amount consistently so he rarely got drunk but was rarely sober either. Even though he'd been detoxed twice, he carried on as if the hospital stays had never happened. It wouldn't have been obvious to anyone outside of our home yet, but we could see the liquor had changed him.

For one, he cursed more frequently and dropped f-bombs like most folks say "the."

Second, he no longer called attention to his drinking. Instead of asking my mother to get him a drink on her way to the kitchen or having me line up his next shot, he now hid his bottles behind the microwave or in the bottom drawer of his nightstand.

Third, he spent the dawn hours opening and closing drawers in the dining room, kitchen, and his tool shed in the yard. We'd hear the squeak of hinges, the clink of drill bits, bullets, batteries, and buttons as his fingers rummaged through, and the eventual slam as he walked away frustrated, still in search of that phantom object. When we asked him what he was looking for, maybe we could help, he'd wave us away and shout, "Ah, fuck it!" and then have a shot of whiskey.

Fourth, anything could set him off at any time, so we hid his guns and kept our voices low when he was arguing with us.

"A cat is a pet, Daddy. Are you really serious right now?" I couldn't stomach trying a rib, but I swiped my index finger over the meat and tasted the barbecue sauce—spicy with a hint of lemon.

"Girl, you better get out of here with that nonsense. We all animals. You too. The sooner you know that, the sooner you'll understand this world. If a bear see your ass in the woods, he ain't gon' spare you because he thinks you cute."

When I was away at college in New York, my mother told me that my father had started "showing out."

"Showing out" was the phrase she'd used when I was ten and my father had gotten so drunk he'd put his key in the front door and fell asleep with that door half-open, one foot in the house and the other on the porch until she'd dragged that "pot-bellied, snaggle-toothed, country nigga" into the house and dried him out.

"Showing out" was the phrase she'd used when he'd fired his pistol into the sky from our backyard and shouted "Happy New Year, Motherfuckas" in the middle of a random June night.

But this time, "showing out" meant Daddy had taken a buyout from the plant, opened up an eighty-thousand-dollar line of credit for a "big, white, deluxe, top-of-the-line" van he'd named "Shiloh," and then he'd arrived home one night in "Shiloh" with a "crackhead, prostitute-looking woman" in tow. My mother had put him out, but was so worried about him once he was gone that she'd called my Uncle Lee to see about him.

Unc, now running his own profitable Creekmore farm but also with his own failed marriage and adult children who hated his guts, rounded up my father's other brothers and sisters, drove to Detroit, tracked Daddy down at the "crackhead, prostitute-looking woman's" house, threw Daddy in "Shiloh," and drove him home to Creekmore.

The "crackhead, prostitute-looking woman" followed my father to Creekmore. How did I find out? Because one afternoon the fall semester of my senior year of college I got a call at my dorm room from a bill collector who said my father was about three months behind on the note for Shiloh. The previous check had been written by Evelyn (a.k.a. "crackhead, prostitute-looking woman") and then another check had been written in my name but with the same handwriting as Evelyn's, and so the credit agency had opened an investigation because, when they'd reached Evelyn by phone, she'd said that "Don's youngest daughter at school in New York" was the true driver of the vehicle. Evelyn also added that if the credit agency wanted to repossess the van, they'd have to take it from me in New York.

I was carrying a full university course load, tending to a work-study job, and a second part-time job, which allowed me to pay my phone bill and get on the subway to go to a glamorous unpaid internship—yes, unpaid, just like the internships had by all of the rich kids at my school—so I could one day have a career and not a job. It cost thirty thousand dollars per year for tuition, so Daddy's van could have paid for nearly three years of school. Yet there were many days I survived morning 'til night on one yam, one apple, and a handful of spinach, because come first semester freshman year my father had cut me off financially.

"You grown, you gone," he'd said when I'd called to tell him I couldn't register for classes because my tuition was unpaid. With his accent, "gone" rhymed with "grown," making the statement into a dark sing-song.

His phone calls to me dried up shortly after his money had, and he called my mother every Sunday to check on her and ask about me. He never missed a Sunday call to my mother. He was confused half the time, my mother said, apparently trying to garner some sympathy from me.

She didn't need to tug at my proverbial heartstrings. Even though I hated him, I loved him. You can't really have the hate in the first place without the love. I remembered the meals of steak and potatoes or baked chicken and rice or pork chops with gravy that he'd cook for me every day after school. And I remembered the sweaters, goose-down jackets, and rhinestone-studded jeans that he'd bought me for Christmases and birthdays. I remembered how he'd made sure his health insurance was used to the fullest for me so I could have eye exams, and dental cleanings, and physicals once a year.

The man who'd allowed some "crackhead, prostitute-looking woman" to forge my name was not my real father. The man who'd let me fend for myself in New York at a time when I was trying to complete my college education was not my real father. If my real father, not the addict-shell he'd become, had known that I was surviving on yams and apples and spinach because my meal plan had been suspended, then my real father not only would have given me some money, but he would have driven to Manhattan himself and cooked up some pork ribs with a side of slaw and pinto beans. I couldn't let real-Daddy suffer for the sins of addict-Daddy, because what if real-Daddy got stronger and beat his addiction? I'd want him at my college graduation. And one day, I'd want him at my wedding, and at the hospital when I had his first grandchild.

"I won't be able to help you with your investigation of my father."

The bill collector actually scoffed in my ear. "But this is fraud, and if you—"

"Excuse me. Did you hear what the fuck I just said? You're barking up the wrong damn tree. I will not help you investigate my father. And, I'm so sorry to be the one to tell you, jack, but you'll probably never see that vehicle or your money again."

When I hung up, I stared at the phone as if I were staring at my father. I didn't care that the phone was the property of the university's housing department. When it rang again, I ripped the cord from the wall, opened the window, and threw the bastard into the airshaft.

—

UNSHOD, CACKLING, AND NAKED

The coroner would have gone to jail if anyone had known he'd wheeled Daddy's naked remains out of the funeral parlor's autopsy room just so I could see my father. "Emphysema," the death certificate would state, only because the coroner was a friend of Grandma Beulah. But I knew, and everyone else knew, that my father had drunk himself to death at fifty-six.

Daddy was draped with a sheet that came just low enough for me to see the autopsy incisions. Hair had grown on his chin and lip in the three days since he'd died.

"Shave him real good." Those were the first words I'd heard Grandma Beulah utter since my mother and I had arrived that morning in Creekmore. According to Uncle Lee, "crackhead prostitute-looking woman" Evelyn had been put out months before when Daddy had caught her taking cash out of his wallet. Grandma Beulah was the one who had called to inform me that Daddy's body had been found on the floor of his Creekmore kitchen by one of his drinking buddies. "And I mean real good. No hair on that chin. My baby never went out without being well groomed."

I stared at Daddy, thinking about his hunting rifle, his fishing poles, his tackle box and his blue pick-up truck. Thinking about those rabbits and cats and fetal pigs. Wondering what he thought of his remains now. Wondering whether he still saw his body the same as he had seen the pig's. It was February and raining in Creekmore, so I wondered, when they put him under the ground would his body get wet.

"I don't eat animals anymore, Daddy." I know Grandma Beulah thought I was crazy. I know my mother, who turned, in tears, and walked out of the room, thought I was crazy. But I hadn't spoken to my father by phone in more than six months and hadn't seen him in person in more than five years, and I wanted him to know. I wanted him to know that once I'd started eating yams and apples and spinach, I stopped missing the taste of meat. I wanted him to know I agreed with him that we were all animals in the end. That he was right. We were neither innocent nor guilty. But he was wrong about one thing. Our bodies mattered. Our flesh mattered. The body of an animal, the flesh of an animal, it mattered. Because my real father had been dead years before his body gave out, but I still clung to his corpse the same. I still honored his remains enough to use the savings I'd made from my first job out of college to buy his burial plot. Because the vessel for his spirit mattered whether he was in it or not. The living had dominion over the dead. And dominion didn't mean violence. Dominion meant care and protection. I stopped eating animals because I loved Daddy, but I wouldn't be him. I wouldn't be Grandma Beulah either.

When the coroner wheeled him back to the autopsy room, just before his body was through the door, the sheet slipped off his foot. Something about the arch of that foot, how slender and delicate and brown it was, how unique it was to him, and not like any other foot I'd seen before or that I've seen since, that foot was the thing that would break me.

I turned to stare in Grandma Beulah's face to see whether she had seen what I'd seen. Did seeing Daddy's naked foot make her stomach pull inward as if it were eating itself? Her eyes looked the way I imagine a woman would look when she's lost her eldest son to alcoholism and realizes he'll never walk barefoot across her living room floor again.

She took my hand. She gripped it. She'd not spoken to or touched me or stared into my eyes in five years, yet she took my hand as if she'd held it every day since I was born. She took my hand as if she were taking my father's hand. We were beyond tears. We were beyond sobbing. We held hands, and with our other palms, we braced ourselves on the nearest things to us—the funeral parlor's red chair, a wooden table with a dim lamp. We held onto each other and to that funeral parlor furniture and to whatever sanity we could muster in the face of loss…and…we…screamed.

I am Goddess

Lira's perfect face was in progress. She was an appointment away from getting her final transformation treatment, and only one thing stood in the way—her husband.

In the corner of her yard, she hung linens, towels, and her husband's work shirts in a neat row of five. A sheet tied between the fence and the back of her one-bedroom house sheltered her from the setting sun as she clipped the final cotton sleeve. Ensuring the sewn-on Fulsom Security badge was not in need of extra stitching, she brought her right hand down too closely to the line and accidentally sliced her right palm.

Three tiny bulbs of blood trembled in her hand. She looked up at the woven threads of hemp-cloth to find the red dots there as well. Her husband had insisted on using twine instead of a regular clothesline because his brother did inventory at Esther's Hardware and had access to "a crapload of free stuff." But how had such a simply twisted fabric managed to cut her so deeply? It was often the things we least expected that hurt us the most.

She checked the work shirt nearest to the twine's stain. It was not bloodied up by her foolishness. Thank God her mishap would not interfere with her ability to make the house perfect for him. With the autumn breezes that had arrived in Medford, she expected his clothes to be dry in a few hours, by dusk, and definitely before he got home. Today, she needed everything to be to his liking so he would agree to the very thing he'd already vetoed. It made her bitter she had to go to such lengths. And she wished it didn't smell like rain because that could ruin everything.

She left the basket on the cement deck, next to the deep freezer filled with his venison. Inside the house, she rinsed her wound under lukewarm water; it throbbed. Deep red oozed from the cut, down her fingers, and across her wedding bands. The engagement ring was filled with a low-quality, three-carat diamond that glowed yellow each time she looked at it, and the wedding band was adorned with two dark channels of the stone. She'd wanted simple white gold, something practical, but he hadn't agreed.

She kept two boxes of bandages in the drawer by the sink. She was clumsy after all. She removed one, set it on the counter beside the notice she'd received from her Transformation Doctor advertising a weekend intensive of "holistic beauty transformations" this upcoming weekend. She'd undergone three treatments with him already.

The doctor was now offering half off his services until the weekend, the letter promised, giving her just two days to convince her husband to use part of their savings—really her savings—for her continued change. She was so close to being the woman she always wanted to be. The fourth treatment was supposed to be the one that changed the bone structure of her cheeks and eyebrows and really created the symmetry her face needed to be perceived as beautiful. She didn't want to be greedy, but she definitely wanted to be the woman her husband deserved.

She washed her hand with dish detergent. The soap burned her gash but the warm water soothed her skin as she rinsed. She thought of how he would soon get off work from double shifts, and she'd have a pork chop, black-eyed peas, and cornbread waiting for him, all the rest of his shirts for the week on the line outside, and a cold beer in the refrigerator. How could he say no?

THE FIRST TREATMENT

She got a ride and walked past the doctor's location three times before realizing he operated out of a shuttered temple. She tiptoed between two sunlit pillared halls and snaked around columns adorned with the concerned faces of women before she made it to the center of the structure. He'd pulled together a massage bed, a tub, chairs, and desks. He even had a curio filled with glass bottles of red, amber, and turquoise elixirs. He asked her to call him Dr. Transformation.

She was not put off by any of this. Quite the opposite. The set-up was what she'd expected when she'd made the three-hour appointment online with the spiritualist, right down to his receding hairline, martial arts wear, bare feet, and the bloodshot eyes from too much marijuana. She'd heard some of his satisfied customers on the radio, and, furthermore, she'd grown up in Medford. To survive in the city, you had to know how to handle yourself on the street, and, anyway, she kept a switchblade in her purse at all times in case things went south.

"We will be cutting your diet," he said, peering into a multicolored series of gems lying on a table next to them. He selected a black one, which seemed to swallow the sunlight flowing through a stain-glassed window.

"Fewer calories?" Clipboard in hand, she paused from signing her waiver and stared at him, wondering whether she should leave. She hadn't known her diet would come under question.

"Added sugar, dairy, land and sea animals, processed food, saturated fats, alcohol, eggs."

"Yes. I eat all those. What about them?"

"You won't eat them anymore."

She laughed.

Dr. Transformation did not.

He spent two hours taking her through a course of facial exercises to tighten her muscles, reduce swelling, and prevent sagging before she aged.

"Preventative," he said. "Better to forestall sagging than to repair it."

They both sat cross-legged opposite each other in the middle of the space, and a draft came through and chilled her as he held up a mirror for her to peer into. The exercises brought a flush to her cheeks and neck, and her skin felt tighter, her nasal passages clear.

When she was lying on the examination table and deep breathing to rid herself of the headache the facial exercises had brought on, Dr. Transformation rang a gong, stood over her, and chanted, "I am goddess," as if he were talking about himself and not Lira. She focused on the drone of his voice as he repeated the mantra, "I am goddess. I am goddess. I am goddess."

Eventually, she entered a trance and only realized it when he placed hot stones on every inch of her face, even covering her nose. He held those in place with warm bandages, and she imagined she looked like a mummy. She stopped breathing for a while, she was aware, and, when she "came to," the skin on her face was free of blemishes, moles, and its uneven tone.

When she made it home, her husband asked, "Are you…are you wearing makeup?"

—

Blood spread across the paper towel as she dried her hand. She rinsed the wound. Patted it again. Taped up her palm. Lit a pomegranate-scented candle and placed it on the counter to overpower the aroma of onions and garlic coming from her cooking.

Even though Lira was a supermarket manager and got off work just two hours before he did, her daytime schedule and exhaustion wouldn't keep her from tending to her husband. Because with him by her side, she felt she'd gotten somewhere in life. Finally, she was no different than her prettier cousin Melva.

Unfortunately, her husband was late again. But never mind. It was just that he could be such a boy at times. Maybe he stopped at the liquor store on his way home to buy cigarettes and get her a cinnamon bun, the way he used to when they were first married. She used to eat those sticky, sugary treats and wonder how she'd gotten so lucky.

Back in high school, she hadn't been what anyone considered pretty. She'd played volleyball and, at six-foot-one was a little "gump-y" as her main tormentor Chaz called her. Or "bucktoothed" or "had a flat butt like a white girl" as Melva had teased her.

A fierce wind arrived, and the back door she'd not closed properly burst open, knocking over the trash bin, sending empty bean cans, plastic cling wrap, and orange onion scraps skidding across the floor. *Not today!*

She scrambled to right the waste can, thinking about how the week after she'd been promoted to assistant manager, her future husband had come to Provincial Foods and had cracked a few jokes about how "no-nonsense" she was in heels, more fit to manage a Fortune 500 company than a regional supermarket, told her he managed security at Medford Hospital, a crumbling medical facility that everyone referred to as Deadford Hospital because you went in alive and came out dead.

With his attention, she felt as if the sun had finally come to warm her plain face. He called her every night as soon as he got home from work, and, every morning, he woke her to say hello. He took her to her first nightclub, her first road-trip outside of the state, he held her hand, caressed the back of it with his thumb, and introduced her to his church-going parents and his divorced brother.

Another gust of wind blew out the candle's flame. The odor of onion had overpowered the sweet fruit's aroma anyway. She picked up the crumpled paper towel and scraps of food from the floor, returned them to the garbage can, and ran from the house when she realized two of his shirts had flipped over the twine and the other three had been completely knocked off the line.

Since the beginning, she kept waiting for him to break up with her or for him to randomly die or get drafted into a war, or to find he was married, or had a boatload of hidden kids, or secretly sold drugs, or for him to say this was all part of some big joke that everyone was playing on her, but the Major Problematic Reveal never came. He paid attention and treated her well. She never bothered to ask about the money missing from her sock drawer, nor from her purse, nor from their joint checking account. She wasn't going to mess up her good thing. She'd never had anyone pay attention to her, let alone spend time with her, let alone want to be with her officially.

He'd proposed to her one Sunday after service at Medford Church of God in Christ. They married at the church's red-carpeted altar, and they invited a hundred fifty people into the basement of that house of worship for the reception. They bought a house, tried for a baby, and settled for an aquarium. He said he'd always wanted piranhas.

Taking stock of the mess the wind had made of his clothes, she knew he'd be furious, with that crease in his forehead which resembled the letter V, and she didn't want that. He was too beautiful to be angry. Especially at her. She bent forward and salvaged what she could.

She could never believe her luck. Tall men called him tall. His muscles filled out his clothes. Even as his skin aged, it still glowed like a child's. His dark eyes seemed to perpetually scrutinize life, and his dimpled smile made women blush when he said hello. The first negative thing she noticed about him was how jealous he became whenever anyone paid attention to her, like the great conversations she had with the unmarried accountant on the next street over—Nelson.

Nelson was a certifiable nerd. And when she passed his house on her way home from the bus stop, she slowed and they talked near Nelson's fence, sharing do-it-yourself house repair tips, and their thoughts on the latest independent film, and they both had read Baldwin and Morrison and Charles Johnson, so there was so much to talk about, and they'd laugh and stand there, with his white picket fence between them as the sun began to set, and the children packed up their balls and bikes and headed in for dinner, and Nelson never invited her in, and she never made physical contact with him even as he lightly touched her wrist or forearm, told her she reminded him of his mother, all until her husband's own bus arrived. Her husband always squinted at her and glared at Nelson as he approached. Until he'd had enough, and her husband put an end to it, saying he "wouldn't have it. None of it." And she'd be lying if she said his jealousy wasn't cute. Because it *was* cute, and she loved it.

She showed her hubby off like a winning sweepstakes check whenever she went with him to the movies to watch his stupid action films, to church, to Melva's house for the family's Sunday dinner. Her family had ignored Lira's high school graduation because they'd all graduated from high school, and her college graduation because she'd gone to a small satellite school so they'd downplayed the significance even though they'd never gotten a degree, and they ignored the fact that she was running the Provincial Foods store and had been invited to become a regional manager of several of the grocery chain's stores. It wasn't until she had her prize—"A man!"—that anyone treated her like a "real" woman. Even Melva, her childhood tormentor and creator of the cackling taunt "Fear-a Lira and her scary teeth!" had to concede, "Some catch, Lira."

Her hands and the bandage were wet from the trash, and she needed to disinfect them, but she didn't want his clothes getting soiled on the damp grass. She couldn't let all her detailed set-up get ruined. She was really putting on extra charm for him today with those crotch-less panties he liked and a lace bra underneath the loose-fitting cotton dress she'd thrown on. All because she wanted a fourth beauty treatment, which normally cost two thousand dollars but was now on sale for one thousand, and even though he'd noticed the improvement in her face, he'd insisted the entire thing was a waste of money. So was a vacation to Miami—she'd never been to the ocean—so he took her to Michigan's upper peninsula, which was not what she'd envisioned when she'd said "beach." Too expensive also were smart phones, so she had a simple flip phone, though he'd gotten the latest iPhone as soon as it was available. Said it was for work, but several hundred dollars had been missing from their savings. He'd said he had to fill out a form to get reimbursed for it, but she had not seen the money come back into the account. She didn't follow up because she didn't want to argue about it until she got her fourth treatment with Dr. Transformation.

She saved his shirts and rehung them carefully on the twine. *Where was he?* He should have arrived thirty minutes ago. Maybe the bus had gotten backed up. She went onto her front porch to see if he would be ambling down the road, but she only saw a vintage red Camaro at the end of the block. The car had been parked in the same spot for the past two weeks. It was there in the mornings when she left for work, was gone when she came back home, but in the evenings when she took out the trash, she'd always find the vehicle had returned. She'd never seen anyone get in or out of it, but, suddenly, the car door opened. She squinted. She couldn't be certain because her vision was bad without her contact lenses, but she could have sworn it was her husband crouching, standing, stretching, slamming the driver's door, and sauntering toward their home.

She raced inside and out back again. Had he rented a car? Was he taking her on a romantic trip? He'd done that before. Once. When they were dating. Had just shown up in a rental and said he was taking her on a getaway to a surprise destination. They'd gone to an amusement park, rode the roller coasters all day and made love all night in the motel. Would he be doing that now?

Lately he was a crumbs-on-the-counter husband, a drop-his-fork-on-the-plate-and-stand-and-walk-away husband, a let-her-wash-and-dry-the-dishes-alone husband, who stepped over clutter on the floor and left his beard shavings in the sink. He seemed to think his only job was having sex with her, which he did almost every night, pawing at her in her sleep, sliding up her robe, and easing inside of her. The lovemaking was gentle and she used to enjoy it, but these days that middle-of-the-night groping was the only attention he paid her so the affection meant less to her than it had before. When she sat close to him on the couch or reached for him at the dinner table, he always made an excuse to get up and walk away, so she was doubtful he was surprising her with a trip, but she hoped he was.

She grabbed the basket again and hung his pants on the twine. Behind her, in the kitchen, the lid clanked down on a pot, and, when she turned, he was standing near the stove, lifting another lid, hunching over the peas, tasting them from the wooden spoon. He helped himself to the dinner the way he helped himself to her body—without asking, as if access to all things belonged to him. His collar was unbuttoned revealing the undershirt she'd selected for him that morning. His work shoes were dull because she'd run out of polish for them. The creases of his pants were not as neat as when she'd pressed them the night before.

She rushed in. Replaced her worry with a large grin. Hugged him from behind, the muscles of his back feeling sturdy against her breasts. Kissed his cheek, savoring the prick of the stubble against her lips and the smell of his pine-scented aftershave. He did not turn from his involved tasting.

"I missed you." She raised her bandaged hand. "I cut my palm on the twine."

He glanced at her hand, then in the direction of her face without making eye contact, then back at the pot of peas, bubbling now in chicken stock. His only words to her were, "Needs more spice."

—

Things were starting to get to her. Even though they both worked for the same amount of money, and, even though she'd had her own financial set-up before she met him, her husband came from a long line of religious men—deacons and pastors and church elders—and she from a long line of church women—deaconesses and first ladies and mothers—who believed the man was the head of the household. Her paychecks went into a joint checking account. A quarter of his paychecks went there and the other three-quarters he put in a private savings account. Or so he told her. She had no way of knowing, and when she was awake at three a.m., she fretted over the unaccounted-for money.

She paid the bills and he contributed a little to the house note. The mortgage was in her name because his credit was bad. She refused to add him to the house note, and she would not back down on this one point, though she had on just about everything else. She'd given up on the idea of a smart phone and a car because he'd pout and give her the silent treatment for weeks until he got his way. She told him satellite television should be given up in deference to her beauty treatments, but he insisted he needed to watch his games on a fifty-six-inch television mounted to the wall, which he did on the rare occasion he was at home in the evening or on the weekend.

Nelson had driven her to and from the treatments when she'd gone, seeming to enjoy their time together and insisting on walking her to her door. But, when Nelson had offered to pay for the treatments her husband had balked at, she'd stopped accepting his help.

"It's no big deal. I have the money. It's important to you. It will be our little secret."

But she'd known that nothing was free, and she'd also known her husband wouldn't approve of her having a secret with Nelson. She declined politely.

"Well, why don't you just buy the treatment yourself?" Nelson seemed hurt over the rejection and perhaps exasperated by her predicament. "You don't need anyone's permission to do what you want."

She'd gotten angry. Nelson had overstepped, and her pursed lips and deep sigh let him know it. But her anger went beyond the crossed boundary. She was embarrassed because Nelson had seen through her and exposed her for the child she sometimes felt herself to be. She'd told Nelson he just didn't understand marriage. That she couldn't make a hefty purchase without first checking with her husband. She'd felt superior when she'd told Nelson, who was three-years divorced with no children, "That's just what married people do. You wouldn't understand."

So, she had to forgo a washer and dryer in her home, and perhaps additional beauty treatments, and a smart phone, and a car to get back and forth to work. She washed their clothes and linens by hand in a tub with a washboard the way Big Mama used to. No separation by color. Just one big load—dirty. And she hung it all out to dry. Her neighbor asked her about it once, and she pretended she had a washer and dryer but liked the clean air smell left on her clothes. The pesky neighbor had pointed out that she could just buy dryer sheets with the same smell, which really made Lira want to throw the entire load on the nosy, old lady, burying her and her questions and comments and unsolicited advice underneath the mound of cotton. Nowadays, when she got off the bus, she walked straight home, merely nodding at Nelson as she passed. He'd always shout, "Hope all is well, Lira. Let me know if you need anything." She'd ignore him and walk faster.

Lira had made so many compromises to keep her husband happy because wasn't that what she was supposed to do to "keep a man?" Wasn't that everything she was taught from toddlerhood when she was given the toy oven, the pretend kitchen, the make-believe broom and dustpan, the plastic vacuum cleaner, the baby doll with the stroller, layette, and bottle? Wasn't that what she was told when she was a young girl? "Keep your legs closed; you're wearing a dress." "Don't scuff your shoes." "Sit up straight. Boys don't like bad posture." "Don't be too loud. Boys like quiet, dainty girls." "Let him open the door for you." "The key to a man's heart is his stomach." She'd followed all those rules, had made sacrifices. She was tired now. She could do without the conveniences if she could have the face she'd dreamed of. The face her man dreamed of.

THE SECOND TREATMENT

Dr. Transformation placed a cotton sheet with attached needles on her face and blew incense around the room as he called upon the "weaknesses" within her to be released.

"I am goddess. I am goddess," he chanted as he stabbed the pins into her flesh.

Her body trembled. At first from the pricks to her skin, but then her muscles seemed to quake in rhythm with his words. She felt both like singing and running from the room.

"Lira means balance," the doctor uttered as he withdrew the final needle. "We're simply restoring you to that place of equilibrium."

Back at home, her husband couldn't figure out what had changed that time, but he said, "Your face looks softer. More feminine."

He smiled when he said it and made eye contact with her, so she knew the treatments were pleasing to him.

"No. And no." Her husband turned and walked to their bedroom, where he removed his work shirt and threw it on the floor. He never had the decency to place it in the hamper. She wanted to curse every time she saw how he cared so little about the cleaning of his clothes and never considered the items themselves. She was the one who had to bend and scrape them from the floor so she could wash them by hand, hang them on the line outside, press them, fold them, and line them neatly in the drawer she'd organized, only for him to snatch them out, throw them on his body, drop ketchup or beer on the fabric, rip them off, ball them up, and throw them, soiled and wrinkled, onto the floor for her again at the end of every night. When the two of them were dating, she'd felt honored that he trusted her to wash the very garments resting against his skin, but when she saw how little he cared for his wardrobe, when she saw how his mother waited on him, his brother, his father, and his uncles like a housekeeper, when she saw how these men felt entitled to service, his laundry became a chore.

"You didn't let me finish either point." The letter was trembling in her hand. The sweat of her fingertips became mixed with the ink on the page, creating a multicolor stain above her bandage. The cut throbbed, the pain reminding her that while injury was quick, healing was slow. Couldn't he see how much more attractive she could become in a short amount of time?

"I already know what you're going to nag about." He walked to the closet. Pulled out his black jeans, the ones she'd ironed with starch so he could have the creases he wanted. He tossed them onto the bed. "So, the answer to both is no. You're not getting more beauty treatments because they're expensive and use up our savings, and, no, I'm not staying in tonight because I promised the fellas I'd swing by and watch the game. I'll eat when I get back."

He grabbed a belt and threw it alongside the pants. He removed a neatly folded undershirt from the drawer and flung it alongside the growing outfit. If he took out white socks, that meant he was going to wear sneakers. But he chose black socks and tossed those over as well, which meant he was going to wear his leather shoes. Since when did he wear leather shoes to watch the game with the fellas? He selected a collared shirt too, which he usually wore to his parent's house or out to dinner. Definitely not game-watching wear. Was it another woman?

She remembered how privately embarrassed she'd been the first time they'd had people over. It was their housewarming and they'd been married for barely a year. He really couldn't keep his hands off her back then, and would brush against her or touch or kiss her whenever she was near. And if she wasn't within range, he'd mouth "Come here" from across the room and she loved that just as much as the touches.

At that housewarming party, on her way from the bedroom where she'd retrieved a photo of her late grandfather to give to her mother, she saw Melva applying lipstick in the hallway mirror, and when Lira's husband walked by her cousin, he checked out Melva's ass, and when Melva looked in the mirror and saw him noticing her rear, the two of them made eye contact in that mirror and chuckled as if they had some private joke. Melva playfully smacked him on the shoulder and he didn't touch Melva at all, but he didn't move away either. He just stared at Melva until Melva closed up her pocketbook and slunk to the bathroom. He continued watching Melva and her sashaying ass as she moved all the way down the hall and closed the door. Lira had remembered how her cousin had told her at the previous family gathering that Black men liked her curves and that Lira could fix her hair, skin, and teeth, but she'd still have a flat ass like a white girl.

Lira returned to the party in the den before he could turn around and notice her. She was humiliated as she handed her mother the photo and sat on the arm of the couch. For the rest of the party, she was quiet and stared beyond him, and he kept asking, "Lira, everything okay?" She said she was fine, and he never looked at Melva the rest of the party. And his lack of acknowledgment of Melva was the thing that bothered her the most. That he'd had two different interactions with Melva, that he could turn his flirtations on and off as he saw fit, that he could show his attraction to the very cousin he'd known had always tormented Lira. What was his angle? she'd wondered. What was he really capable of?

"I will pay for the treatment myself. They've never been this cheap, and I'm not missing out on the deal." She held up the letter for him to examine.

He took it from her, balled it up, and threw it in the wastebasket. "With what money, Lira?" He had a smirk now. Was he laughing at her anger? Something sprang up inside her that hadn't been there before when they'd quarreled. This was more than anger.

I am goddess.

"You think throwing away that letter is going to stop me?" The more she spoke, the angrier she became. "It wasn't a coupon, you know. The treatments are just on sale this weekend. I've been saving my own money. I don't need your permission to make my life easier."

It wasn't lost on her that she'd used Nelson's reasoning, the very person her husband despised. But Nelson had been right. Where her husband was concerned, she needed to stop asking and start telling, just like she did at work.

I am goddess.

"Permission? Who said anything about permission? I think you're trying to pick a fight with me so you can start crying the way you always do and then guilt me into staying at home with you. But I'm not going to argue with you. Not tonight. You want your crazy treatments, go on and pay for it yourself."

"Oh, I plan to."

He smirked again. She realized he had smirked when they'd first met. That charming smile that attracted all the ladies, including her, wasn't a kind smile. It was smug. As if he were smarter than the person he spoke to. She wanted to dig her nails into his left cheek and tear across to the right, thereby removing that simper from his mouth. Who did he think he was?

I am goddess.

"That's fine. Whatever you want, Lira. Where's my Raiders jersey?"

She folded her arms across her chest. She did not answer and had no plans to. She could sit on the bed straight-backed like a wall all night if that's what it took to keep him home. She wasn't going to help him leave. And he didn't even see how ridiculous it was that he—a grown man—needed to ask her where his favorite jersey was. She knew how important that jersey was to him. He and his grandfather had matching jerseys, and his grandfather had died the previous year, imbuing the shirt with even greater meaning. She'd washed it and left it in the laundry basket on the back deck, but she'd keep that detail to herself.

"You're really trying me right now, Lira. You're really trying me. You're not the only one who can save money, you know."

"Yeah. It seems you've saved a lot with that new Camaro you just stepped out of."

He looked caught, and she was unhappy that he looked caught. This was not an argument she wanted to win.

"I can't talk to you, that's why I didn't tell you. Because you always whine about stuff that's not important. Beauty treatments from fake doctors. Washers and dryers. And the beach when we don't live near the ocean. And always eating dinner at home when restaurants have better food and atmosphere. The really important stuff, like having a car, I have to go out and do that stuff on my own. You think small. You wanted to get some small, ugly, no-name, used car, and I would rather take the bus than ride around in something that looked like that."

"Here I've been asking you about the purchase of my final treatment when you went out and secretly bought a car. A car! And you've been driving it for at least two weeks while I've been riding the bus. You go out and get a flashy, expensive car that we can't afford so you can look flashy and expensive? That's why you pulled out your black socks and are about to put on your flashy leather shoes, because you care about what people think?"

"That's not it, Lira. You never understand me."

He'd said that to her before. And he was right. She didn't understand him. He dreamed of cars, basketball games, beer, and parties, and she liked none of those things and she and her husband had nothing in common, and it hit her at that moment that she had been so delighted someone had finally noticed and chosen her that she'd never put any thought into who she would have chosen. A man who cared what kind of car he drove was not whom she would have chosen. She was a simple person, like Nelson. Nelson had a plain black car that drove well and only had fifteen thousand miles. Practical. And she didn't like going to get beauty treatments, but she felt she needed them to keep her husband's interest. She needed to compete with Melva or whomever he was seeing.

"That's exactly it, isn't it? It's just occurring to me now. These rings. Your fifty-six-inch television, surround sound, leather shoes, official Raiders jersey, this brand-new car, your bad credit score. You care about appearances."

"I do not. You just want a lapdog and not a husband."

"This is not about me. Stop trying to turn this back on me. This is about you. Just admit it. You don't care about what's important to me. You don't care about what's important to this house. Our finances. Our future. You care about appearances, and having fun, and that's it."

"Dammit, Lira. If I cared about appearances, I wouldn't have married you."

The air left the room and the breath left Lira's chest in a gasp. There it was. There it effing was. She had finally arrived at the Major Problematic Reveal. The entire evening, perhaps their entire relationship, had been leading to this one moment. She felt the tears on her cheeks before she even realized she'd been crying. She'd been cut with the twine again, but this time across her chest. If she had that cord, she'd wrap it around his neck and squeeze, just enough to scare him. She wanted to throw things. She wanted to break something. Smash a fragile plate and stare at the tiny shattered bits on the floor. She wanted to rip at her hair and stomp on something until it died. But she just sat there on the end of the bed, staring beyond him, down the hallway.

"I didn't mean it that way, Lira." His voice was soft and lacked all the rage from a moment ago. He was in his boxers, and he dropped to his knees in front of her. He looked as wounded as she felt. "Don't cry, Lira. Please. That's not what I meant. I just…"

Was this what he meant when he said she'd guilt him into staying? Because he could go. She actually wanted him to go now. Had he been using her all this time? She always ignored Melva's "Why does he want you?" questions even though her cousin wasn't the only person to ask. They'd all seemed to have suspicions about his motives—the mothers in the church, her family members—but she'd always told herself they were envious, they were making a commentary about what they thought of her looks and not what he thought of her looks. He was able to see her beauty because he was the only person able to see her, she'd thought. And now she knew they'd been right all along. Even Nelson had tried to warn her. She'd been used by her husband and humiliated and here he was burying his face against her chest and holding her around her waist as if she should be comforting him.

"Get off of me."

"Lira, baby, look." He kissed her breasts, noticing the lace bra and reaching inside her dress, inside her bra and stroking her nipple.

"Get off of me." She pushed his hands away.

He returned them to her waist and slipped them under the dress, glancing underneath and seeing the crotch-less panties. She felt like an idiot being done up for him while he'd been dressing to go out. He slid his fingers down the panties. It was an intrusion and she smacked his arm and ripped his grimy paws off of her.

"You have to believe me, baby." His breath was on her neck. "Just let me show you, Lira. Like I always show you."

And he did always show her. That's what he'd done after she told him she'd seen the secret glances between him and Melva. He said he'd simply had too much to drink, that Melva was not attractive to him. That he only wanted Lira, and she'd let his vigorous lovemaking stand in for his respect. No more.

I am goddess.

"I said, 'Get off of me.'" She shoved his shoulders. As she stood, he lost his balance and fell back onto the carpet. Standing over him, she thought of bringing her foot down on his nose, crushing it beneath her sole, but she caught herself, barely.

"Lira. What I was trying to say—"

She turned and left him on the floor. She walked to the backyard. The rain had finally come, and, with the wind, the thick, long droplets were falling in a sideways pattern. Clip by wooden clip, she pulled his clothes from the twine and threw the shirts, pants, and t-shirts into the mud. The wind was howling now, and even though it was dark outside, she could see by the lamppost near their garage and the full moon above her. She yanked each godforsaken thing down and threw it to the earth. Now wearing his carefully selected outfit of jeans and collared shirt, he walked behind her and picked up his muddy clothes.

"The hell are you doing, Lira? Stop."

Her hair was drenched and the rain had pasted her sexy dress to her crotch-less panties, lace bra, and oiled up skin. When she was done taking down his clothes and emptying what was left in the hamper into the muddy grass, she went into the garage, removed the garden sheers, and cut down the twine, the long rope dropping to the middle of the yard.

"I've spent thousands of dollars on this house, on these bills, on your satellite television since we've been married. Got painful fertility injections that I couldn't afford and didn't need. Paid all of our tithes and offerings to your uncle's church. And you and I make the same amount of money." She was shouting. The nosy neighbor turned on the light to her back porch. The dog from across the alley began barking.

"You've only spent what you felt like spending during the same period and that hasn't been worth a piss. How do I know this? Because I pay all the bills. I do all the cooking, the laundry, the taking-out of trash, the yard work, and I order all the repair work. What do you do? You give just enough to keep a roof over your head and food in your belly and the rest you spend god knows where, and now you show up in a car without checking with me and I can't get a damn treatment with a doctor? A damn washer and dryer? A damn smart phone?"

She didn't usually curse. 'Damn' felt sinful in her mouth, but she was done being prudent.

I am goddess.

She picked up a Fulsom Security shirt, threw it into the air, and, as it floated back down to the ground, she hacked its middle with the garden shears. She frightened herself by imagining him in the shirt, his skin inches from the blades.

"Lira. That's my work shirt! They'll dock my pay for that."

"They *should* dock your pay! I should dock your pay as well." Her throat burned as the shouts came out.

She tossed up another shirt. *Snip*. Right in the middle. The two halves fell to the ground. He didn't move. He stood in place and held out his arms to her with disbelief on his face. "Lira!" But he didn't move his feet. She must have looked as mad as she felt. Not angry-mad. Out-of-control mad. She hated him but she hated herself more for letting him be such a shit to her. She was smart. *Snip*. Had a degree. *Snip*. A salary. *Snip*. Was a manager. *Snip*. Another shirt up. *Snip*. Another. *Snip*. The last. *Snip*. When all five of his work shirts were cut in half in the middle of the yard, she grabbed the heap of his pants and was about to toss those up as well, but he grabbed her arm, right along her triceps.

"Enough, Lira."

She snatched her arm away and grabbed his Raiders jersey. It would break his heart if she cut it. She tossed up the jersey. He snatched it, but the timing was off, so she ended up slicing his forearm with the shears.

"I am goddess!" Her words echoed off her home's brick and all down their street. The dog barked faster and louder. More neighbors turned on lights in the backs of their homes.

A bolt of lightning appeared in the sky, brightening the blood on his skin, allowing her to see how quickly it flowed out of him. He moaned, shuddered, and fell to the grass holding his arm. She felt light, otherworldly, as if she were floating above herself watching the sheers come to rest on the grass, witnessing the raindrops rinse the blood from the blade.

The old Lira would have gone to him, with apologies flowing as profusely as his blood, and she would have wrapped his wound in the fabric of her dress, and gotten him into the house, seen whether he needed stitches and taken him to urgent care or called for a paramedic. But all she could hear was, *Dammit, Lira. If I cared about appearances, I wouldn't have married you.* She did not buy into the idea that a woman's value was in her looks, but everyone else did, and it therefore made for a constant reminder to measure her looks against other women. Was his co-worker pretty enough for him to want? What did he think of the woman who delivered their mail? And then there was, of course, Melva.

"Lira?" It was Nelson's voice. He was in their yard, standing behind her in the rain still in business casual from work. He bent slowly, picked up the sheers as if he were removing a wounded bunny from a lion pit. Nelson grabbed her husband around the waist and helped him stand. "Can you get me some bandages, Lira?" Nelson stared at her and then at her husband. He said, "It's all right, man. Just hold it this way to slow the blood."

She moved sluggishly, with one leaden foot stepping slowly in front of the other, as if she were traversing a tightrope, until she was back in the house. Perhaps they thought she was going to fetch those bandages or some tape or a piece of fabric. Instead, she sat at the dinner table, and ate her husband's meal, savoring the saltiness of the pork chop and black-eyed peas, the sweetness of the cornbread, the bitterness of his cheap, drugstore-bought wine. Finished and satisfied, she dropped her fork in the middle of the plate and stood. It felt good to not be responsible for anything. She saw why he enjoyed that role so. She ripped his satellite box out of the wall and threw it into the backyard, where he and Nelson were on the deck in the downpour unsuccessfully wrapping his wound with the twine and strips of shredded clothes.

After twenty minutes of her sitting on the couch staring at the remains of their stomped-on wedding photo, she heard the backdoor creak open, slow, stumbling footsteps, jagged breathing, and her husband appeared in the archway to the living room pale-faced, with twine dragging behind him, blood running through the fabric dressing, dripping down his arm and onto the rug. Nelson was not with him. Her husband must have told Nelson, "I'm good, man," and sent him home. Her husband leaned against the wall, leaving his bloody handprint there, and handed her his car keys.

"I need stitches."

"Have one of the fellas take you in your new car."

"Please, Lira." His voice quivered. He was on the brink of tears. "I need you. Please."

THE THIRD TREATMENT

Dr. Transformation put her to sleep using an anesthetic he gave her through a vein on the back of her right hand. She woke without pain, but covered in blood. When he held up a mirror, she found her nose was tiny like a doll's. Her eyes were wider and brighter; her chin prominent, not weak and sunk against her throat the way it usually was.

He explained the blood was not her own, but he also wouldn't say whose it was. She didn't like that she'd become lighter-skinned, with thinner features, and daintier edges to her visage—did pretty mean more like white people? she asked herself—but he made her promise to chant, *I am goddess*, when waking up and before going to bed until her next treatment.

After about four months of chanting and healing, she still wasn't quite at the P word, but one day, when she dismounted the bus and strode by his home, Nelson said she "sure" looked "nice."

―

The Camaro did not have that new car smell. When she cranked the ignition, it didn't turn over easily. The ride to Deadford was rough and smelled of gasoline. His taste in cars were like his taste in rings—flashy on the outside but lacking quality within. She thought of putting him out of the vehicle when she saw he'd spent God knows how much money on a heap of unleaded-fuel junk, but if he didn't make it to the doctor to get stitches, what would happen to him? Blood had soaked his shirt, pants, and shoes. Might he die and she'd be charged for cutting him and leaving him in the rain?

He didn't speak during the fifteen-minute ride, but he did glance at her behind the wheel several times as if he were about to say something and then decided it was best to keep quiet. She pulled close to the emergency room's front door.

"You're not coming with me?"

"No, I'm not coming with you. You need me to talk for you too? Call your mother if you need one."

She wondered then whether the treatments had actually done anything to her physically. What if it was just her perception Dr.

Transformation had changed? Maybe he'd reprogrammed her core. Maybe the "goddess" she had been chanting about was the part of her that was no longer willing to be trampled on. She *was* a goddess. The mantra had made her able to see herself clearly, and therefore able to see her husband clearly as well.

He did not look angry. He looked as if he were finally hearing her. But he also didn't look afraid to lose her. Perhaps it was the maid-mother-ATM-easy-sex part of her he'd been worried about losing, and now that she'd cut him—literally and justifiably—the deal didn't seem as sweet as it once had.

He got out. She parked and waited in the car. It was two hours of fidgeting and moving against that squeaky leather seat—because cloth seats would have been too cheap for his expensive tastes—before he emerged stitched-up and walking with his head down. The waiting time had not cooled her off. He got in. She drove them home in silence.

In bed she cried until the morning. When she woke, her neck, chest, and stomach ached. He must have sat up all night on the couch in his blood-stained clothes because when she went to the kitchen to make breakfast, for herself only, she found him sitting, with his head resting on the back of the couch and his mouth open, snoring. She clanged two pots together, jolting him awake with a snort.

"I want you to move out."

He cleared his throat and stared at her.

"I'm done being your charity case or your bank, whichever it is. So, take your hunk-of-junk car and leave."

He didn't respond and didn't move. He just sat there, eyes wide, as if he were seeing her for the first time.

She added, "Now! Before I cut you again!"

THE FOURTH TREATMENT

At her final treatment that weekend, Dr. Transformation said her husband had paid for everything ahead of her arrival.

"I don't have a husband," she mustered as she walked behind the curtain, removed her clothes, and pulled on the medical gown. She was angry he'd intruded on a day that was supposed to be about her.

She ended up not needing the gown because the final treatment was a meditation. The doctor told her to envision herself standing in the open ocean, hugging herself, caressing her arms, her hair, her face. He told her to imagine loving herself so completely, with pure kindness and not an ounce of haughtiness, that her self-love would one day burst from her body so ferociously it would cause a wake in the water large enough to capsize ships.

When she returned home, she stood in her bathroom mirror for an hour, analyzing her nose, eyes, skin color, cheeks, and she grinned when she realized her face had never really changed.

—

And that should have been the end. She should have gone on a date with Nelson, and they should have gotten married and had kids. But that wasn't the end of Lira's story, rather the beginning.

She found herself sitting in the park on a bench after dark staring into Melva's apartment window. Her cousin lived on the third floor, and she never closed her drapes, and was prancing back and forth in front of the window in lace undergarments.

Melva seemed to be preparing for a visitor because she lit candles on her dining table, chopped vegetables at her kitchen counter, turned on the music on her television, and poured wine into two glasses.

Wind blew, but Lira didn't notice as she shoved her hands deep into her pockets and touched the tip of her blade. She glanced up and down the street to ensure it was deserted. This was the industrial part of town near the bottling plant, with tanker trucks parked at the end of the block and warehouses ringing the building. Not much activity on a Sunday night after nine p.m.

Melva threw open her door and flung her arms around a male visitor, and when he walked over to the chair near the window and removed his sweater, Lira saw that it was her husband—soon to be ex-husband. He showed off the bandage from where the doctor had stitched up his arm, and Lira reveled in knowing he had lost so much skin and blood thanks to her.

Lira sat for five hours watching her cousin and her husband drink an entire bottle of wine, spoon-feed each other from the plates Melva had made for them, cuddle on the couch in front of the television, make out until they were fully undressed, rise from the cushions on wobbly feet, and tiptoe to the bedroom still kissing and groping, careful not to bump his bandage.

Lira was patient as she caressed the edge of her blade and waited for the lights to go out. She knew he'd be finished, having washed up in the bathroom, and asleep in less than half an hour. She even gave him an extra thirty minutes in case he behaved differently for Melva than he did for Lira.

It was easy getting into Melva's building. Lira had the code from when she first helped her cousin move in. Getting into the unit would have been tricky if she hadn't hidden around the corner earlier in the day. She'd snuck in to get the extra key from the kitchen drawer while Melva had been busy bringing in grocery bags to prepare dinner for Lira's husband—soon to be ex-husband.

Lira removed her shoes before stepping into the foyer. She was beside her cousin's bed in less than three minutes. She silently unscrewed the light bulbs from the lamps on the nightstands, pulled on a medical mask, tightened her skull cap, removed the blade from her pocket, and, using the moonlight and streetlamp to see her snoring husband and her cousin, who was lying on her back with her long locks splayed on the pillow and on the shoulder of Lira's husband—soon to be ex-husband—Lira pointed the sharp edge at Melva's left cheek, pressed in, and ripped across the flesh, bumping her nose, and tearing across the right.

As Lira turned to dash out, she felt hot blood on the back of the hand holding the knife. She placed it and the blade back in her pocket, and heard her cousin give off an ear-piercing scream. As expected, the lamps came crashing down as one or both of them unsuccessfully tried to turn them on. Lira dropped a note just outside the front door that read, *I Am Goddess*, and was in the hallway heading for the stairwell when she heard, "My face!"

Lira made it to the street and was so high on adrenaline she skipped the bus and walked the four miles home. She had heard of slashers before. Watched them in horror movies, read about them in books. And she wondered whether she could really be one if she only maimed her victims. What if she never actually killed anyone, just opened their flesh, and made them feel alive?

—

Chaz, her adolescent tormentor, was harder to get to. He'd moved to Chicago, and she'd had to take a train, track him to a high-rise near the Navy Pier, and figure out how to enter the building when it was managed by a doorman. But it was easier than she'd thought.

She wore a hat, sunglasses, all black clothing and gloves because it was chilly, and purchased a fancy floral arrangement, then pretended to be the person to deliver it. She entered at the busiest time of day, when the revolving doors were moving non-stop, and the lobby was filled with folks returning from work, dropping off packages, arriving with take-out orders that were hot, some dripping sauce, and when residents were coming and going to walk their dogs.

"You can leave it here," the exasperated but friendly doorman said to her.

"I have to sing with this."

"I didn't know anyone did singing telegrams anymore."

"That's why I'm wearing the glasses. I'm supposed to be one of the Beatles."

He chuckled, said, "The Thirty-fourth floor," and buzzed open the inner doors that led to the elevator bank.

She rang Chaz's doorbell, and, when he answered, she handed him the sunflowers and zinnia arrangement. He looked exactly how he had in high school, only twenty pounds heavier, with lines around his mouth, and a weathered look in his eyes.

"What is this?" he asked as she stared down into the bouquet. He reached for the card, and when he brought it up to eye level, Lira removed her knife and sliced across his forehead.

She was calm as she dropped the note near his door and descended the elevators, as if she'd been born to do this work. To make people feel alive. To make them feel the pain they caused her. But feel it on their face, where people usually showed their pain. She wished he had a trophy from her outings. Should she be removing a slice of skin? No, she thought. That would require her to stay for too long. And it would leave a trail of blood. Maybe collect newspaper clippings when her outings were reported? She had kept the one from Melva's. That had even included a grainy image of Lira leaving Melva's building. Lira had gotten a real chuckle out of that. She'd basically been a blurry black shadow. No one would ever find her.

She waved to the man at the front desk on her way out. He had the landline phone up to his ear, covered the mouthpiece with his hand, and said, smiling, "What song did you sing up there?"

UNSHOD, CACKLING, AND NAKED

Just before going through the revolving doors, and careful to keep her back to the lobby's security camera, she grinned, and said, "*Maxwell's Silver Hammer.*"

—

All the way back to Michigan she laughed about her answer to the doorman's question. The bit about *Maxwell's Silver Hammer* turned up in all the Windy City papers. Never mind that she hadn't used a hammer. The song title was mentioned in every article about the attack.

The police even made an arrest. Some homeless woman who frequented the area around Chaz's building. Apparently, the bag lady sang Beatles songs for money, and, like Lira, she was Black, so everyone assumed the woman in the security video from the lobby was the woman who lived on the street.

Chaz had gotten twelve stitches, would live, so they didn't even put her in prison. Just made her go to a treatment program.

When Nelson had phoned and texted her half a dozen times with no return call, he finally knocked on her door.

"Can we talk?" he asked, seeming concerned and angry.

She let him in. Sat him at her breakfast table, where she used to put down her husband's plate filled with sausage, pancakes, and scrambled eggs. She made Nelson a gin and tonic. She hadn't served a man in months and was glad that part of her life was over. She never wanted to go back to being powerless and obsequious.

"How is your cousin doing?" he asked, sipping from the glass and then staring at it, as if he were surprised it was so good. The trick was that she mixed a sweet club soda with the dry tonic before adding the gin and lime.

"My cousin?"

"Yes. Melva. I saw in the papers she'd been attacked."

"Oh." She suddenly felt suspicious. Nervous. She tried to

remember when she'd ever spoken to Nelson about her cousin. "I don't know."

"You don't talk to her? I just remember she was at your party when you guys first moved here."

She'd forgotten Nelson had been at their housewarming. Back then, her husband wasn't suspicious of Nelson, so he had no problem with Nelson coming around.

"No. I don't talk to her. But I'm guessing she is okay. Lots of stitches, I think."

Lira sipped the drink. She had not added gin to hers. Only to Nelson's.

"Where have you been? I saw you went out of town."

"Are you snooping when I leave the house?"

"No." He looked embarrassed and then met her eyes again. "But I do notice you. Saw you leave with a large bag. You were gone for a few days."

"Visited a family member."

"You don't have to say anything, Lira. But I wanted to talk to you about your husband. And your cousin."

"What about them?"

"I just wanted to say, don't let them change you. Don't let anyone change you. I've always liked and cared for you. And I know they hurt you. But what I saw out there in your yard that night…" The memory seemed painful to him. "That wasn't you, Lira."

It wasn't? She wasn't so sure. Her outsides had been called ugly enough times that she wondered whether it hadn't changed her insides. Or perhaps when her outsides had gotten prettier, it made her insides unwilling to put up with the mistreatment she'd endured. *I Am Goddess.*

Nelson's words opened a flood in Lira's chest. One tear escaped her eye, then several more fell, until she was a mess of wet cheeks and upper lip.

Seeming satisfied he'd gotten the reaction—the breakthrough—he'd come for, he stood, got her to her feet, and held her. He kept her close to him until she was calm again, and he said, "Call me if you ever need anything. Or want to talk."

He returned home, and by nightfall, she was ready to talk to Nelson. She didn't call, just rang his doorbell. He invited her in, surprised she was ready to open up so quickly. And she told him everything, from her childhood to Chaz's building in Chicago. He listened without judgment.

"You have to go to the police," he told her, holding her face.

"You hate me," she said.

"I don't hate you. I'm scared for you. If you step forward, admit what happened and why, I don't think any judge will be too hard on you. But if they hunt you down and find you, well, I think you'll end up in prison."

"You're right. But I'm only willing to tell them if you come with me. Hold my hand. I'm only doing this because of you. Because I…"

"What, Lira?"

"It's silly now after everything I've told you."

"No, it's not. My feelings for you haven't changed because of what you've said. You're as much the victim in all this. You've been bullied. Non-stop. And taken advantage of."

"I hoped you and I would have a future together."

His answer was to make love to her. In his bed, gently, and with more adoration than she'd ever felt in her life. And, after, when he was on his side, snoring, and the gentle breezes were flowing through the window, pushing the curtains in and out like ghosts, Lira was reborn. Her old ways of opening the skin were no longer needed.

She reached into her bag, pulled out her blade, and plunged it into the back of his neck. She went deeper into the flesh and muscle than she'd ever done before, and when she, on her hands and knees, couldn't plunge the knife any further, she turned it, feeling a spray of hot liquid across her bare breasts. She laughed, and shouted, "I am goddess!"

The news article about Nelson changed tone and language from the ones written about Melva and Chaz. For, in Nelson's case, the journalists spoke of the "manhunt" and asked the public to call in with any tips. And Lira was delighted to see that in at least one, the author referred to her as "The Medford Slasher."

UNSHOD, CACKLING, AND NAKED

Abduction Near Knife Lake

They'd left the wedding reception at midnight. Though they were headed for drinks at the bar, the mood in the rental car was less festive-laughter and more anxious-whispers, because no one knew how to get back to the hotel.

The storm had ended hours before, but oil-slick rainwater still coated the pavement, and caked-up mud dimmed their headlights. Luckily, the full moon lit their path.

Samiah served as navigator for their fifteen-mile journey along Michigan's backroads, but she had a poor sense of direction on a good day. As maid of honor, she rode shotgun, while she and Will, the best man-turned-chauffeur, squinted at road signs, peered into their phones, and consulted a paper map the concierge had given them on the way out that morning.

She didn't like being up north. This section of the state, not far from Lake Huron, was the site of several unsolved killings. For the past decade, bodies kept turning up in the woods, clawed to death and bitten, like an animal had gotten to them.

The city of Knife Lake leaned into its infamy. The bride and groom, Gwen and Seth, had had their first date at the local Halloween hayride, and the couple thought an early-October, haunted farmhouse wedding was a beautiful commemoration. In the backseat, the pair oscillated between hiccups and light snores, filling the car with the odor of whiskey.

Samiah was inebriated too. Will had described himself as "buzzed" while taking the keys from her, and she'd remembered the freeway sign back home in Detroit that read, "Buzzed Driving is Drunk Driving." She'd intended to admonish him, but it had slipped her mind.

Neither of them slurred their words, so that was worth something. Yes, her ears were ringing, but she could hear. She might vomit at some point, but that was likely from the Chilean sea bass at dinner, not the three glasses of champagne nor the two gimlets she'd downed with Will. The group hadn't even done shots yet.

Hoping to get information on where in the bejesus they were exactly, she squinted at a digital road sign, but when the bright orange dots melded into words, she saw it was an Amber Alert.

Child Abduction/Knife Lake/Suspect Vehicle: White Ford Mustang.

She typed the license plate number—*L-C-M-7-2-X-3*—into the note-taking app on her phone. Her stomach sank.

"This makes my heart hurt."

Will responded that the abductor was probably someone who knew the child. "You know, a custody thing."

She thought his optimism was misplaced, but that fish dinner threatened to come up, so she kept her mouth shut.

"We're gonna have to stop and ask someone where we're going." Will seemed to be sobering. His goofy grin from earlier in the evening was gone. She was impressed at how grown-up they'd been to each other. They'd had a bitter break-up back in college, but since this wedding weekend, it almost seemed like she'd dreamed up those older versions of themselves. They laughed easily now, were excited about the other's successful career, and had even made out after the rehearsal dinner. "We should have been there already. Plus, reception's spotty." He mostly was speaking to himself, but she nodded anyway.

The gas station didn't belong in her imagined version of rural Michigan. The ramshackle building seemed to have no brand for its

UNSHOD, CACKLING, AND NAKED

fuel. It just said, *Gas*, and the letter A was missing. A row of restrooms sat to the right, and dark elm trees surrounded both structures, giving the area a feeling of desolation.

The fuel spot was empty, save the lone convenience store attendant, whom Samiah could see through the large windows. The young woman with a sandy-blonde French braid peered into a tablet device as if she didn't have customers outside.

When Will went inside to ask for directions, the woman pointed toward the road they were already on, in the direction they were already headed, all while keeping her eyes on the tablet.

Samiah's cell phone vibrated. She looked down. An alert for the child abduction popped up, only this one had a photo and a description of the victim:

Last seen: city of Knife Lake; Gender: Girl; Age: eight; Height: four feet 9 inches; Weight: fifty-eight pounds; Answers to 'LeeLee;' Wearing blue t-shirt and red Mickey Mouse shorts.

Samiah studied the picture, and the face gazing back reminded her of Gwen at eight. Same deep brown skin and curly hair. Eyes big and sad, even when she was smiling.

Samiah's stomach dropped, and not from the sea bass. She didn't share Will's thinking that this was a family abduction. But it was impossible to know from the alert what was happening to the girl. Trafficked? Raped? Killed? Her mother must be worried sick.

When Will was back at their vehicle pumping gas, Samiah rolled down her window and showed him the photo. Cold, damp air filled the car. The rainfall had made the night chilly.

"Last seen in Knife Lake?" Will seemed concerned now. "See? We need to get out of here."

Another car pulled into the station, its engine revving. Will didn't seem to notice as he stared at Samiah's phone. Samiah barely looked up, herself. She was mesmerized by the girl's picture. What type of animal would take a child?

Will returned the fuel dispenser to its cradle and was back in the driver's seat. He touched her thigh, reminding her of their kiss the previous night.

"She said we're headed in the right direction. Two more exits on this highway, and we're there."

Samiah's reception went out again so they'd have to rely on the attendant's words. She put away her phone. Rolled up her window. And, as Will pulled off, she checked on the bride and groom in the backseat—blissfully snoring—then stole a glance at the gas station.

A white car sat at the tank but no one had exited. The body of the vehicle reflected the moonlight as if it had just been waxed. The hubcaps twinkled. Its headlights were off, and the idling thing sounded like a race car waiting for the flag. She squinted, her eyes darting across the bumper where the metallic, galloping pony emblem seemed to leap out at her.

"That's the car!" Samiah hit Will's arm.

"What car?"

"From the Amber Alert."

He slowed the rental and dipped his head to look out her window. "Same license plate?"

She searched the rear of the Mustang, where the blue and white letters should have been. "It's missing."

Heart thumping, palms sweating, she stared inside the Mustang's tinted windows as Will brought their rental car to a complete stop. She could only make out the shadow of a person who seemed to be sitting still. Waiting, perhaps, for them to drive off.

"We have to go back."

"You mean, we have to go to the police station."

"We don't know where the police station is, and there isn't enough time."

"We're not cops. We can call the cops."

"With what reception? The time it takes to figure this out could be life or death for her. And she's Black. You know the police won't track her down like they do these white girls. It probably won't even make the news."

Will sighed. The old Will would have driven off, and the two of them would have shouted at each other all the way back to the hotel. But the new Will nodded, removed the bowtie from his collar, and checked his rearview. He threw their car in reverse, gunned it back to the station, and eased the rental next to the tank they'd just left. Their Toyota Camry sat parallel to the Mustang again. Will turned off the ignition. "Okay, Sam. What's the plan?"

"I'll walk up to the window and look inside. See if she's in there." She unbuckled her seatbelt and turned on her phone's flashlight app.

Will covered the screen with his palm and forced the device onto her lap.

"Sit tight. Lock the doors. I'll go in and tell the attendant to call the police."

As Will got out, he whistled the way a person would on a normal night when they'd perhaps forgotten something in the station's store. With his hands in his tuxedo pockets, he strolled nonchalantly back inside.

With a broad, fake smile, he spoke to the attendant, who slowly, cautiously put down her tablet and stared up at him with her mouth hanging open. Will must have told her not to look out the window. Not to let the Mustang driver know they were calling the cops.

The white car, which was now off and silent, jerked as if someone inside were moving. On the other side of the fuel machine, between the nozzles and the metal garbage can, a car door opened. A tall, shadowy figure rose and stood easily six and a half feet tall.

"Where are we?" Gwen's voice made Samiah jump.

"Gas station," Samiah whispered, taking in the thousand-watt grin on the face of her lifelong best friend. Gwen had just had the wedding of her macabre dreams, to the rock band-guitarist love of her life, and the newlyweds were headed for Jamaica in the morning. Samiah couldn't bring herself to explain the murderous sideshow mere feet away from them. "Go back to sleep."

Gwen rummaged around in her purse and retrieved a tampon. "I need to pee." She opened her car door and left her handbag behind.

"Wait," Samiah hissed, reaching for Gwen's thin, white honeymoon dress. "Stay in—"

But Gwen was out, slamming her door and stumbling across the oil-stained concrete before Samiah could finish the word 'inside.'

Seth stirred, the car jerking as he roused.

"Same." He threw open his door and got out, tossing his tuxedo coat on the backseat.

"You can't—"

The other car door slammed. Samiah was alone, and she'd lost sight of the shadowy figure. With thick, trembling fingers, she locked the doors. She faced forward and folded her arms across her chest so the Mustang driver wouldn't know she was on to him. Her heart was pumping like she'd just finished a race. She had the urge to pee as well, but she knew it was adrenaline coursing through her body.

From her peripheral vision, she could see the Mustang driver coming around the gas pump towards the Camry. She searched the floor near her feet for some sort of weapon but came up short.

She held her breath. Stared at her blank phone. He walked past her car. *Thank God!* With a pronounced limp and filthy hands, he followed Gwen and Seth to the row of bathrooms. She couldn't make out much, but she could see the hulking figure was dripping blood.

Blood!

Samiah repressed a scream and tried to clear her jumbled mind. What was her plan? She wished she weren't still drunk. *Think!*

Okay, she could rush to the bathrooms and warn Gwen and Seth that they may or may not be in danger from the bloody freak and then come back out and save LeeLee. Or she could go inside the station and tell Will she would phone the police while he went to warn Gwen and Seth, and, when police confirmed they were on their way, she'd run out and save LeeLee.

But those options did not satisfy Samiah. If it were eight-year-old Gwen trapped in that car, she would want someone to intervene right away. She decided it was now or never. The universe had handed her this moment, and she would seize it.

She glanced into the station. Will was using the landline, and the attendant was staring at him, seeming as freaked out as Samiah felt.

Samiah got out, but didn't close her door. If the bloody Mustang driver were listening from the restrooms, she didn't want him to hear the slam and know she'd exited. Ignoring the goosebumps on her flesh and the pit in her stomach, she tiptoed around the gas machine, turned on her phone's flashlight app, and peered into the backseat. It was empty.

Of course, it was. Kidnappers wouldn't leave their victims all out in the open at a gas station, even a dimly lit one and especially when they were taking a bathroom break. She needed to open that trunk.

She ducked into the Mustang's backseat, noticing a pool of blood on the floor as well as the smell of cigarettes and sweat. If the driver returned, she was a goner, so she checked the rear window to make sure he wasn't on his way. She moved quickly. She reached over the driver's seat and found the lever to pop the trunk.

It creaked open, as if it had been amplified by a mic. She rushed out and around back. Sure enough, she found a whimpering child wedged between a duffel bag and a spare tire, gagged with a horse muzzle, her ankles and wrists bound with twine. The trunk smelled of urine. A tiny brown face with eyes big as saucers peered out. The girl was smallish, with a dark shirt.

Samiah ripped off the ties, unbuckled the muzzle, and lifted the girl like a baby from her prison. She closed the trunk quietly, ensuring it snapped shut before she scurried away.

Samiah's strapless bridesmaid's dress hugged her frame as she clicked her high heels across the concrete and stuffed the feather-light girl into the rental car in the front passenger seat. She waved down Will, mouthing, *Let's go*, and she squeezed into the front, her body pressed against LeeLee's.

The girl stared at Samiah with confusion and fear. Tears filled the girl's eyes, and, with the muzzle gone, the girl's sunken cheeks and slight tremor became apparent. The child looked sick, and with something more serious than a cold.

"It's going to be okay, LeeLee. You're safe now."

Will exited the store with quick, short steps, no longer whistling, and the bell above the frame jingled as he left.

The Mustang driver stalked across the station lot and began to fill his tank.

As Will returned to the driver's seat and closed his door, he shouted, "What the hell?"

"She was tied up in the trunk. I pulled her out."

The driver must have heard Will's shout because the figure leaned down, saw the girl in the rental car, turned, and popped the Mustang's trunk. He stared into that empty space for all of a half-second before knocking over the trash can and sending it clanging across the ground on his way to the Camry.

"Shit." Will started up the car. It was slow to turn over.

Samiah got a good look at the creep as he tugged on the door's handle. It's like she was seeing double. He wasn't so much a man as he was a monster, but two creatures fused into one. He wore a cap that covered his face and a long coat that resembled a cape. Dirt covered his skin. Thick gashes and blood-splattered lacerations snaked up his neck.

He banged on Will's window, smearing blood across the glass, and he shouted, but she couldn't make out what he said. Something like, "Everybody killed," and "wrong." As Will shifted to drive, the hulking, double-monster pulled down the 91-octane gas nozzle and cracked open Will's window. Glass exploded into the car along with gasoline and blood.

"Oh-my-god-he's-going-to-kill-us-Oh-my-god-Oh-my-god!" Samiah covered the girl's eyes and strapped the two of them into the seatbelt.

The abductor reached across Will and snatched at the girl, but Will whacked him in the nose with his cell phone, shoved the abductor's head and arms back out, and floored it out of the gas station, throwing the shadowy figure to the ground.

Amid pants and gasps, and exclamations of, "Ohmygod," Samiah checked her side-view mirror. The Abductor rose, yanked the hose from the Mustang's fuel tank letting the nozzle drop to the ground, and slammed the trunk with both hands, as if he were trying to break the thing in two. He hopped in the vehicle and flew out of the station before even closing his door.

When that Mustang sprang to life, and that ton of monstrous metal got out on the road, it was like their rental car was being chased by fire.

Samiah needed to upchuck that sea bass. There was no way on God's vehicular earth that their rented Toyota Camry, which didn't have navigation but boasted an in-dash CD player, would outrun that souped-up, vintage Mustang from horsepower hell.

Will checked his rearview then turned to look over his shoulder at the car-beast closing in on them. "Where are Seth and Gwen?"

"Dammit!" Tears burned Samiah's eyes. She'd completely forgotten the bride and groom in the gas station bathroom. "They went to pee." She imagined them exiting, wondering where the car was, and hopefully going inside to talk to the attendant.

Will pushed the car faster than it had probably ever driven, and it rattled at the increased speed, threatening to break apart if they pressed it more.

"What was that thing back there?" Samiah was asking Will, but she was kind of asking LeeLee as well. The girl snapped her eyes shut and whimpered.

"You mean the baby-snatcher chasing us?"

With Will's busted window, wind whipped around the car tossing Samiah's hair into her eyes. The girl burrowed into Samiah's side.

"It's going to be okay, LeeLee."

The Mustang roared as it blasted down the empty, two-lane highway. Before Samiah knew it, the white car was on their tail, ramming into their bumper and honking. The driver had also turned on the high beams, blinding them. Will couldn't possibly see the road because Samiah couldn't even make out the dashboard in front of her.

"Shit. Shit. Shit." Will swerved, trying to duck the Mustang, but the pursuing vehicle would not let up. Will stepped on the gas harder. The car jerked forward, throwing Samiah's head against the top of her seat. The rental pulled ahead of the Mustang, but only for a few seconds and the white car was back on their ass.

The Abductor was laying on the horn too. The top of Samiah's bridesmaid's dress became wet. When she looked down, she realized the girl was crying and shivering something awful.

Will hit a curve and hugged it, never letting off the gas. Their tires tore up rock and brush as they went slightly off-road, but he managed to straighten out the car. They came to a hill, and the momentum sucked them down like soda in a straw. Samiah's insides shot up to her throat the way they did on roller coasters.

The Mustang cut its lights, eased off the horn, but continued its pursuit. They were plunged into pitch darkness, and the rental fishtailed as their eyes adjusted. The Mustang pulled to the left of the Camry, seemingly toying with them because it wasn't even traveling at its top speed.

The Abductor rolled down his window and Samiah leaned forward to peer inside. A scream left her body before her mind processed what she was seeing.

"Gun!" The word burned her throat as she shouted over the wind.

A loud pop, a flash of light, and Will slammed on the brakes.

Seth's tuxedo coat flew from the backseat and skidded across the windshield before sliding down and landing at Samiah's feet. Gwen's bejeweled purse careened into the front, spitting lipstick and credit cards onto the gearshift. Samiah placed her hand on the dashboard to stop herself and the girl from flying forward as the rental skidded across the concrete and violently stopped. The Mustang was a whole football field away before it slammed on its brakes.

Will put his hand to his cheek. Blood gushed from his flesh.

"I..." His face muscles slackened. His blood-soaked hand went limp and dropped to the console between him and the girl. His head fell forward and landed on the horn, which bleated a cry of panic.

"Nononononononono. You can't be dead."

Samiah squinted down the road at the Mustang. Its engine revved. Its glistening body quaked. She yanked the lever under Will's seat, pushing it mostly in the back. She leaned Will onto his headrest, thereby snapping off the horn's scream. She sat on his lap and shifted the car back into drive. Shuddering from the cold and adrenaline coursing through her body, she popped a U-ie and floored their vehicle back in the direction of the gas station.

"The police should be there by now." She was talking to herself, though she glanced at LeeLee too.

"You hear me? You're going to be safe."

The girl's eyes were half-closed, as if she were struggling to stay awake. There was something odd about the way her body twitched. She moved like a fiend, whose drug was electricity that shocked her from inside. What had that monster done to her?

Samiah checked her rearview where the Mustang was navigating a U-turn. She snapped on her high beams. That made a world of difference. She could make out the trees lining the two-lane highway, the yellow lines in the middle of the concrete, the boulders to the right of where she drove, and the places where the rocks gave way to a ditch.

The Mustang slammed into her bumper, but Samiah kept the wheel steady. Then the white car pulled to Samiah's left and she peered into its open window, bracing for the shadowy figure to fire another shot.

She got the idea to open the glove compartment and throw something, anything, to try to injure him, but as soon as she reached for the handle, the Mustang rammed into her car.

The impact pressed the door frame against the side of Samiah's body, the airbags exploded into her face and chest, and the rental veered to the right. LeeLee screamed.

Another slam from the Mustang and Samiah's wheels were no longer on the concrete. The rental was smacking into rock and brush. Her teeth slammed together when the Camry hit the guardrail and crashed into the ditch. The rental groaned as it leaned and flipped. Will's head flew forward and banged into the back of hers. The car rolled and tumbled down the embankment into the woods. The little girl screamed, the sound resembling a howl.

—

When she came to, pain throbbed across the back of her head. Frigid wind sent shivers through her body. Her ears rang. She tasted blood. A radio delivered local news updates; the volume barely audible.

"You're listening to WJXF Radio. If you're just joining us, we have an update on that Amber Alert from earlier in the evening. Knife Lake Police, in conjunction with the County Sheriff, have confirmed they've located the child just outside of town. Her abductor is in custody, and the eight-year-old has been reunited with her parents at a local hospital, where she was taken for observation."

Samiah heard the words flowing from the bass-heavy speakers but didn't register their meaning. Whimpers nearby drowned out the broadcast, and she searched her clouded mind to figure out where she was. Hospital? She smelled gasoline, so probably not.

When she opened her eyes, she was staring through the half-cracked, half-blasted-out windshield at a full and high moon. She hung upside-down in the car, her seatbelt taut across her torso and hips, the deflated airbag and her curls dangling around her head.

Will moaned. *Thank the Lord Almighty!* He wasn't dead. He'd ended up crumpled on the bottom of the car, which was really the top. Samiah looked around and found the girl tethered to the seat by her belt as well, crying, her shoulders shuddering violently. Was she having a seizure?

Samiah tried to speak, but her chest and ribs ached when she breathed. How the hell was she going to get out of this mess?

Somewhere, far away but close enough to hear, a car turned off.

"LeeLee?" she whispered. "Will? We have to get out of here."

Will groaned, but seemed to have his wits about him as he sat and stared at her. Blood dripped from his face, but it also had clotted on his cheek. His hands were slow but deliberate as he unstrapped Samiah and eased her out of the upside-down driver's seat.

Being right-side-up took the pressure off her throbbing head. There was still that stabbing feeling in her torso, but she couldn't think about that now. She scooped up LeeLee, and the trio slithered through the busted-out driver's window, crunching glass as they broke free.

Samiah's eyes immediately went up the rock-strewn ditch and came to rest on the road, where the Abductor stalked toward them, his long rifle hanging from a shoulder strap, his coat flapping behind him in the wind. The Abductor wasn't running, but he wasn't strolling either.

She was unsteady on her feet, and, as they ran away from the Camry, its radio whispering and its seatbelt-reminder chiming, they slid farther down the embankment into knotted trees and thick brush. She tasted vomit; that sea bass must have come up at some point.

LeeLee didn't have any cuts or bruises, but her body shook. Unblinking, the girl stared at the moon and needed to be carried.

Twigs snapped behind them.

"Get down." Will grabbed Samiah and LeeLee and tucked them all into a spot behind a wide trunk.

At some point, Samiah had lost her shoes. Insects bit at the flesh near her ankles, but her chest didn't hurt as much as it had.

LeeLee shivered against Samiah's torso. The night was cool but the girl was warm. Will and Samiah panted as they caught their breath. She checked his face in the light of the moon and saw that the bullet had torn off a chunk of skin but had not entered him.

About twenty yards away, branches snapped. LeeLee grew hot as she gripped Samiah's waist. Samiah stared down at the girl and noticed her shirt wasn't actually blue. It was green. And she wasn't wearing red Mickey Mouse shorts, rather a tattered pair of jeans. Samiah shook her aching head, wondering when the girl had been kidnapped. Where were her blue shirt and red shorts?

"She's burning up," she whispered to Will. "I think she has a fever."

And no wonder. The girl was barefoot and had the appearance of someone who'd been starved. Wind blew, and the girl's shivering grew steadier, rhythmic.

With wide eyes, Will placed his finger to his lips, silently shushing Samiah. A gunshot cracked against the trunk, spitting bark around their heads, and, in one motion, the three of them sprinted deeper into the woods, Samiah carrying LeeLee's upper body and Will the lower.

Large stones with jagged surfaces appeared around them. The boulders formed a circle and were the kind of rocks typically at a shore, not buried beneath heavy brush.

LeeLee thrashed Samiah's cheek as she convulsed. Samiah released the girl's body, frail and weightless, and LeeLee fell to the ground, her muscles twitching. The child rolled onto her side and drew her arms and legs into the fetal position. She cried out in agony. Panicked, Samiah searched Will's face.

"Shhhhhh," he covered LeeLee's mouth, and checked over his shoulder. LeeLee only screamed louder. "We have to go, Sam."

Will grabbed Samiah's hand, but she snatched it back.

"I'm not leaving her."

Brush broke and leaves rustled as the Abductor, aware of their position now, drew closer. Will reached for Samiah again, but a claw shot up and sliced across his arm.

He screamed, and when Samiah looked down, she was no longer seeing LeeLee. Something was there in the girl's place. A mound of fur, a longer, more muscular frame, with cat-like eyes.

Another claw shot through the air and swiped at Will's stomach. The impact was hard enough to toss him ten feet away and knock Samiah on her bottom.

It was Samiah's turn to scream. She scooted back, once, twice, three times to stay just outside of the claw's grasp. But she couldn't move any farther; she'd backed into a downed log.

The moon peeked between the tree canopy, and the fur rose to its full height above her. Unable to make out the figure against the dark background, Samiah kept her eyes open and pulled her forearms up to guard her face. The claw rose in the air, preparing to come down on Samiah's head, when a shot rang out, and the fur was gone.

The Abductor stood in the moonlight with his rifle pointed and steady in front of him. He glanced toward Samiah and Will. His hat was gone, and she saw his face.

He was a man after all. And his previous monstrous nature she realized was owing to her blood-alcohol level. He had deep brown skin, dark circles beneath his eyes, grooves beside his nose and sagging cheeks. She'd put his age at sixty, though the fierceness of his glare made him seem younger.

He could shoot Samiah and Will. Could end both their lives, easily. But instead, he turned and dashed into the trees in the direction of the fur and cat-like eyes. Feeling great shame as her mistake in judgment was solidified before her, Samiah squinted, but could only see blackness and fog.

Nearby, Will gasped, struggling to take in air, and Samiah inched towards him, the moon lighting the brush around them. She followed the trail of blood until she reached his outstretched hand, and, in the distance, she heard a gunshot. Then another report from the rifle. Seconds later, a noise somewhere between a human scream and an animal's guttural cry. The shriek pierced the night. Then another. Samiah lifted Will, limped with him toward the road, silently though, as the trees swallowed the sound of the deafening howls.

TAMIKA THOMPSON

About

Tamika is a writer, producer, journalist, and author of *Salamander Justice* (Madness Heart Press). She is co-creator of the artist collective POC United and fiction editor for the group's award-winning anthology, *Graffiti*. Her work has appeared or is forthcoming in several speculative fiction anthologies as well as in *Interzone, Prairie Schooner, The New York Times,* and *Los Angeles Review of Books,* among others.

She received a Bachelor of Arts in Political Science from Columbia University and a Master of Arts in Journalism from the University of Southern California. She lives in the San Francisco Bay Area. Find her online at tamikathompson.com.

"Bridget Has Disappeared" appeared in *Interzone 292/293* by TTA Press
"Under the Crown" appeared in *Prairie Schooner*
"The Bats" appeared in *Typhon: A Monster Anthology, Vol 2* by Pantheon Magazine
"These Parts" appeared in *Shifters* by Hazardous Press
"Angry Slash of Blood" appeared in *The Monsters We Forgot, Vol 2* by Soteira Press
"Mannequin Model" appeared in *Glass Mountain*
"She By the Sea" appeared in *Horror USA: California* by Soteira Press
"And We Screamed" appeared in *Orca*
"I Am Goddess" appeared in *If I Die Before I Wake, Vol 7* by Sinister Smile Press

www.ingramcontent.com/pod-product-compliance
Lightning Source LLC
LaVergne TN
LVHW010846230125
801937LV00049B/703